FLESH-RIPPII
OF LONDON

Scorpionic

FLESH-RIPPING GHOULS OF LONDON

J M Rymer, Thomas Prest & Others

ISBN 978-1-902197-51-7

A Scorpionic Book

Published 2012 by Creation Oneiros

Copyright © Creation Publishing

III : SHORT TALES

INTRODUCTION

The "penny blood" came into being through a process which began with higher standards of general education and literacy in England at the beginning of the 19th century, and continued with the invention of fast and efficient printing presses and cheap paper production. These combined elements simultaneously created a new, mass market for literature, and fed that market with new, affordable product. The gothic novel, popular amongst a rarefied class of literary readers, duly gave way to sensationalistic, graphic shockers for the masses.

The most popular forms of publication during this period were chapbooks and broadsheets; broadsheets, favoured by the poor reader, usually contained an illustrated ballad based on some (often scandalous) item of news. In 1818 James Catnach, one of the major London broadsheet publishers alongside John Pitts, was gaoled for producing an exceptional gruesome sheet telling the story of a cannibal butcher. But even more relevant to this study are the "gothic chapbooks" – illustrated booklets of either 36 or 72 pages – which began to proliferate at the turn of the century, and presented new literary form in a new physical template; typical titles would include *The Secret Oath, or Blood-Stained Dagger* (1802) and *The Cavern Of Horrors, or, Miseries of Miranda* (1802). Among the main publishers of these chapbooks were Dean And Munday and Thomas Tegg; they sold their wares at sixpence for 32 pages, and one shilling for 72 (hence the term "shilling shockers"). By condensing the contents to a series of gory and macabre highlights, reinforced by graphic woodcuts, these pamphlets were an early forebear of the penny papers to come.

A typical example of the transition from gothic literature to populist pulp is Edward Montague's *The Demon Of Sicily*, a book first published in London in 1807, and reprinted with lurid illustrations in 1839 by William Dugdale, a noted pornographer and publisher of *The Exquisite* erotic periodical (1842-44). Basically, Montague's novel takes the most outrageous elements of gothic works such as *The Monk*, ramps them up to new levels of sex, violence and gore, and delivers them in a literary form more accessible to the then-putative "mass market":

At the decayed bridge Leonardi alighted, he conducted the trembling form of Isabella through the broken portals. Well knew the Knight the subterraneous recesses of the castle; within its tottering walls his own arm had perpetrated dark deeds of horror.

Down many a step which seemed to be a passage to the bowels of the earth, he forced the wretched Isabella, till at length they entered a dungeon.

"Now, lady," said he in harsh accents, "'tis like thou mayest repent of the deep insult you have offered me. No longer a suitor, I command thee to yield to my wishes; dreadful indeed will be the punishment of disobedience, for my soul yet burns with the remembrance of the injury I have received."

The soul of Isabella rose above the horrors of her situation; she seized the dagger that glittered in the girdle of the gloomy Leonardi.

"Barbarian," said she, "I fear thee not; in a moment I can put myself beyond thy infamous design. Powers of mercy, receive my soul!"

The dagger she had directed to her bosom here interrupted her; she fell to the ground, her pure blood dyed her garments.

Furious grew Leonardi at being disappointed of his expected prey; he looked blackly on the prostrate Isabella; she still lived, for the wound was not mortal.

"Since not my desires, I can however yet satiate my revenge; the pangs of death from my hand shall torture thee."

Thus said, he drew his glaive; he divided the lovely head of Isabella from the convulsed body; he caught it by the beautiful long black tresses, and strode away with it to another chamber; he set it on a piece of a broken column, and contemplated with a demoniac satisfaction the features once so lovely, so interesting, but now ghastly with the agonies of death. "Those eyes," said he, "will no longer look indignant on me; neither will that mouth further insult me. Would I could have increased the torture of death; gladly would I have done it; for her groans were comfort to my soul."

Some days he continued indulging his black revenge; at length a new thought struck him; "I will go," said he, "to the cell where her body lies, and take from it her proud heart; I shall find pleasure in trampling on it."

Other sub-gothic melodramas of this period included *The Witch of Ravensworth* (1808), by George Brewer; *The Mysterious Hand, or, Subterranean Horrors!* (1811), by Augustus Jacob Crandolph;

Manfrone, or, The One-Handed Monk (1809), by Mary Anne Radcliffe; and *Rosalviva, or, The Demon Dwarf* (1824), by Grenville Fletcher.. By 1826, macabre literary material of this type – dealing with witchcraft, deformity, depravity, insanity, sadism and gore – could be found in *Legends Of Terror*, a 40-part omnibus of supernatural tales, and later in *The Casket*, a weekly publication which touted itself as "the first of the penny papers". Published through the auspices of the *Ladies Penny Gazette*, *The Casket* regularly contained such tales as *The Ice-Witch*, *The Devil's Ducat*, *The Evil Eye*, *The Fiend Of The Heath*, *The Skeleton Count*, and *Vampires Of London*, completing the transition from gothic novel to mass-produced pulp horror. Such weeklies, usually of eight pages in length, tightly typeset in double columns, cheaply printed and illustrated by gruesome woodcuts, were produced in vast numbers from then until around 1850; this was the golden age of the "penny blood".

As early as 1823, horrific material was also available in various proto-"true crime" periodicals, serial publications such as *The Tell-Tale* (1823-4), *Legends Of Horror* (1825-6) and *The Terrific Register* (1825-7); packed with illustrated accounts of violent robbery, murder, cannibalism, dismemberment, torture and execution, these had their roots in such 18th century book anthologies as Captain Johnson's *A General History Of The Robberies And Murders Of The Most Notorious Pirates* (1724) and *The Newgate Calendar* (1774), a compendium of crimes, trials and hangings which appeared in numerous editions and even spawned a separate literary sub-genre, the "Newgate novel" as epitomised by William Harrison Ainsworth's *Rookwood* of 1834. The *History And Adventures Of That Famous Negro Robber, "Three-Fingered Jack", The Terror Of Jamaica* (1822) was a one-off, 24-page "crime romance" in this tradition which described itself as a "penny misery". Later penny crime weeklies would include William Strange's *Calendar Of Crime* (1832) and George Drake's *Calendar Of Horrors* (1835, notable for its serial *Geralda, The Demon Nun; or, The Charmed Bracelet*). The *Calendar Of Horrors* was edited by one Thomas Peckett Prest, a key figure in the history of pulp fiction. Prest, who also edited *The Horrors Of War* (1936) for Drake, was soon turning his hand to writing serial fiction, and over the ensuing decade would produce a huge volume of work notable for its grotesquerie and gore.

It was Edward Lloyd, a bookseller turned publisher, who detonated the penny-pulp market with the inauguration of a new line of sensationalistic mass-produced bloods, his career starting in 1936 when he took over *The History and Lives Of The Most Notorious Highwaymen, Footpads, Murderers, Brigands, Pickpockets, Thieves, Banditti, and Robberies of Every Description* and *The History Of The Pirates Of All Nations* (both originally published by George Purkess). Although these were published monthly, ran for around 24 pages and sold for sixpence, Lloyd soon realised that the format favoured by *The Casket* – weekly, 8 pages, and retailing at just one penny – was the way to reach the masses. Running stories in a multi-episode, serial format also ensured repeat custom. Supplementing his income by low-rent plagiarisms of Charles Dickens, Lloyd soon built up a raft of weekly publications, including *Lloyd's Entertaining Journal, The Penny Sunday Times, Lloyd's Companion To The Penny Sunday Times, Lloyd's Penny Weekly Miscellany, Lloyd's Penny Atlas, Lloyd's Weekly Miscellany,* and *The People's Periodical.* By 1843 he had moved to new premises in Salisbury Square, introducing new high-speed printing presses, and was even manufacturing his own paper. He also employed a pool of writers-for-hire in order to cover the immense anmount of work needed to fill his weeklies; chief amongst these were the aforementioned Thomas Prest, one James Malcolm Rymer, and one E.P. Hingston.

Besides short stories with such lurid titles as *Confessions Of A Deformed Lunatic* or *The Madhouse Of Palermo*, Lloyd's journals were primarily driven by the serials, largely written by either Prest, Rymer, or a combination of both with other writers – it remains almost impossible to absolutely verify which of them wrote what. Some of the most successful and notorious serials published by Lloyd include: *Mary Bateman, the Yorkshire Witch* (1840), *Adeline, or, The Grave of the Forsaken* (1840-41), *The Death Grasp, or, A Father's Curse* (1841), *Vileroy, or, The Horrors of Zindorf Castle* (1841-42), *Ada, The Betrayed, or, The Murder at the Old Smithy* (1842), *Almira's Curse, or, The Black Tower of Bransdorf* (1842), *The Maniac Father, or, The Victim of Seduction* (1842), *The Black Monk, or, The Secret of the Grey Turret* (1843-44), *The Lady in Black, or, The Wanderer of the Tombs* (1844), *The Black Mantle, or, The Murder at the Old Ferry* (1845-46), *Newgate, A Romance* (1845-47), *Varney the Vampire, or,*

The Feast of Blood (1845-47), *The Death Ship; or, The Pirate's Bride and the Maniac of the Deep* (1846), *The Black Pirate, or, The Phantom Ship* (1846), and *The String of Pearls, or, The Barber of Fleet Street* (1846-47).

Other notable penny publishers were the aforementioned George Purkess, the aforementioned William Strange (whose *Penny Story-Teller* was launched in 1832), the aforementioned William Dugdale, the aforementioned George Drake, Thomas White, John Thomas Dicks (*Reynolds's Miscellany*), George Biggs (*The Family Herald*), Henry Lea, William Caffyn, George Vickers (*London Journal*), William Clarke, and Benjamin Davy Cousins (*The London Pioneer, The London Entertaining Magazine*). They, and a host of smaller presses, were responsible for thousands of penny serials and articles throughout the 1840s, ranging from Thomas Frost's *Alice Leighton, or, The Murder at the Druids' Stones* (Caffyn, 1848) and Eugène Sue's "uncensored" *Mysteries Of Paris* (Dugdale, 1844) to more obscure items such as *The Old Tar And The Vampire* (1843), *The Mysteries Of Bedlam* (1847), or *The Mysteries Of The Dissecting-Room* (1846, complete with horrific images of human evisceration and dismemberment). One of Lloyd's most successful rivals, both as an author and later as an editor and publisher, was G.W.M. Reynolds, whose grim 1845 serial *Mysteries Of London* (inspired by Eugène Sue) was immensely popular, selling many thousands of copies per week; in 1846 Reynolds started his own journal, *Reynolds' Miscellany*, launched with a new serial shocker by Reynolds himself, *Wagner The Wehr-Wolf*.

But by the 1850s, the golden age of the penny bloods was waning; the reading public seemingly grew tired of horror and gore, and the most popular new serials were those featuring dashing highwaymen, outlaws, and other romantic outsiders; such titles as *The Black Mask, or, the Mysterious Robber* (1850), *Black Bess, or, The Knight of the Road* (1861), or *Starlight Nell! Queen of the Highwaymen, and The Red Riders of Hounslow Heath* (1865) were exemplars of a new genre, the "penny dreadful". This trend increasingly caused penny weeklies to be aimed at a younger readership, and juvenile anti-heroes such as burglar *Charley Wag, The New Jack Sheppard* (1860) were at the vanguard of a new "Wild Boys" genre, of which the early classics include *Wild Boys of London,* or *The Children Of The Night* and *The Wild Boys of Paris, or The Secrets of the Vaults of Death* (both 1866). (These would later prove a seminal influence on the 20th century author William S. Burroughs, who viewed his own work as very much in the tradition of criminal and outsider literature.)

Inevitably, these penny dreadfuls were blamed for problems of delinquency, and in time would succumb to changing social and moral attitudes, being reviled by public and police alike, and by the 1870s the penny market was overtaken by sanitised boys' adventure papers. But the thirst for gore and sadism remained in some quarters, if driven underground, and would continue to be sated, especially through the importing and reprinting of so-called "dime novels" from the USA. The equivalent of England's penny bloods, these were mostly Western adventure but contained high levels of bloody violence and cruelty; the following example comes from a story entitled *Wild Ivan or, The Brotherhood Of Death* (originally published in 1878), re-published in London by the Aldine Publishing Company and drawing particular criticism:

"And I'll murder you by inches!" hissed the colonel, savagely, bending over the helpless girl, and glaring at her with the ferocity of some enraged beast. "I'll have you cut to pieces and strung on a rope for public exhibition before you shall cheat me out of that treasure!"

"You may do all of that and more!" replied Red Kit's girl firmly, "but I shall never – never – never tell you, nor any of your band, where to find the treasure!"

"We'll see!" said Blood grimly, straightening up - "we'll see. Blue Bob, you generally are a pretty fair carver, and carry sharp tools. Cut off the little finger of that girl's left hand!"

As this order came from the chief's lips, all eyes were centred upon Blue Bob. He was known to be a cruel, heartless instrument of torture in the hands of the Brotherhood, and was never known to shirk a duty. But the old man hesitated now, and his hand sought his belt slowly and reluctantly.

"Go on, you old devil!" yelled Colonel Bill, grasping a revolver from Sandusky's belt, and cocking it, "go on, or I'll bore a hole through your thick skull, and throw you into yonder stream!"

Apparently frightened at his superior's harsh language, Blue Bob crawled forward and dropped upon his knees by the side of the fair prisoner.

"Off with the little finger of her left hand!" repeated the colonel, sharply. "no flinching, you old buzzard but off with it, I say!"

Blue Bob bent forward, and then there was a piercing shriek of pain, a grating, crunching sound, after which the old ruffian leaped to his feet, holding aloft a severed white finger from Alice La Rue's hand.

"Good! Now, will you tell us the hiding-place of the treasure?" demanded Colonel Bill, with a grin of exultance.

"No! no!" almost screamed the girl, her blue eyes flashing darkly. "You can cut off every finger I have, and then my head, but I'll not tell!"

"We'll see you young she-cat – we'll see about that. I've handled worse cases than that. You, Blue Bob, cut off and unjoint her foot at the ankle – the left foot!'

A murmur of horror escaped the outlaws' lips. This was even beyond their limit to horror.

Blue Bob knelt again, knife in hand, and was preparing for the terrible deed, when suddenly the whole heavens were illuminated with a blaze of fire, there was a frightful clap of thunder, and a fresh deluge of rain.

Involuntarily the ruffian started forward with a cry of alarm, for they saw Colonel Blood totter away and fall in a heap upon the bank of the stream, blood streaming from a hole in his forehead.

And ere they could reach him the flood with restless fury had swept his corpse away.

"Heaven's hand!" a wild voice cried, and turning, the startled ruffians beheld a youthful figure standing in the light of their camp-fire. "Such is the vengeance He had meted out to your captain, with His fiery hand."

The present collection, which focuses on the "golden age" of the penny bloods, starts with a selection of gruesome true crime stories from *The Tell-Tale*, *The Terrific Register*, and *The Calendar Of Horrors*; the first of these, *Horrible Murder And Human Pie-Makers*, published in 1825 in *The Tell-Tale*, may be the piece which inspired the creation of Sweeney Todd, cut-throat barber of Fleet Street, who later featured in Edward Lloyd's celebrated serial *The String Of Pearls*. Another case history included here, that of the Scottish cannibal-killer Sawney Beane, would (much) later provide the basis for Wes Craven's exploitation-horror movie *The Hills Have Eyes* (1977).

Part II of this anthology presents a selection of episodes from some of the best-written penny serials, starting with the aforementioned *Skeleton Count*, believed to have been written by Elizabeth Caroline Grey, who later became secretary to Edward Lloyd and contributed to several of his serials, possibly including *Vileroy, or, The Horrors of Zindorf Castle*. The "Vampire Bride" episode of *The Skeleton Count* reproduced here stands as one of the earliest examples of vampire fiction, and perhaps the first ever written by a woman. The two episodes from *Vileroy* next reproduced are typical of the sub-gothic romance; variously attributed to Grey, Prest and Rymer, *Vileroy* is an epic of midnight murder, ghosts, skeletons, dungeons, and females in distress. Much more horrific was *Varney The Vampire*, again attributed to either Prest or (more likely) Rymer; streaked through with gore and passages of pulp poetry, *Varney* ran for over 100 episodes and remains probably the second most famous (after *Dracula*) of all epic vampire tales. The four episodes reproduced here feature elements of the vampire attack, vampire resurrection, and vampire-hunting.

The next three serials represented are somewhat different; moving away from the gothic and the supernatural, they feature horror of a different kind – the horror of everyday life in the poorest, most crime-infested quarters of London. Published by George Vickers in 4 52-part volumes, *The Mysteries Of London* was partly a plea for social reform by its author G.W.M. Reynolds, a committed Chartist. The four episodes here reproduced vividly convey the horrors of child slavery, grave-robbing, and execution. Published a year later, Edward Lloyd's *The String Of Pearls* gave us one of literature's most enduring villains, Sweeney Todd, the demon barber who murders and robs his victims before having their corpses turned into meat pies, thereby making unwittingly cannibals of half the population of East London. Again attributed to Prest and Rymer, this is another epic of realistic horrors, complete with scenes in the madhouse, and shot through with wicked black humour. Another Lloyd publication by Prest or Rymer was *Newgate, A Romance*; the story concerns a man morbidly obsessed with the infamous prison, and its grotesque opening sequences, reproduced next in this section, involve a crippled dwarf beggar and an infernal descent into a butcher's basement.

The final serial featured is this section is G.W.M. Reynolds' *Wagner The Wehr-Wolf*, a return to the supernatural milieu of *Varney*. As in *The Skeleton Count*, the story concerns an old man who is granted youth in a pact with the Devil, but must pay with a nightly transformation into a creature of horror. Reynolds, who also wrote a serial version of *Faust*, created many powerful sequences for *Wagner*; those included here feature Wagner's initial encounter with Satan, a murderous nocturnal rampage, and an atmospheric episode of a young woman condemned to a subterranean cell of penitent, self-flagellating nuns.

Part III closes this anthology with two self-contained short stories of the supernatural; *The Demon Of The Hartz*, attributed to Thomas Peckett Prest, first appeared in *Legends Of Terror* (1826) and must be one of his earliest published works – a tale set in German mountains haunted by witchcraft and demons, an evocation of ancient legends, and a warning to the greedy. *The Rosicrucian*, by Edwin F. Roberts, was first published in *Reynolds' Miscellany* around 1848. Roberts, who also wrote tales such as *The Vampyre's Bride*, was one of George Reynolds' main staff writers, and an expert on the occult. *The Rosicrucian* is a tale of the Illuminati, resonant with elements of alchemy, demonology, and cosmic horror.

PART I
THE CRIMINAL ANNALS

HORRIBLE MURDER
AND HUMAN PIE-MAKERS

In the Rue-de-la-Harpe, which is a long dismal ancient street in the faubourg of St Marcell, is a space or gap in the line of building upon which formerly stood two dwelling-houses, instead of which stands now a melancholy memorial, signifying, that upon this spot no human habitation shall ever be erected, no human being ever must reside!

Curiosity will, of course, be greatly excited to ascertain what it was that rendered this devoted spot so obnoxious to humanity, and yet so interesting to history.

Two attached and opulent neighbours, residing in some province, not very remote from the French capital, having occasion to go to town on certain money transactions, agreed to travel thence and to return together, which was to be done with as much expedition as possible. They were on foot, a very common way even at present, for persons of much respectability to travel in France, and were attended, as most pedestrians are, by a faithful dog.

Upon their arrival at the Rue-de-la-Harpe, they stepped into the shop of a *peruquier* to be shaved, before they would proceed to business, or enter into the more fashionable streets. So limited was their time, and peremptory was their return, that the first man who was shaved, proposed to his companion, that while he was undergoing the operation of the razor, he who was already shaven would run and execute a small commission in the neighbourhood, promising that he would be back before the other was ready to move. For this purpose he left the shop of the barber.

On returning, to his great surprise and vexation, he was informed that his friend was gone; but as the dog, which was the dog of the absentee, was sitting outside of the door, the other presumed he was only gone out for the moment, perhaps in pursuit of him; so expecting him back every moment, he chatted to the barber whilst he waited his return.

Such a considerable time elapsed that the stranger now became quite impatient, he went in and out, up and down the street, still the dog remained stationed at the door. "Did he leave no message?" "No"; all the barber knew was, that when he was shaved he went away. "It was certainly very odd."

The dog remaining stationed at the door was to the traveller conclusive evidence that his master was not far off; he went in and out, up and down the street again. Still no signs of him whatever.

Impatience now became alarm; alarm became sympathetic. The poor animal exhibited marks of restlessness in yelps and in howlings, which so affected the sensibility of the stranger, that he threw out some insinuations not much to the credit of the barber, who indignantly ordered him to quit his boutique.

Upon quitting the shop he found it impossible to remove the dog from the door. No whistling, no calling, no patting would do, stir he would not.

In his agony, the afflicted man raised a crowd about the door, to whom he told his lamentable story. The dog became an object of universal interest, and of close attention. He shivered and he howled, but no seduction, no caressing, no experiment, could make him desert his post.

By some of the populace it was proposed to send for the police, by others it was proposed a remedy more summary, namely to force in and search the house, which was immediately done. The crowd burst in, every apartment was searched, but in vain. There was no trace whatever of the countryman.

During this investigation, the dog still remained sentinel at the shop-door, which was bolted within to keep out the crowd, which was immense outside.

After a fruitless search and much altercation, the barber, who had prevailed upon those who had forced in to quit his house, came to the door, and was haranguing the populace, declaring most solemnly his innocence, when the dog suddenly sprang upon him, flew at his throat in such a state of terrific exasperation, that his victim fainted, and was with the utmost difficulty rescued from being torn to pieces. The dog seemed to be in a state of intellectual agony and fury.

It was now proposed to give the animal his way, to see what course he would pursue. The moment he was let loose, he flew through the shop, darted down-stairs into a dark cellar, where he set up the most dismal howlings and lamentations.

Lights being procured, an aperture was discovered in the wall communicating to the next house, which was immediately surrounded, in the cellar whereof was found the body of the unfortunate man who had been missing. The person who kept this shop was a *patissier*.

It is unnecessary to say that those miscreants were brought to trial and executed. The facts that appeared upon their trial, and afterwards upon confession, were these:

Those incautious travellers, whilst in the shop of this fiend, unhappily talked of the money they had about them, and the wretch, who was a robber and murderer by profession, as soon as the one turned his back, drew his razor across the throat of the other and plundered him.

The remainder of the story is almost too horrible for human ears, but is not upon that account the less credible.

The pastry-cook, whose shop was so remarkable for savoury patties that they were sent for to the Rue-de-la Harpe from the most distant parts of Paris, was the partner of this *peruquier*, and those who were murdered by the razor of the one were concealed by the knife of the other in those very identical patties, by which, independently of his partnership in those frequent robberies, he had made a fortune.

This case was of so terrific a nature, it was made part of the sentence of the law, that besides the execution of the monsters upon the rack, the houses in which they perpetrated those infernal deeds, should be pulled down, and that the spot on which they stood should be marked out to posterity with horror and execration.

THE HORRIBLE MURDER
OF A CHILD BY STARVATION

The annals of crime scarcely furnish a more diabolical instance of cruelty than the one we are about to record; but the circumstances of the murder are eclipsed, in the point of hardened depravity, by the means taken to conceal it.

In July, 1762, Sarah Metyard and Sarah Morgan Metyard, mother and daughter, were placed at the bar of the Old Bailey for the murder of Ann Nayler, a girl, thirteen years of age, by shutting up and confining her, and starving her to death. There was also a second indictment for the murder of Mary Nayler, her sister, aged eight years. The unfortunate child (Ann) it appeared, had been apprenticed to the elder prisoner, and it was principally on the evidence of her own apprentices that she and her daughters were convicted. They deposed that about Michaelmas, 1758, Ann Nayler attempted to escape, she was used so ill; being frequently beaten with a thick walking-stick and a hearth- broom, and made to go without her victuals. The day she endeavoured to run away, a milkman who served the family stopped her, as she was running from the door, and brought her back to the prisoners. The daughter dragged her up stairs, and while the mother held her head, beat her cruelly with a broomstick. She was then tied up with a rope round her waist, and her hands fastened behind, so that she could neither sit nor lie, and in this position she remained for three days, without food. During this period she never spoke, but used to stand and groan. At the end of the three days, the witness observed that she did not move; she hung double; and when this was mentioned to the daughter, she said she'd make her move. She ran up stairs, and struck her with a shoe, but there was no animation in her. The mother came up, laid the child across her lap, and sent one of the girls for some drops. The girls were ordered down stairs, and the unhappy victim was never afterwards seen by them. In the order to remove the suspicion of her death from the minds of the apprentices, by leading them to imagine she had made her escape, the old woman two days after this left the garret door open, and the street door ajar, and sent one of the girls up stairs to tell Nayler to come down to dinner. The girl returned with the intelligence of the door being open, and Nayler missing. The old woman made answer, 'She is run away. I suppose she ran away while we were at dinner.' The girl replied, 'Then she has left her shoes behind her.' 'O!' returned the other, 'she would not stay for her shoes.'

Richard Rooker deposed that he lived in the prisoner's house about three months, which was long since the child had been missing. He observed the children were very ill used, and had very little food. When they had any, they were not allowed more than five minutes to eat it. The old woman's disposition was so violent that he was obliged to remove; and out of compassion to the daughter, who was repeatedly beaten by her, he took her into his service. The mother, however, would not suffer her to remain in peace. She came almost every day, insulting the witness and the daughter. On one occasion he heard the cry of murder; and going into a little room, he found the girl in agonies, struggling with the old woman. She had driven her up into a corner, and had got a sharp-pointed knife in her hand, with which she was attempting to stab her. During the altercation he heard the daughter say to the mother: 'Mother, mother, remember the gully-hole.' Some time after, he questioned the girl as to the meaning of those words, when with great reluctance she told him that the child and her sister had both been starved to death. That a few days after Ann Nayler's death, the body was carried up into a garret, and locked up into a box, where it was kept upwards of two months till it became putrefied, and maggots came from her. The mother then took it out of this box, cut it into pieces, cut off the arms and legs, and burnt one of the hands in the fire, cursing her that the bones were so long consuming! Saying the fire told no tales. Then she tied the body and head in a brown cloth, and the other parts in another, being part of the bed-furniture. She carried them to Chick Lane gully-hole, and threw them in. Her mother told her that, as she was coming back, she saw one Mr Ineh, who kept a public house near Temple Bar, who cried out, 'what a stink there is!' to which she replied, that he had it all to himself, for she smelt none. She called for some brandy and went away. In consequence of this confession, Rooker wrote a letter to the officers of the parish where he dwelt, acquainting them with the particulars.

Thomas Lovegrove, overseer of St Andrew's, deposed that on the 12th of December, at near twelve at night the constable came to him with two watchmen, and told him there were parts of a human body lying at the gully-hole in Chick Lane. He went with them to the spot, and the smell of the body was so offensive, that the watchmen were unwilling to remove it. It was at length taken to the work-house; the parts were washed, and laid upon a board; a coroner's inquest set upon it, and returned a verdict of wilful murder. In the meantime, in consequence of Rooker's letter, the mother and daughter were apprehended.

Some other witnesses were examined, who corroborated the essential parts of the above evidence. The mother, when asked for her defence, told a lame story of the girls running away, and called one or two witnesses to prove that she used her apprentices well, and gave them sufficient food, but in this they failed. One of them said he had he had never been in her house at meal-times, and never saw the children have any. He described the place in which they worked to be a little slip room, two yards wide at the widest part, and tapering at the end.

The daughter denied all participation in the murder excepting the concealment; and threw all her odium on her mother. 'When the girl was dead,' she said, 'I desired my mother to apply to the parish to have her buried. She said I was a fool, for if she did, every body would see the girl had been starved; and if the girls were asked, they could tell how long she went without victuals. I then asked her to get the other girls not to say how long she had been kept without food: but this, she replied, would be useless, as it would be discovered on opening the body. She told me if I would stay with her 'till she was out of danger, I should go to service. When I thought she was out of danger I begged to go to service, as she proposed. She said, no, I should not; I should with her while she was in the house. She said I might and be damned; for if I did, she would swear I killed and that she secreted my crimes. The body was never buried. She wanted me one night to help her in dividing the body in pieces, and said I need not be afraid of her now she was dead, for she would not bite me. This was two or three months after the girl died. I told her, indeed I could not. I was then with her up in the room; I offered to go out; but she told me I must help her. I got out of the room; and she caught hold of my clothes. I cried. She said, what would the girls think, seeing me cry so? How could I be such a cruel brute as to leave her? I told her she had brought it on herself, and must get out of it how she could. After that, she told me she had done the limbs up in one bundle, and tied the body and the head up in another. She tried to take the head off, but could not. She brought them down stairs, and first took the limbs out, and carried them to the gully-hold in Chick-lane. She said she tried to fling them over the wall, but could not. Then she came and took the other bundle, which she said she carried to the same place, and found the other parts lying there. One night, after the children were gone to bed, she brought down the hand which had a stump finger, which she said she would make away with in the fire, because "the fire concealed every thing".'

Here the elder prisoner interrupted her daughter, by saying it was all false; and that if she had burnt any part, she might as easily have burnt it all. To which the other replied, 'that she said she would destroy it all by fire, but it would make a smell, and alarm the neighbours.' The daughter called a few witnesses to character; but both prisoners were found guilty. 'Death.'

The interval between their condemnation and execution was spent in mutual recrimination. When they were visited in their cell, no pen can describe the anguish of soul and horror visible in both their countenances. Both equally persisted in denying the guilt of the murder; but the daughter, in the vigour of youth, was most averse to die, to avoid which she had pleaded most pathetically for a little respite, and after this a legal plea of pregnancy had been set aside by a jury of matrons. The whole night previous to their execution, the mother had continued in a fit, speechless, and without any motion, except strong convulsions, which were ascribed to her long and obdurate fasting, with a view to destroying herself before execution. But being put into the cart, the mother was laid along at the bottom, in a state of insensibility, and when they arrived at Tyburn, she continued in a fit, scarcely seeming to breathe or move, except now and then with a convulsive twitch, her breast appearing greatly swelled, and heaving. She was obliged to be supported till she was turned off. The daughter still persisted in her innocence of all but the concealment, and added that she died a martyr in her innocence.

THE MONSTER OF SCOTLAND

Sawney Beane was born in the county of East Lothian, about eight miles east of Edinburgh, in the reign of James VI. His father was a hedger and ditcher, and brought up his son to that same laborious employment. Naturally idle and vicious, he abandoned that place, along with a young woman equally idle and profligate, and they retired to the deserts of Galloway, and took up their habitation by the sea side. The place which Sawney and his wife selected for their dwelling, was a cave of about a mile in length, and of considerable breadth; so near the sea that the tide often penetrated into the cave above two hundred yards. The entry had many intricate windings and turnings which led to the extremity of the subterraneous dwelling, which was literally 'the habitation of horrible cruelty'.

Sawney and his wife took shelter in this cave, and commenced their depredations. To prevent the possibility of detection, they murdered every person that they robbed. Destitute also of the means of obtaining any other food, they resolved to live upon human flesh. Accordingly, when they had murdered any man, woman, or child, they carried them to their den, quartered them, salted and pickled the members, and dried them for food. In this manner they lived, carrying on their depredations and murder, until they had eight sons and six daughters, eighteen grandsons and fourteen grand daughters, all the offspring of incest.

But, though they soon became numerous; yet, such was the multitude who fell into their hands, that they often had superabundance of provisions, and would, at a distance from their own habitation, throw legs and arms of dried human bodies into the sea by night. These were often thrown out by the tide, and taken up by the country people, to the great consternation and dismay of all the surrounding inhabitants. Nor could any discover what had befallen the many friends, relations, and neighbours who had unfortunately fallen into the hands of these merciless cannibals.

In proportion as Sawney's family increased, every one that was able, acted his part in their horrid assassinations. They would sometimes attack four or six men on foot, but never more than two upon horseback. To prevent the possibility of escape, they would lay an ambush in every direction, that if they escaped those who first attacked, they might be assailed with renewed fury by another party, and inevitably murdered. By this means, they always secured their prey, and prevented detection.

At last, however, the vast number who were slain, raised inhabitants of the country, and all the woods and lurking places were carefully searched; and though they passed the mouth of the horrible den, it was never once suspected that any human being resided there. In this state of uncertainty and suspense, concerning the authors of such frequent massacres, several innocent travellers and inn-keepers were taken up on suspicion; because, the persons who went missing had been last seen in their company, or had last resided heir houses. The effect of this well-meant and severe justice constrained the greater part of the inn-keeper in these parts, to abandon such employments, to the great inconvenience of those who travelled through that district.

Meanwhile, the country became depopulated, and the whole nation was surprised, how such numerous and unheard of villainies and cruelties could be perpetrated, without the least discovery of the abominable actors. At length, Providence interposed in the following manner to terminate the horrible scene: one evening, a man and his wife were riding home upon the same horse from a fair which had been held in the neighbourhood; and being attacked, he made the most vigorous resistance; unfortunately, however, his wife was dragged from behind him, carried to a little distance, and her entrails instantly taken out. Struck with grief and horror, the husband began to redouble his efforts to escape, and even trod some of them under his horse's feet. Fortunately for him, and for the inhabitants of that part of the country, in the meantime, twenty or thirty in a company came riding home from the same fair. Upon their approach, Sawney and his bloody crew fled into a thick wood, and hastened to their infernal den.

This man, who was the first that had ever escaped out of their hands, related to his neighbours what had happened, and shewed them the mangled body of his wife, which lay at a distance, the blood-thirsty wretches not having time to carry it along with them. They were all struck with astonishment and horror, took him with them to Glasgow, and reported the whole adventure to the chief magistrate of the city.

Upon this intelligence, he wrote to the king, informing him of the matter.

In a few days, his majesty in person, accompanied by four hundred men, went in quest of the perpetrators of such cruelties: the man who had his wife murdered before his eyes went as their guide, with a great number of bloodhounds, that no possible means might be left unattempted to discover the haunt of these execrable villains.

They searched the woods, traversed, and examined the sea-shore; but though they passed by the entrance of the cave, they had no suspicion that any creature resided in that dark and dismal abode. Fortunately, however, some of the blood-hounds entered the cave, raised up an uncommon barking and noise, indicating that they were about to seize their prey. The king and his men returned, but could scarcely conceive how any human being could reside in a place of utter darkness, and where the entrance was difficult and narrow, but as the blood-hounds increased in their vociferation, and refused to return, it occurred to all that the cave ought to be explored to the extremity. Accordingly a sufficient number of torches were provided. The hounds were permitted to pursue their course; a great number of men penetrated through all the intricacies of the path, and at length arrived at the private residence of these horrible cannibals.

They were followed by all the band, who were shocked to behold a sight unequalled in Scotland, if not in any part of the universe. Legs, arms, thighs, hands, and feet, of men, women, and children, were suspended in rows like dried beef. Some limbs and other members were soaked in pickle; while a great mass of money, both of gold and of silver, watches, rings, pistols, cloths, both woollen and linen, with an inconceivable quantity of other articles, were either thrown together in heaps, or suspended on the sides of the cave.

The whole cruel brutal family, to the number formerly mentioned, were seized; the human flesh buried in the sand of the sea-shore: the immense booty carried away, and the king marched to Edinburgh with the prisoners. This new and wretched spectacle attracted the attention of the inhabitants, who flocked from all quarters to see this bloody and unnatural family as they passed along, which had increased, in the space of twenty-five years, to the number of twenty-seven men, and twenty-one women. Arrived at the capital, they were all confined in the Tollbooth under a strong guard; they were next day conducted to the common place of execution in Leith Walk, and executed without any formal trial, it being deemed unnecessary to try those who were avowed enemies to all mankind, and of all social order.

The enormity of their crimes dictated the severity of their death. The men had their privy-members thrown in the fire, their hands and legs were severed from their bodies, and they were permitted to bleed to death. The wretched mother of the whole crew, the daughters and the grandchildren, after being spectators to the death of the men, were cast into three separate fires, and consumed to ashes. Nor did they, in general, display any signs of repentance or regret, but continued with their last breath, to pour forth the most dreadful curses and imprecations upon all around, and upon all those who were instrumental in bringing them to such well-merited punishment.

A MOST EXTRAORDINARY
AND DIABOLICAL MURDERER

Tom Austin was born of very respectable parents, who left him a farm worth about eighty pounds per annum, and he received with his wife eight hundred pounds per portion; but, instead of improving his farm by the cash which he had received, he spent it in every species of debauchery. Nor was it long before he was constrained to mortgage his own property.

Thus reduced to poverty, he betook himself to the highway, robbed Sir Zachary Wilmot, betwixt Wellington and Tauntondean, and barbarously murdered him for making some resistance. His booty was forty-six guineas, and a silver-hilted sword. His money being spent, he went to visit his uncle, who lived about a mile distant.

He found that his uncle was absent, and sitting down to keep the family company until his return, he shortly seized a hatchet, cleft the scull of his aunt, cut the throats of five small children, laid them all in heap, and robbed the house of sixty pounds. Returning to his wife, she observed some drops of blood on his neckcloth, and inquired the cause. He said, 'I will show you the manner of it,' and pulling out the bloody razor, cut her throat from ear to ear. Then he ripped up the bowels of his two children, the eldest of whom was not three years old. Scarcely had he completed these diabolical cruelties, when his uncle accidentally came to visit him, who, beholding the horrible sight, instantly seized the monster, and carried him before a magistrate, who committed him to Exeter jail. And if the feelings of the uncle were severely wounded at beholding the first deed of blood, how agonizing must they have been, when he went home, to behold all his own family weltering in their blood!

The mind shudders at the relation of such unheard-of barbarity, to the perpetration of which nothing appears to have excited the unnatural wretch, but the gratification of his own inhuman temper. Austin suffered death for his atrocities, and continued sullen and hardened in an extraordinary manner. When the halter was about his neck, the Ordinary asked him if he had any thing to say before he died.

'Nothing, only there's a woman yonder with some curds and whey, and I wish I could have a penny-worth of them before I am hanged, because I don't know when I shall see any again.'

MUTUAL MURDER

A man by the name of Hesketh, living at Hollingwood in Lancashire, was possessed of some property, and had several children (one only then living) by the deceased woman, who dwelt with him in the double capacity of house-keeper and mistress. Frequent quarrels happening between them, accompanied with blows, the neighbours seldom interfered, Hesketh's house standing at some distance from any other; and on the evening which produced this horrid catastrophe, although a great noise was heard by several persons passing, no one thought it proper to go in.

The next morning early, a stream of blood was observed running under the door; an alarm was given, and a passage forced into the kitchen, where Hesketh was extended near the fire-place, with a pair of tongs in his hand, much bent; and by the side of him his child, about three years old, wrapped in the shades of death, over which his arms were thrown, either for defence, or from an effort of affection. The woman was lying at a small distance from them, not quite dead, still grasping a poker; but she did not survive above a few minutes, thus drawing an impenetrable veil over the particulars of the transaction; little doubt, however, remains, that the man and woman had fought with the poker and tongs, till loss of blood exhausted their strength, that during the affray the child had continued for some time to scream, and was at length silenced by violence, as the poor innocent's tongue was nearly torn out, and its body much bruised.

THE UNNATURAL HUSBAND

In the year 1652, there lived in the island of Thanet, in Kent, Adam Sparckling, Esq. who had twenty years before married Katherine, the daughter of Sir Robert Leukner in Kent. This Sparckling had a large estate, but had greatly exhausted it; by drinking, gaming, whoring, etc. At last, some executions were issued out against him, and he was obliged to keep at home, and made his house his prison. This filled him full of rage, so that his wife was constrained many times to lock herself up from him.

On Saturday night, Dec. 15th, 1652, he came to a resolution of doing his wife some mischief, and being in his kitchen, about ten o'clock, he sent for one Martin, a poor old man, who was then in bed, to get up and come to him; so there were in the kitchen, Sparckling and his wife, one Ewell, and this Martin; Sparckling ordered Martin to bind Ewell's legs, which Ewell let him do, thinking it had been one of the odd whims of his master. Then he began to rave against his wife, who sat by him, and gave him no other than very good words; yet he drew his dagger, and struck her over the face with it, which she bore very patiently, though she was greatly hurt in the jaw. He still continued to rage at her, and she being very much frightened, got from her seat, and went towards the door; her husband followed her with a chopping knife in his hand, with which he struck at her wrist, and cut the bone asunder so that her hand hung down only by the sinews and skin. No help was near; Ewell was bound, and Martin being old and weak durst not interpose, fearing his own life, and only prayed his mistress to be quiet, hoping all would be well; and getting a napkin bound her hand with it.

After this, towards the morning, Sparckling still raging at his wife, he dashed her on the head with an iron cleaver. Upon her knees, she cried, and prayed God to pardon her own and her husband's sins, hoping God would forgive him as she did; but while she was thus praying, her bloody husband chopped her head in the middle, so that she fell down and instantly died. Then he killed six dogs, and threw four of them by his wife; and finding she was dead, he chopped her twice on the legs, compelled Martin to wash Ewell's face with her blood, after which he washed Martin's face, and his own with it.

He was soon after carried to Sandwich gaol, and tried at the Assizes for the said murder, found guilty, and was hanged on the 27th of April, 1653, dying very desperately, not suffering either minister or friend to speak to him after his condemnation.

SINGULAR DISCOVERY OF A MURDER

A woman living in St Neots, in 1740, returning from Elsworth, where she had been to receive a legacy of seventeen pounds that was left her, for fear of being robbed, tied it up in her hair. As she was going home, she overtook her next door neighbour, a butcher by trade, but who kept an inn, and who lived in good repute. The woman was glad to see him, and told him what she had been about. He asked her where she had concealed the money? She told him in her hair. The butcher finding a convenient opportunity, took her off her horse, and cut her head off, put it into his pack and rode off. A gentleman and his servant coming directly by, and seeing the body moving on the ground, ordered his servant to ride full speed forward and the first man he overtook to follow him wherever he went. The servant overtook the butcher not a mile off from the place, and asked what town that was before them? He told him St Neots. Says he, 'My master is just behind, and sent me forward to inquire for a good inn for a gentleman and his servant.' The murderer made answer that he kept a good inn, where they should be well used. The gentleman overtook them and went in with them and dismounted, bidding his servant take care of the horse whilst he would take a walk in the town and be back presently. He went to a constable and told him the whole affair, who said the butcher was a very honest man, and lived there a great many years in good reputation; but going back with the gentleman, and searching the pack, the constable, to his great surprise, found it was the head of his own wife! The murderer was sent to Huntingdon gaol, and shortly after executed.

THE LUNATICS

The following horrible occurrence took place in France a few years since at the House of Refuge for Lunatics, established at Charite-sur-Loire, in the department of the Nievre.

The Sieur Mangue, an apothecary of Sancerre, and the Sieur Leonard Pousscrean, a mason of Lucry de Bourg, had been placed in the house as insane patients. Among other proofs of madness, Mangue continually manifested a strong dislike of life, and endeavoured to prevail on the different inmates of the house to murder him. Unfortunately the proposal was made to Pousscrean, who laboured under a most incurable kind of insanity, and he willing undertook to perpetrate the horrid act.

The two lunatics immediately descended the stair-case leading to the kitchen, where they found a wooden horse. Mangue suddenly stopped, coolly took off his coat and cravat, turned down his shirt collar, and laid his head on the horse. They now wanted an instrument, and Mangue pointed to the kitchen chopper. Pousscrean ran to fetch it, returned, and finding his companion still in the same attitude, beheaded him with a single stroke, without any one having heard or observed the preparations for this horrible execution.

The event was, however, soon discovered by the loud fiendish laughter of the maniac, and by the bloody stains with which he was covered. On being questioned, he confessed without the least emotion, that he had yielded to the repeated entreaties of Mangue; that the latter had bequeathed to him a valuable document (which, on being produced, proved to be merely a piece of waste paper), and that he would perform the same office to any one who asked him politely! The maniac was afterwards ordered into solitary confinement, and in a short time died.

THE DEAD DEVOURED BY THE LIVING!

Instances of extraordinary and depraved appetites may be found in the writings both of ancient and modern authors; and there are also many cases on record, in which it will be seen that the horrible disease has reached to a most astonishing height; but not one of them can parallel the following disgusting narrative. We have some recollection of reading an account of a brutal Englishman, whose depraved and unnatural appetite could only be appeased by human flesh; but even this case was not attended with such diabolical circumstances of depravity and horror as will be found on perusal of the following:

The police of Paris a short time since apprehended and lodged in the Bicetre, a man named Antoine Langulet, who, they were given to understand, had been for a long time past in the habit of satisfying an unnatural appetite with food of the most repulsive and disgusting description. It appeared that animal substances in the highest state of putrefaction, and even the human body itself were regarded by this miserable wretch as very delicate *morceaux*. He usually stayed within doors the whole of the day till sunset, when he would walk forth, and parade up and down the dirtiest lanes and alleys of Paris; and noting where a piece of stinking carrion lay floating in the kennel, he would return at midnight, and, seizing it, convey it to his lodgings, and feast on it for the next day's meal. In this manner he kept up his wretched existence for years, until, by a refinement in his appetite, he at length found his way to the burial grounds; and after many attempts (with some rude instrument his ingenuity had formed for that purpose) he at length succeeded in pulling out of the graves several of the bodies of the recently interred. His appetite was so ravenous that he would feast upon them on the spot, and covering the remains with mould, would return for several successive evenings to finish the repast, as he states he was at first fearful of being seen carrying anything from such a place as a cemetery. What is still more extraordinary he would feast himself upon the intestines in preference to any other part of the body; and when he had thus regaled himself, he would fill his pockets with as much as they would conveniently hold of this horrible material for a future meal.

At length he found this plan inconvenient, as it took up too much time; he therefore determined on running the risk of discovery, and conveyed his darling article of food to his lodging, which was a miserable hay loft. This he attempted, and actually conveyed, at several times, the whole of the body of a young female which had been entombed a week before. Here he was discovered regaling on this truly horrible repast; and the terrific appearance which the whole scene presented struck the beholders with unspeakable horror.

When interrogated on the subject of this dreadful depravity, he said that from a child he had always been fond of what other people denominated loathsome food, and then expressed his surprise and wonder that any one could attach the least blame to him for a taste so natural. Nor did he appear to consider that he had committed any crime in endeavouring to satisfy that appetite in the way he had done.

His answers to whatever questions were put to him were precise and rational, although there appeared at times a little incoherence in his manner. He acknowledged that he had sometimes felt the greatest inclination to devour children of a tender age, but that he never could summon sufficient courage to kill them. He has ever since been incarcerated in the prison at the Bicetre for fear of the consequences which might result from his horrible propensities.

The above report was communicated to the conductors of the Archives by Dr Berthollet, and every reliance may be placed on its authenticity.

This horrible account cannot possibly be equalled. We, however, present our readers with the following specimen of an unnatural appetite, which has been not unaptly termed by medical practitioners the 'Bulimis, or Canine Ravenous Fever', and the disease is always beyond the power of medicine to relieve in any way.

There was a Polish soldier, named Charles Domery, in the service of the French, on board the *Hoche* frigate, which was captured by the squadron under the command of Sir J. Borlace Warren, off Ireland, in 1799. Domery was 21 years of age, and stated that his father and brothers had been remarkable for their voracious appetites. He began when he was 13 years of age. He would devour raw and even live cats, rats, and dogs; besides bullock's liver, tallow candles, and the entrails of animals. One day (September 17, 1799), an experiment was made of how much this man could eat in one day. This experiment was made in the presence of Dr Johnson, a commissioner of sick and wounded seamen, Admiral Child, and Mr Forster, agents for prisoners at Liverpool, and several other gentlemen. He had breakfasted at four o'clock in the morning on four pounds of raw cow's udder; at half past nine o'clock there were set before him five pounds of raw beef and twelve tallow candles of one pound weight, together with one bottle of porter; these he finished by half past ten o'clock. At one o'clock there were put before him five pounds more of beef, one pound of candles, and three bottles of porter. He was then locked up in the room, and sentries were placed at the windows to prevent his throwing away any of his provisions. At two o'clock he had nearly finished the whole of his candles, and great part of the beef. At a quarter past six he had devoured the whole, and declared he could have ate more; but the prisoners on the outside having told him that experiments were being made upon him, he began to be alarmed. Moreover, the day was hot, and he had not had his usual exercise in the yard. The whole of what he had consumed in the course of the day amounted to – raw cow's udder, 4lb.; raw beef, 10lb.; candles, 2lb. – total, 16lb.; besides five bottles of porter. The eagerness with which this man attacked his beef when his stomach was not gorged, resembled the voracity of a hungry wolf; he would tear off large pieces with his teeth, roll them about his mouth, and then gulp them down. When his throat became dry, from continued exercise, he would lubricate it by stripping the grease off a candle between his teeth; and then wrapping up the wick like a ball, would send it after the other part at a swallow. He would make shift to dine on immense quantities of raw potatoes or turnips; but by choice would never taste bread or vegetables. He was in every respect healthy; six feet three inches high, of a pale complexion, grey eyes, long brown hair, well made, but thin; his countenance rather pleasant, and he was good tempered. His perspirations were profuse, to which Dr Johnson, and other medical men, have ascribed the rapid dissipation of the ingesta, and his incessant craving for fresh supplies of food.

THE DEAD ALIVE;
OR, THE MENDICANT ROBBER OF ORLEANS

In 1747, a man was broke alive upon the wheel at Orleans, for a highway robbery, and not having friends to take care of his body, when the executioner concluded he was dead, he gave him to the surgeon, who had him carried to his anatomical theatre, as a subject to lecture on. The thighs, legs, and arms of this unhappy wretch had been broken; yet, on the surgeon's coming to examine him, he found life reviving, and by the application of proper cordials, he was soon brought to his speech.

The surgeon and his pupils, moved by the sufferings and solicitation of the robber, determined on attempting his cure; but he was so mangled that his two thighs and one of his arms were amputated. Notwithstanding this mutilation and loss of blood, he recovered, and in this situation the surgeon, by his own desire, had him conveyed in a cart fifty leagues from Orleans, where, as he said, he intended to gain his livelihood by begging.

His situation was on the road side, close by a wood, and his deplorable condition excited compassion from all who saw him. In his youth he had served in the army, and he now passed for a soldier, who had lost his limbs by a cannon shot.

A drover returning from market, where he had been selling cattle, was solicited by the robber for charity, and being moved by compassion, threw him a piece of silver. 'Alas,' said the robber, 'I cannot reach it – you see I have neither arms nor legs,' (for he had concealed his arm which had been preserved behind his back) 'so for the sake of heaven put your charitable donation into my pouch.'

The drover approached him, and as he stooped to reach up the money, the sun being shining, he saw a shadow on the ground which caused him to look up, when he perceived the arm of the beggar elevated over his head, and his hand grasping a short iron bar. He arrested the blow in its descent, and seizing the robber, carried him to his cart, into which having thrown him, he drove off to the next town, which was very near, and brought him prisoner before a magistrate.

On searching him a whistle was found in his pocket, which naturally induced a suspicion that he had accomplices in the wood; the magistrate, therefore, instantly ordered a guard to the place where the robber had been seized, and they arrived there within half an hour after the murder of the drover had been attempted.

The guard having concealed themselves behind different trees, the whistle was blown, the sound of which was remarkably shrill and loud: and another whistle was heard from under ground, three men at the same instant rising from the midst of a bushy clump of brambles, and other dwarf shrubs. The soldiers fired on them, and they fell. The bushes were searched, and a descent discovered into a cave. Here were found three young girls and a boy. The girls were kept for the offices of servants, and purposes of lust; the boy, scarcely twelve years of age, was son to one of the robbers. The girls in giving evidence deposed, that they had lived nearly three years in the cave, had been carried there by force from the high road, having never seen daylight from the time of their captivity; that dead bodies were frequently carried into the cave, stripped and buried; and that the old soldier was carried out every dry day, and sat by the road side for two or three hours.

On this evidence the murdering mendicant was condemned to suffer a second execution on the wheel. As but one arm remained, it was to be broken by several strokes, in several places, and the *coup de grace* being denied, he lived in torture nearly five days. When dead, his body was burnt to ashes, and strewed before the winds of heaven.

PART II
THE SERIALS

THE SKELETON COUNT

THE VAMPIRE BRIDE

Count Rodolph, after his impious compact with the prince of darkness, ceased to study alchemy or to search after the elixir of life, for not only was a long lease of life assured him by the demon, but the same authority had declared such pursuits to be vain and delusive. But he still dabbled in the occult sciences of magic and astrology, and frequently passed day after day in fruitless speculation, concerning the origin of matter, and the nature of the soul. He studied the writings of Aristotle, Pliny, Lucretius, Josephus, lamblicus, Sprenger, Cardan, and the learned Michael Psellus; yet was he as far as ever from attaining a correct knowledge of the things he sought to unveil from the mystery which must ever envelope them. The reveries of the ancient philosophers, of the Gnostics and the Pneaumatologists, only served to plunge him into deeper doubt, and at length he determined to pass from speculation to experiment, and put his half-formed theories to the test of practice.

After keen study of the anatomy of the human frame, and many operations and experiments on the corpse of a malefactor who had been hanged for a robbery and murder, and which he stole from the gibbet in the dead of night, and conveyed to Ravensburg Castle, with the assistance of two wretches whom he had picked up at an obscure hostelry in the town of Heidelberg, he resolved to exhume the corpse of some one recently dead, and attempt its reanimation. The formula of the necromancers for raising the dead did not suffice for their restoration to life, but only for a temporary revivification; but in an old Greek manuscript, which he found in the library of the castle, was an account of how this restored animation might be sustained by means of a miraculous liquid, for the distillation of which a recipe was given.

Count Rodolph gathered the herbs at midnight, which the Greek manuscript prescribed and distilled from them a clear gold-coloured liquid of very little taste, but most fragrant odour, which he preserved in a phial. Having discovered that a peasant's daughter, a girl of singular beauty, and about sixteen years of age, had died suddenly, and was to be buried on the day following that on which he had prepared his marvellous restorative, he set out on that day to Heidelberg to obtain the assistance of the fellows who had aided him in removing the corpse of the malefactor from the gibbet, and then returned to Ravensburg Castle, to prepare for his strange experiment.

At the solemn hour of midnight he departed secretly from the castle by a door in the eastern tower, of which he retained the key in his own possession, and bent his step to the church-yard of the neighbouring village. It was a fine moonlight night, but all the rustic inhabitants were in the arms of Morpheus, the leaden-eyed god of sleep, and the violator of the sanctity of the grave gained the churchyard unperceived. He found his hired associates waiting for him in the shadow of the wall, which was easily scaled, and being provided with shovels and a sack to contain the corpse, they set to work immediately. The fresh broken earth was soon thrown off from the lid of the coffin, which the resurrectionists removed with a screw-driver, and then the dead was disclosed to their view.

The corpse of the young maiden was lifted from its narrow resting place, and raised in the arms of the ungodly wretches whom Rodolph had hired, who deposited the inanimate clay on the margin of the grave, which they hastily filled up, and then proceeded to enclose in the sack the lifeless remains of the beautiful peasant girl. Having removed every trace of the sacrilegious theft which they had committed, one of them took the sack on his shoulders, and when he was tired his comrade relieved him, and in this manner they reached the castle. Count Rodolph led the way up the narrow stairs which led to his study chamber in the eastern turret, and having deposited the corpse upon the floor, and received their stipulated reward, the two resurrectionists were glad to make a speedy exit from a place which popular rumour began to associate with deeds of darkness and horror.

Having lighted a spirit lamp, which cast a livid and flickering light upon the many strange and mysterious objects which that chamber contained, and made the pale countenance of the corpse appear more ghastly and horrible, Count Rodolph proceeded to denude the body of its grave-clothes, which he carefully concealed, lest the sight of them, when the young maiden returned to life might strike her with a sudden horror which might prove fatal to the complete success of his daring experiment. He then placed the corpse in the centre of a magic circle which he had previously drawn upon the floor of the study, and covered it with a sheet. He had purchased some ready-made female apparel in the town of Heidelberg, and these he placed on the table in readiness for the use of the young girl, whom he felt sanguine of resuscitating.

Bertha had been, as was evidenced by her stark and cold remains, a maiden of surpassing symmetry of form and loveliness of countenance; no painter or sculptor could have desired a finer study, no poet a more inspiring theme. As she lay stretched out upon the floor of the study she looked like some beautiful carving in alabaster, or rather like a waxen figure of most artistical contrivance. Her long black hair was shaded with a purile gloss like the plumage of the raven, and her features were of most exquisite proportion and arrangement. But now her angelic contenance was livid with the pallid hue of death, the iron impress of whose icy hand was visible in every lineament.

Count Rodoiph then took in his hand a magic wand, one end of which he placed on the breast of the corpse, and then proceeded to recite the cabalistic words by which necromancers call to life the slumbering tenants of the grave. When he had concluded the impious formula, an awful silence reigned in the turret, and he perceived the sheet gently agitated by the quivering of the limbs, which betokened returning animation. Then a shudder pervaded his frame in spite of himself, as he perceived the eyes of the corpse slowly open, and the dark dilated pupils fix their gaze on him with a strange and stolid glare.

Then the limbs moved, at first convulsively, but soon with a stronger and more natural motion, and then the young girl raised herself to a sitting posture on the floor of the study, and stared about her in a wild and strange manner, which made Rodolph fear that the object of his experiment would prove a wretched idiot or a raving lunatic.

But suddenly he bethought him of the restorative cordial, and snatching the phial from a shelf, he poured down the throat of the resuscitated maiden a considerable portion of the fragrant gold coloured fluid which it contained. Then a ray of that glorious intellect which allies man to the angels seemed to be infused into her mind, and beamed from her dark and lustrous eyes, which rested with a soft and tender expression on the handsome countenance of the young count. Her snowy bosom, from which the sheet had fallen when she rose from her recumbent position on the floor, heaved with the returning warmth of renewed life, and the Count of Ravensburg gazed upon her with mingled sensations of wonder and delight.

As the current of life was restored, and rushed along her veins with tingling warmth, the conscious blush of instinctive modesty mantled on her countenance, and drawing the sheet over her bosom, she rose to her feet, with her long black hair hanging about her shoulders, and her dark eyes cast upon the floor. Count Rodoiph then directed her attention to the clothing which he had provided, so sanguine of complete success had the daring experimentalist been, and then he withdrew from the study while the lovely object of his scientific care attired herself.

When the Count of Ravensburg returned to his study, Bertha was sitting before the fire, attired in the garments he had provided for her, and he thought that he had never beheld a more lovely specimen of her sex. She rose when he entered, and kissed his hand, as though he were a superior being, and would have remained standing, with head bowed upon her bosom, as if in the presence of a being of another world, had he not gently forced her to resume the seat from which she had risen, and inquired tenderly the state of her feelings upon a return to life so strange and wonderful. But he found that she retained no remembrance of a previous existence, and all her feelings were new and strange, like those of Eve on bursting into conscious life and being from the hand of the Omnipotent. In her mysterious passage from life to death, and from death to new life, she had lost all her previous ideas and convictions, all her experience of the past, all that she had ever acquired of knowledge; and had become a child of nature, simple and unsophisticated as a denizen of the woods, with all the keen perceptions and untrained instincts of the untutored savage.

The young girl had braided up her flowing tresses of glossy blackness, and on her cheeks dwelt colour that might test a painter's skill, so rich yet delicate its hue, like the rosette tinge of some rare exotic shell, or that which a rose would cast upon an alabaster column. The young count felt himself irresistibly attracted towards the maiden, whom his science had endued with such a mysterious and preternatural existence, and she, on her part, regarded the handsome Rodolph with the wild, yet tender passion of frail humanity, mingled with the gratitude and devotion which she deemed due to one who stood to her in the position of her creator.

Thus the feelings which had so rapidly sprung up in her heart towards the only being of whom she had any conception, partook of a nature of a religious idolatry, but mingled with the grosser feelings of earth, like those which agitated in the bosom of the vestal whose sons founded Rome, or the virgin of Shen-si who was chosen from among all the women of the celestial empire to become the mother of the incarnate Foh.

'Thou art gloriously beautiful, my Bertha!' exclaimed the enamoured count, pressing her in his arms. 'Say that thou wilt be mine and make me thy happy slave; thou should'st be loving as thou a loveable, beautiful child of mystery!'

'Love thee!' returned Bertha, a soft and tender expression dwelling in the clear depths of her dark eyes. 'I adore thee, my creator; my soul bows itself before thee, yet my heart leaps at thy glance, though I fear is presumptuous for the work of thy hands to look on thee with eyes love.'

'Sweet, ingenuous creature!' cried the Count of Ravensburg, kissing her coral lips and glowing cheeks. 'It is I who should worship thee! Thou art mine, Bertha, now and for ever. Henceforth I live only in thy smile!'

'For ever! Shall I remain with thee for ever? Oh, joy incomparabe! My heart's idol, I adore thee!' and the beautiful Bertha wound her white arms about his neck, and pressed her lips to his, for in the new existence which she now enjoyed her feelings knew no restraint, she yielded to every impulse of her ardent nature.

'Come, my Bertha,' said the enraptured Rodolph, 'this solitary turret must not be thy world; come with me, thy Rodolph, and be mistress of Ravensburg Castle, as thou art already of its owner's heart.'

Passing his arm around the taper waist of the mysterious maiden, Rodolph took up the lamp, and quitting the eastern turret, they proceeded with noiseless steps to his chamber, where the first faint blush of day witnessed the consummation of their desires, nor did the torch of Hymen burn less brightly because no priest blessed their nuptial couch.

The presence in Ravensburg Castle of this young girl, which Rodolph, with that contempt for the opinion of the world which usually marked his actions, took no pains to conceal, became the engrossing topic of conversation in the servants' hall throughout the day, and as Rodolph had never before indulged in any intrigue, either with the peasant girls of the neighbouring village or the courtezans of Heidelburg, the circumstance seemed the more remarkable. But the beautiful Bertha seemed quite unconscious of the equivocal nature of her position in reference to the young count, and though her views on human nature became every moment more enlarged with the sphere of her existence, she still regarded Rodolph as a being of superior mould.

When night again drew his sable mantle over the sleeping earth, Rodoiph and the mysterious Bertha sought their couch, and never had shone the inconstant moon on a pair so well matched as regarded physical beauty, or we may add as regarded their strange destiny – one gifted with almost superhuman powers of mind, yet in a few days to undergo so horrible a transformation, and far removed by that strange fate from ordinary mortals; the other endowed with such singular beauty yet doomed to the dreadful existence of one who had passed the boundaries of the grave, and returned to life!

With sonorous and solemn stroke the bell of the castle clock proclaimed the hour of midnight, and then Bertha slowly raised herself from her lover's body and slipping from the bed, attired herself in a half-unconscious state, and stole noiselessly from the room.

Her cheeks were pale, and her eyes had the wild and stolid glare which Rodliph had observed when she awakened from the slumber of he grave; she quitted the castle, and after gazing around her, as if uncertain which way to go, she proceeded towards the village.

She stopped opposite the nearest cottage, and then advanced to the window, and shook the shutters; the fastenings being insecure, they opened with little trouble, and a broken pane of glass enabled Bertha to introduce her hand, and remove the fastenings of the window. Then she cautiously opened the window, and entered the room – she ascended the stairs on tiptoe, and entered a chamber where a little girl was in bed and fast asleep. For a moment she shuddered violently, as if struggling to repress the horrible inclination which is the dread condition of a return to life after passing the portals of death, and then she bent her face down to the child's throat, her hot breath fanned its cheek, and the next moment her teeth punctured its tender skin, and she began to suck its blood to sustain her unnatural existence!

For such is the horrible destiny of the vampire race, of whom we have yet further mysteries and secrets to unfold; and such a being was she whom Count Rodolph had taken from the grave to his bed!

Presently the child awoke with a fearful scream, and its father, leaping from his bed in the next room, hurried to her succour, but Bertha rushed past him in the dark, and escaped from the house. The peasant found the little girl much frightened, and bleeding at the throat; but she had suffered no vital injury, and having ascertained this fact, he snatched up his match-lock, and hurried after the aggressor.

'A vampire!' exclaimed the peasant, turning pale with horror, as he distinctly saw, by the light of the moon, a young female hurrying from the village at a rapid pace.

The man gave chase to the flying Bertha, and gradually gaining ground, came within gun shot, just as she reached the shelving banks of the river, when he raised his weapon to his shoulder, and fired. The report echoed along the banks of the Rhine, and Bertha screamed as the ball penetrated her back, and tumbled headlong into the stream. The peasant hastened back to the village, satisfied that the horrible creature was no more, and the corpse of the vampire floated on the surface of the moonlit river.

The moon was that night at the full, and shed a flood of pearly light over the picturesque scenery of the Rhine, which, throughout its whole course, is a panorama of scenic beauty, every bend revealing some object interesting either for its historical reminiscences or legendary associations. There was the village, but now the scene of a horrible outrage – the castle, thrown into alternate light and shadow by the passing of the light fleecy clouds over the face of the moon – the town of Heidelberg, sloping from the Castle of the Palatine, and spanning the river with its noble bridge – and the Rhine, here shaded by the dark rocks which overhung the opposite bank, and there reflecting the silver light of the moon. The corpse of the vampire floated down the stream for some distance, and then it became arrested in its course by the bending of the river, and lay partly out of the water on the shelving bank.

And now commenced another scene of strange and startling interest – another phase in the fearful existence of the vampire bride! For as the beams of the full moon fell on the inanimate form of that being of mystery and fear, sensation seemed slowly to return, as when the magic spells of the Count of Ravensburg resuscitated her from the grave; her eyes opened, her bosom rose and fell with the warm pulsations of returning life; her limbs moved spasmodically, and then she rose from the bank, and shuddering at the recollection of what had occurred to her, she wrung the water from her saturated garments, and ran towards the castle at a pace accelerated by fear.

Having admitted herself into the castle, she sought the count's chamber with noiseless steps, and having taken off and concealed her wet clothes, she returned to his bed without his being aware that she had ever quitted it. The count was surprised to find that his mistress took no refreshment throughout the day, but he was led to consider it as one of the natural laws of her strange existence, and thought no more about it.

But in the village, the utmost excitement prevailed when it became known that the cottage of Herman Klaus had been visited by a vampire during the night, and his little daughter bitten by the horrible creature. All day long the cottage of the mysterious visitation was beset by the wondering villagers, who crossed themselves piously, and wondered who the vampire could have been, and the services of the priest were called into requisition to prevent the little blue-eyed Minna becoming a vampire after death, as is supposed to be the case with those who have the misfortune to be bitten by one of those horrible creatures, just as a person becomes mad after the bite of a mad dog or cat.

According to the terms of the compact which had been entered into between Count Rodolph and the demon, its conditions did not come into operation until seven days after the signing of the dreadful bond, and as day after day flew on, Rodolph dreaded the necessity of acquainting Bertha with the terrible transformation which he must rightly undergo. But he knew how impossible it would be to keep his hideous and appalling metamorphosis a secret from his mistress, and he reflected that if he made her the confidant of his terrible fate it could be the more likely to remain unknown to the rest of the world. He accordingly nerved his mind to the appalling revelation which he had to make, and on the seventh day after his compact with Lucifer, he disclosed to her his awful secret.

'Bertha,' said he, in a sad and solemn tone, 'I am about to entrust thee with a terrible secret; swear to me that thou wilt never divulge it.'

'I swear,' she replied.

'Know, then,' continued the count, lowering his voice to a hoarse whisper, 'that, by virtue of a compact with the infernal powers of evil and of darkness, I am endowed with a term of life and youth – amounting almost to the boon of immortality; but to this inestimable gift, there is a condition attached which commences this night, and which I almost tremble to impart to thee.'

'Fear not, my Rodolph!' exclaimed his beautiful mistress, twining her round white arms about his neck, 'thy Bertha can never love thee less, and her soul the rather clings to thee more intensely for the preternatural gift which links thy destiny more closely to my own. For mine, too, is a strange and fearful existence, which I owe to thee, and therefore shall I cling to thee the more fondly for the kindred doom which allies us each other while it lifts us far above ordinary mortals.'

'Then prepare thy ears for a dread revelation, Bertha,' returned the Count of Ravensburg. 'Each night of my future existence, at the hour of sunset, my doom divests me of my mortal shape, and I become a skeleton until sunrise on the morn ensuing. Now, thou knowest all, my Bertha, and be it thy care to prevent the dreadful secret from becoming known.'

'It shall, my brave Rodolph!' exclaimed Bertha, her eyes glittering with a strange expression, as she thought of the facility which her lover's strange doom would allow for her nocturnal absences from the castle. 'No eye but mine shall witness thy transformation, and I will watch over thee until thy return to thy natural shape.'

'Thanks, my Bertha!' returned Rodolph, embracing her. 'The hour draws nigh when I must relinquish for the night my mortal form; come, love, to our chamber, and see that no prying eye beholds the ghastly change.'

Bertha and her lover accordingly repaired to their chamber, and when the luminary of day sank below the horizon, leaving the traces of his splendour on the western sky, the Count Rodolph shrunk to a grisly skeleton, and fell upon the bed. Bertha shuddered as she witnessed the horrid transformation, and they lay down on the bed until midnight, the necessity of secrecy overcoming any repugnance she might otherwise have felt to the horrible contiguity of the skeleton, but when the castle clock proclaimed the hour of midnight with iron tongue, she rose from the bed, and locking the door of the chamber which contained so strange a guest, she stole from the castle to sate her unnatural appetite for human blood.

The moon rode high in the heavens on that night of unfathomable mystery and horror, and her silver beams shone through the chamber window of Theresa Delmar, one of the loveliest maidens in the village of Ravensburg, revealing a snowy neck, and a white and dimpled shoulder, shaded by the bright golden locks which strayed over the pillow. The maiden's blue eyes were concealed by their thin lids and their long silken fringes, and her snowy bosom gently rose and fell beneath the white coverlet as the thoughts which agitated her by day, mingled in her dreams at night. Silence reigned in the thatched cottage, and throughout the village was only occasionally broken by the barking of some watchful house-dog.

But soon after midnight the silence was broken by a slight noise at the chamber window as if someone was endeavouring to obtain an entrance, and the flood of moonlight which streamed upon the maiden's bed was obscured by the form of a woman standing on the windowsill. Still Theresa slumbered on, nor dreamed of peril so near, for the woman had succeeded in opening the window, and in another moment she stood within the room.

With slow and cautious step she softly approached the bed whereon the maiden reposed so calmly, little dreaming how a dread visitant was near her couch, and then she shuddered involuntarily as she bent over the sleeping girl, and her long dark ringlets mingled with the masses of golden hair which shaded the white shoulder, and the partially exposed bosom of Theresa Delmar. Her lips touched the young girl's neck, her sharp teeth punctured the white skin, and then she began to suck greedily, quaffing the vital fluid which flowed warm and quick in the maiden's veins, and sapping her life to maintain her own!

Still Theresa awoke not, for the puncture made in her throat by the teeth of the horrible creature was little larger than that which would he made by a leech, and the vampire sucked long and greedily, for her long abstinence from blood had sharpened her unnatural appetite. Suddenly Theresa awoke with a start, doubtless caused by some unpleasant transition in her dreams, but she did not immediately cry out, for she felt no pain, and as yet she was scarcely conscious of her danger. But in a few seconds she was thoroughly awake, and her surprise and horror may be more easily imagined than described, when she found bending over her, and sucking her blood, the horrible creature that had but a few nights previously attacked Minna Klaus, and which the child's father thought he had destroyed.

Spell-bound by the glittering eyes of the vampire, she lay without the power to scream, until the appalling horror of her situation became too great for endurance, her quivering nerves were strung to their utmost power of extension, and a wild shriek burst from her lips. Even then the horrible creature did not leave its hold, but continued to suck from her palpitating veins the crimson current of her life, until footsteps were heard hastily approaching the chamber, and the lovely Theresa, whose screams seemed to have broken the fascination which had bound her in its thrall, struggled so violently that Bertha was compelled to relinquish her horrid banquet. Springing to the window, she effected her escape, just as heavy blows resounded on the door of the chamber, and her affrighted victim sank insensible on the bed.

'What is the matter, Theresa? Open the door!' exclaimed her terrified parents; but they received no answer.

Then Delmar broke open the door, and he and his wife rushed into the room and found their daughter lying insensible on the bed, with spots of blood on her throat and bosom, and the window wide open.

'The vampire has come to life again, and has attacked our Theresa!' exclaimed her mother. 'See the blood-marks on her dear neck! Raise the village, Delmar, to pursue the monster.'

'Oh, dear! where am I? Has it gone, mother?' inquired Theresa, as she recovered from her swoon, and gazed in an affrighted manner round the room.

'Yes, it has gone now, dear,' said her mother. 'What was it like?'

'Aye, what was it like?' added old Delmar. 'Perhaps it was not the same one that neighbour Klaus shot at the other night.'

'Oh, yes! it was a young woman, and as much like Bertha Kurtel ever one pea was like another,' replied the young girl, shuddering.

'Holy virgin!' exclaimed her mother, crossing herself with a shudder. 'Bertha Kurtel a vampire, and returned from the grave to prey upon our Theresea! Oh, horrible!'

Delmar hurriedly dressed himself, and catching up an axe, he hastened to call up Klaus and others to pursue the vampire, and in few minutes the whole village was in commotion. About twenty men armed themselves with whatever weapon came first to hand, and followed the direction which the vampire had taken when chased by Herman Klaus on a former occasion. They searched every bush all round the village, to which they returned at sunrise without having found any trace of the object of their search. Delmar found his daughter somewhat faint from fright and loss of blood, but not otherwise injured by the vampire's attack. The greatest excitement prevailed in that usually quiet village, and all the morning, groups of men stood about the little street, or clustered round Delmar's cottage, conversing in low and mysterious whispers of the dreadful visitation which the village had a second time received.

'What a shocking thing it would be if a pretty girl like Theresa Delmar was to become a vampire when she dies,' observed one. 'And who knows what may happen now she has been bitten by one of those horrible creatures?'

'And poor little Minna Klaus,' said another.

'Ah, and we do not know how long the list may be if we do not put a stop to it,' added one of the rustic group. 'I have heard Father Ambrose say that they generally attack females and children.'

'Who can it be? That is what I want to know,' said old Klaus.

'Why, Theresa declares it was just like Bertha Kurtel,' returned another, shaking his voice to a whisper.

'Bertha Kurtel!' repeated a youth who had loved her who once bore that name. 'Bertha a vampire! Impossible.'

'It is easily ascertained,' observed the gruff voice of the village blacksmith. 'We have only to take up the coffin and see if she is in it, as she ought to be. If we do not find her we shall know what's o'clock.'

'If it was not for her parents' feelings I really should like to be satisfied whether it is Bertha,' remarked old Delmar.

'Feelings!' repeated the smith, in a surly tone. 'Have we not all got our feelings? Are we to have our wives and children attacked in this manner, and all turned into vampires, and let other people's fine feelings prevent us from having satisfaction for it?'

'There is something in that,' observed Delmar, scratching his head with an air of perplexity.

'I would make one if anybody else would go,' said Herman Klaus, after a pause.

'And I will be another,' exclaimed the smith, looking around him. Now who will go and have a peep in the churchyard to see whose coffin is empty?'

Several expressed themselves ready, and others following their example the smith proceeded to the churchyard, backed by about twenty of the most resolute of the villagers, to reenact the scene which had taken place there but a few nights since. On arriving at the churchyard the smith and another immediately set to work to throw the earth out of the grave, which was soon accomplished, and amid the most breathless silence the smith proceeded to remove the lid of the coffin.

'Look here, neighbours,' said he, turning pale in spite of himself. 'The lid has been removed, and the coffin is empty!'

'So it is!' exclaimed Herman Klaus.

'Then is it not plain that Bertha is the vampire – the horrible creature that sucked the blood of Theresa Delmar and little Minna Klaus?' said the smith, looking round upon the throng which had been swelled during the work of exhumation by idlers from the village.

'But where is she now? That is the question,' observed Herman Klaus.

'This must be investigated,' said the smith. 'We must keep watch for the vampire, and catch it; then we must either burn it, or drive a stake through the creature's body, for they say those are the only methods that will effectually fix a vampire.'

The wondering group of peasants returned to the village, and great was the grief of the Kurtels at the horrible discovery that their daughter had become a vampire, and the youth who had so loved Bertha in her human state became delirious on hearing the confirmation of the suspicion which Theresa's assertion had first excited. The ordinary occupations of the villagers were entirely neglected throughout the day, and nothing was talked of but vampires and wehr-wolves, and other human transformations more terrific and appalling than any recorded in the *Metamorphoses* of Ovid. Towards the evening the venerable seneschal of the Count of Ravensburg arrived in the village and had an interview with the Delmars, after which he visited the cottage of Herman Klaus, and a vague rumour spread like wildfire from house to house, to the effect that the vampire was an inmate of Ravensburg Castle.

The communication made by the seneschal to Delmar and Klaus was to the effect that, on the morning following the interment of Bertha Kurtel, a young female exactly resembling her in form, features, voice, and every individual peculiarity, had appeared in a mysterious manner at the castle, and had resided there ever since in the capacity of the count's mistress. No one knew who she was, where she came from, or how she obtained admission into the castle; and the occurrences in the village having reached the ears of the count's retainers and domestics, accompanied with the suspicion that the vampire was the revived Bertha Kurtel, the seneschal had hastened to the village to report his observations. The abstinence of the count's mistress from food was deemed corroborative of the suspicion that she was a vampire, and the seneschal's report caused the utmost excitement among the villagers. Symptoms of hostile intentions soon became visible, and in less than half an hour, more than a hundred men were proceeding in a disorderly manner towards the castle, armed with every imaginable weapon, and swearing to put an end to the vampire.

Count Rodolph and his beautiful mistress were sitting at a window which commanded a view of the road for some distance, the small white hand of Bertha locked in that of her lover, and whispering words of tenderness and love, when their attention was drawn to the disorderly mob approaching from the village.

'What can this mean?' said Rodolph, rising.

'Oh, this is what I have dreaded!' exclaimed Bertha, turning pale, and clasping her hands in a terrified manner: 'your studies have caused you to be suspected of necromancy, my Rodolph; they come to attack the castle.'

'I fear thou art right, dearest,' said the count: 'but we will give them a warm reception. Ho! a lawless mob menaces the castle with danger: make fast the gates; bar every door; bid my retainers man the battlements to repel the attack.'

'And sunset is approaching,' exclaimed Bertha, with a meaning glance at her lover.

'Do thou retire, sweet love, to thy chamber,' said Rodolph; 'fear not for me; I bear a charmed life, and neither sword nor shot will avail against it. If this lawless rabble be not dispersed when the dread moment comes all hope will be lost, and they shall behold the grisly change. Perhaps they may be struck with a sudden panic, and we may be enabled to fly into another country.'

Bertha retired after embracing the count, and shut herself up in her chamber. Preparations were immediately made to resist the attack of the insurgent villagers, who continued to advance upon the castle, yelling like savages, and breathing vengeance against the vampire mistress of Count Rodolph.

'Down with the vampire!' was the hoarse and sullen cry which rolled like distant thunder from a hundred throats, and then the mob drew up before the castle gates, and the smith struck them heavily with his ponderous hammer.

The count took an arquebus and fired at the mob, very few of whom were provided with fire-arms; one of the peasants was wounded, and with a shout of rage and defiance a volley of shot, arrows, and stones was directed against the beleaguered castle. The smith continued to batter away at the gate, aided by several stalwart fellows with axes, and though several of the mob were killed by the fire of the men-at-arms, those who were endeavouring to force the gate were protected by the overhanging battlements, and continued to ply their implements with unwearied energy.

Could Rodolph turned pale, and shuddered as he listened to the wild cries of the assailants, not from fear, for apart from his invulnerability he was inaccessible to that feeling, but from the horrible ideas engendered from these shouts, having reference to the beautiful Bertha Kurtel. Had her resuscitation from the grave endowed her with the horrible nature of the vampire? Could that lovely creature sustain her renewed existence with the blood of her former companions? Horrible! Yet, had she not hinted at something of the kind when he revealed to her the horrors of his own strange doom? It must be so, then; and he shuddered violently at the appalling idea.

'Down with the vampire!' was still the menacing cry which rose from the assailants, who at length succeeded in breaking down the gates, and rushed tumultuously into the court-yard, shouting and brandishing their weapons.

Undismayed by the fire from the battlements, they commenced an attack on the doors and windows of the castle, and now they were all crowded in the courtyard, Count Rodolph thought the moment favourable for a sally. Drawing his sword, and commanding a score of his armed retainers to follow him, he suddenly opened a door leading into the court-yard, and fell furiously on the flank of the assailants. For a moment they were thrown into confusion, but they quickly rallied, when Count Rodoiph and his little party were surrounded and compelled to act on the defensive. The ruddy beams of the setting sun were already purpling the distant hills when the peasants marched upon the castle, and as his broad disk sank below the horizon, the aspect of the Count of Ravensburg suddenly underwent a marvellous change, and much as the insurgents had wondered to see arrows glance off from his body, and their swords rebound as if their stroke fell on a giant oak, how much greater was their astonishment when they beheld him suddenly transformed into a fleshless skeleton!

'It is some devise of Satan! – he is a sorcerer!' cried the stalwart smith, brandishing his huge hammer. 'Come on, mates – down with the vampire!'

'Down with the vampire!' echoed from the mob, and the count's retainers giving way on all sides, as much appalled as the peasants at this horrible metamorphosis, the assailants rushed into the castle by the open door, and marched from room to room, looking in every closet and under every bed, while the terrified Bertha flew from one apartment to another, until she at length sought refuge in the highest apartment of the eastern turret, that chamber which had witnessed her return from death to her renewed state of strange and horrible existence. She had locked and bolted the door of the study, but what availed these obstacles against a furious mob, animated by their success in gaining the castle, and bent upon destruction and revenge? The door cracked, yielded, was forced open, and several men rushed into the little chamber.

'Here she is! – here is the vampire!' cried the foremost, and despite her piercing shrieks and earnest supplications for mercy, the wretched Bertha was dragged out of the study, with her long black hair hanging in wild disorder about her shoulders, and her beautiful countenance pale with overpowering terror.

'Mercy, indeed! What mercy can we feel for a vampire?' cried the peasants, and the terrified creature was dragged down the turret stairs by one or two of the boldest, for few would venture to come in contact with the dreaded being.

As they reached the foot of the stairs a volume of smoke rolled along the passage, and the crackling of burning wood told them that some of their companions had set fire to the castle.

'Now what shall we do with the vampire?' said her remorseless captors.

'Throw her into the Rhine!' suggested one.

'Tie her up and shoot at her!' said another.

'What will be the use of that?' objected a third. 'Nothing but fire or a sharp stake will destroy a vampire. Let us shut her up in the castle, and burn her to ashes!'

'Yes, yes! Burn the vampire!' shouted a score of voices.

'No, no! – I say, no!' cried the smith. 'Let us carry her to the churchyard, put her in her coffin again, and peg her down with a stake, so that she can never rise again.'

The suggestion of the smith was approved of, and the wretched Bertha was half-dragged and half-carried, more dead than alive, towards the village church. The flames were bursting forth from all parts of the castle when the lawless spoilers left it, and a red glow hung over its ancient towers; the work of destruction was rapid, and in a few hours nought but the bare and blackened walls were left standing.

On the destroyers of Ravensburg Castle reaching the churchyard, the almost lifeless form of Bertha Kurtel was dragged to the grave, which had been left open, and flung rudely into the coffin. Then a sharp pointed stake was produced, which had been prepared by the way, and the smith plunged it with all the force of his sinewy arms into the abdomen of the doomed vampire. A piercing shriek burst from her pale lips as the horrible thrust aroused her to consciousness, and as her clothes became daubed with the crimson stream of life, and the smith lifted his heavy hammer and drove the stake through her quivering body, the transfixed wretch writhed convulsively, and the contortions of her countenance were fearful to behold. Thus impaled in her coffin, and while her limbs yet quivered with the last throes of dissolution, the earth was replaced and rammed down by the tread of many feet.

But those strange and terrible scenes were not yet ended. A young peasant of equal curiosity and boldness, and who had been engaged in the attack upon the castle and the horrible tragedy which followed it, was anxious to know more of the strange affair of the skeleton, which had been left in the courtyard where it fell, none of the villagers caring to interfere with so ghastly an object. He therefore stole away a little before midnight, and went towards the castle, where the fire was dying out, though a fiery glow was still reflected from the mouldering embers of beams and rafters. He advanced cautiously through the broken gates of the castle, and shuddered slightly as he perceived the skeleton of the Count of Ravenhurg still lying on the pavement of the courtyard.

He determined to watch until daylight, and see what became of the grisly relics of mortality, which a few hours before had been the young and handsome Count of Ravensburg. The hours passed slowly on from midnight to the dawn of another day, and when the rising sun tinged the eastern sky with crimson and gold, a strange spectacle was witnessed by the solitary watcher in the court-yard of Ravensburg Castle.

The skeleton rose slowly from the pavement, and assumed the form of Count Rodolph, just as he appeared at the moment preceding his transformation on the evening before. A cold perspiration bedewed the brow of the peasant, and his hair stood erect with terror, witnessing this sudden metamorphosis. The count looked up at the dilapidated walls and towers of his castle, and shuddered violently, and crossing the court-yard, passed through the broken gate.

The peasant then hastened to the village, and reported what he had seen, which was a source of much marvel to the rustic inhabitants. The story of the skeleton count, and his vampire mistress, quickly spread all over Germany, but the villagers were no more molested by vampires, for Bertha Kurtel was securely fixed in her coffin, and no ill effects ensued from her attacks upon Theresa Delmar and little Minna Klaus.

VILEROY

THE AVENGER OF BLOOD

Most anxiously had Caroline listened for every sound which might indicate the return of Claudio to the turret.

A hundred times she passed through the panel, and bent her head to listen for the least noise which might proclaim his presence.

Now the shadows of evening were crowding around her. Darkness was rapidly approaching, and each moment her anxiety became more and more intense.

'Why,' she said, clasping her hands, 'why did I send him on this errand? His life, perhaps, even now, has been sacrificed to my wishes. All the fearful dungeons of those gloomy vaults now flash across my brain. Oh, Claudio, Claudio, have I sent you to destruction? Have I sacrificed the life that was dearer to me than my own?'

She sat down in her solitary chamber, and gave vent to her feelings in floods of tears of agony and self-reproach.

'Those fearful dungeons,' she cried, with horror in her tones. 'Those abodes of hopeless misery! I have sent him to them, and he is lost! He, even he talked of them with shuddering. Oh, Claudio, Claudio, what would I not give to hear your voice again! One word, but one word of yours would now lift me from despair to such a height of pure felicity, that–'

Caroline suddenly started to her feet, and a radiant smile played upon her ruby lips, while her sparkling eyes betrayed the blest feelings of her heart.

''Tis he!' she cried, ''tis he! Thank Heaven 'tis he. I know his lightest footstep. He is safe – safe.'

She flew to the panel and bounded like a young fawn up the turret-stairs. She opened the door.

'Claudio, Claudio,' she cried, and in another moment was clasped to the breast of her lover. It was the first embrace. His lips imprinted for the first time a kiss upon her glowing cheek.

She now gently, and with a profusion of blushes, disengaged herself from the arms of him who could have held her to his heart forever.

'Oh Claudio, Claudio,' she cried, covering her glowing face with her hands; 'you will not think lightly of me. I – I thought you were lost. I did not mean–'

'Nay, dearest, adored Caroline,' he cried, 'blame not yourself that you obeyed the first impulse of your pure heart. Were it possible that I could love you more than I do, it would be for that innocent candour of the guileless soul which you, dearest Caroline, possess above all others.'

'I – I knew not what I did, Claudio.'

'Ah, Caroline, let our hearts ever thus be bound to each other, and the world shall know no truer joys than ours.'

'Never again,' said Caroline, 'oh, never again, Claudio, will I tempt you to revisit the dungeons of Zindorf.'

'There was no danger, love, and little to alarm.'

'I have, perhaps, suffered more myself,' said Caroline, 'in self-reproaches, for urging you and our friend Maurice on such an expedition at all.'

'I only regret, as far as we ourselves are concerned, Caroline,' said Claudio, 'that in the main object of our enterprise, we have been disappointed.'

''Tis most strange,' said Caroline.

'It is,' answered Claudio. 'But, with our utmost vigilance, we can discover no low passage similar to the one you mention as leading to the ancient and venerable prisoner's dungeon.'

'We are all in the hands of Providence,' said Caroline. 'Unhappy prisoner! What human means could accomplish, has been done to rescue thee. We may mourn our failure, but it is not in our power to avert it.'

'Again and again,' said Claudio, 'I would most willingly return to the search, but I am almost without hope. There is some inexplicable mystery in the whole affair, which, time alone, I fear, has the power to unravel.'

'If I could again get possession of the manuscript,' said Caroline, 'from whence I read the particulars of the lonely imprisonment of the hopeless being I sent you, Claudio, in search of, I might, perchance, arrive at some better clue to the place of his confinement. All aid now, is, I fear, however, much too late to preserve the life, or sweeten the bitterness of death of so old a man.'

'I wish much,' said Claudio, 'to see that manuscript. You tell me my poor brother is mentioned in it?'

'He is,' said Caroline, sighing.

'And his fate?'

'Alas!' cried Caroline; 'to keep you in suspense, Claudio, is cruel.'

'Oh, tell me all, Caroline, from your lips I could hear it best.'

'Vileroy fell a victim to the baron's jealousy,' said Caroline.

'My heart told me as much,' said Claudio, mournfully. 'Oh, Caroline, he had the gentlest, bravest heart – I – I–'

Claudio's feelings overcame him, and he turned to the narrow casement of the turret, to weep unseen.

'Oh, Claudio,' said Caroline, 'I should not have told you this.'

'Yes, Caroline, yes,' answered Claudio, in a more composed voice, ''tis fitting I should know all. The pang is now past.'

Caroline wept in sympathy with Claudio's deep distress.

'Another time, Caroline,' he said, 'tell me all. All you know of my poor murdered brother. This baron shall pay dearly for his crime.'

'He is a monster,' said Maurice, struggling with his emotions.

'Until we know such men,' said Claudio, 'we may well doubt the fact of their existence. He is scarcely human.'

'Be cautious,' said Caroline, 'for my sake, Claudio. For all our sakes, let not your just resentment hurry you to some careless act of vengeance.'

'To punish the murderer of my brother,' said Claudio, 'I look upon as a sacred duty, and, believe me, Caroline, I will not hazard the fulfilment of my vengeance of that foul deed by any indiscreet attempt. I must not fail when once I have decided upon the means of bringing this ferocious and demoniac Baron Zindorf to that justice he has so long evaded.'

'The manuscript I mentioned,' said Caroline, 'is in the room occupied by the wicked and false-hearted Count Durlack.'

'He, too,' cried Claudio, 'is a blackened villain.'

'He destroyed my parents,' said Caroline.

'Dear Caroline,' cried Claudio, 'we have both suffered the most frightful injuries from these men, but be of good cheer. The termination of this career of vice and foul wickedness is near at hand.'

'They have, indeed, done us fearful wrong, Claudio.'

'Sir Gaston de Beauvais,' continued Claudio, 'will drag them from this stronghold of their villany, and they may yet perish with ignominy upon a scaffold.'

'It is hard,' said Caroline, 'for one, who, like myself, has suffered so much, to forgive them, but may God have mercy upon them.'

'You are ever too good and gentle,' said Claudio.

'The night is waning on apace,' said Caroline, rising; 'I will leave you to seek that repose which I am sure you so much require.'

'For a brief space, dearest, farewell,' said Claudio. 'Sleep in security; I will watch the while. The least alarm shall bring me to your side.'

'Nay,' said Caroline, 'do you rest, Claudio, there is little danger.'

'Heaven give you blest repose, lady,' said Maurice.

'I thank you kindly,' answered Caroline. 'Farewell to both.'

She tripped lightly down the turret stairs, and entered her own chamber.

Eleven now sounded from the castle clock, and Caroline, trimming her lamp, sat down for a few moments, lost in a pleasing reverie concerning her affection for Claudio, which had sprung up so strangely amid confusion, difficulty, and oppression.

'Shall I repine,' she thought, 'at the decree of Providence that brought me to this gloomy abode? No – no. Have I not here met the one being, who, with a kindred soul, has taught my heart to love?'

After a time, a feeling of dread and intense suffering seemed slowly to creep over her mind. In vain Caroline tried to shake off the oppression of her spirits. It seemed to her as if she was upon the eve of some occurrence which had cast a gloomy shadow before upon the pure sunshine of her soul.

She rose and trimmed her lamp, and then holding it high above her head, she looked, she knew not why, suspiciously around her chamber.

A deathlike stillness seemed to reign throughout the whole castle. Caroline stood trying if, by the utmost attention, she could catch the least sound; but nothing met her ears.

She walked to the panel, and bent all her energies to discover if there was any one in Count Durlack's apartment; but there, too, all seemed perfectly still, and she became satisfied that either he was not there, or had retired to rest for the night.

'All is still,' she said, in a low tone. 'What an awful wrapt repose seems to pervade the castle; one might imagine oneself in a mansion of the dead.'

Caroline's first thought was to endeavour by placing the furniture, or such of it as she could move, in such a position as regarded the panel and the ante-room, that she would be secure from any sudden or silent intrusion.

With this determination, she placed, one upon another, two of the heavy oaken chairs up against the panel, in such a position that no one could enter by that way without either moving them or throwing them down.

The ante-room door, which opened inwards, she proceeded to secure in the same manner against any noiseless visitor.

She dragged a heavy, high-backed chair to the spot, and placed it against the opening side of the door.

As she was retiring back to her own chamber, her eye caught a slip of paper, which was lying upon the ground close to the door.

Caroline raised it, and read upon it these words:

'Lady, beware! Sleep not to-night. There is danger at hand. Face it bravely, and it is innoxious; shrink, and you are lost.
–THE AVENGER OF BLOOD.'

Caroline stood for a few moments gazing upon the slip of paper in utter bewilderment of spirit. Her brain seemed to swim round, and she grasped with convulsive energy the arm of the chair for support.

'It is true, then,' she said; 'my forebodings were not vain. Something terrible is about to occur. Where, oh, where shall I seek protection? Claudio, yes, Claudio will aid me. And, yet, may not this warning be a trick of my worst enemies? Alas! I know not what to think. Unhappy Caroline. Was not the fate of thy parent's misery enough for thee to hear without accumulated sorrows and persecutions of thine own? Sleep! no, no, I can never sleep in Zindorf Castle.'

Again and again Caroline perused the brief but mysterious billet which had so entirely awakened all her worst fears, and she racked her imagination to conceive in what form or manner the threatened danger would present itself.

Many times she formed the resolution of immediately proceeding to the turret chamber, and throwing herself upon the immediate protection of Claudio; but as often was she checked by the thought, that, by so doing she might be the direct means of ensuring his destruction.

'No,' she cried, 'no, Claudio, rest in peace. I will myself face this threatened danger, and, at least, judge of its character before I summon thee to share it with me. It may be that I myself may ward it off without compromising thy dear safety, Claudio. What says the note? "Face it bravely, and it is innoxious." I will face it for thy sake, Claudio. Hark!'

Twelve o'clock now sounded solemnly from the castle clock. Caroline stood still as a statute till the last sound had died away.

''Tis midnight,' she said; 'midnight – that unhallowed hour, when, 'tis said, the spirits of the dead can, for a brief space, re-visit the dwellings of man. Can such things be true? 'Tis not at such an hour that human reason can decide on such a fearful question. I will not think. Now is the hour for any deed of violence.'

She cast her eyes round the room with a feeling of intense anxiety.

Suddenly her cheeks became deadly pale, and her frame trembled. She fixed her eyes upon the ante-room door. A dull, rattling sound came from the lock of the door.

Caroline's breath came thick; she tried to speak, but she could only say faintly, 'Claudio, Claudio, help me, Claudio!' when the ante-room door was flung suddenly open and the chairs fell down with a loud crash.

AN APPARITION

They had now arrived in a long gallery from which many doors opened to different apartments in the castle, and in traversing which, lay their greatest danger of being observed or suddenly discovered by some one coming from some of the rooms.

Euphoric placed his finger on his lips, enjoining silence, and with as quick a step as caution would permit the use of, they proceeded along the gallery.

One half the distance was accomplished, and even Claudio began to hope that all would be well, when Euphoric suddenly drew back, and laid his hand upon Claudio's arm, while his usually pale face became still paler.

'Hush!' he said. 'Retire within this doorway. I hear footsteps.'

They were close to an arched and elaborately sculptured doorway, the porch of which would with ease have contained a party of double the number.

Claudio and Caroline now both distinctly heard the sound of footsteps from the further end of the gallery, approaching, apparently, towards them.

'Hush!' said Euphoric, in a hoarse whisper. 'I know that step well. I should know the shadow of that man.'

'Who is it?' whispered Claudio.

'The count,' said Euphoric. 'It may be that his hour has come.'

'What mean you?' said Claudio.

'He may come this way,' answered the page.

'What then?'

'We shall be seen. It will be but for a moment, though.'

As he spoke, Euphoric drew from his breast the glass dagger, and a wild and unearthly fire seemed to sparkle in his eyes.

The footsteps now suddenly ceased, and a door was heard to close.

'The danger is passed,' said Claudio.

'It is,' answered Euphoric, putting up the dagger. 'Let us proceed.'

They walked forward in silence till they came opposite a door, at which Euphoric paused.

'We must enter here,' he said. 'This is the commencement of the suite of apartments which terminate at your chamber, lady.'

He gently opened the door and looked in. Then beckoning his companions, they all left the gallery and found themselves in a spacious room, hung round with ancient tapestry, and furnished in a costly style of former splendour.

'This way,' said Euphoric, 'will lead us direct to the Count Durlack's apartment. Our alarm in the gallery has at least assured us that he is not there, for he left the gallery by a door on the other side.'

'Then we are comparatively safe,' said Claudio.

'We are,' answered Euphoric. 'I do not think we are likely now to meet with any obstruction.'

They passed through several rooms of considerable extent, and all betraying the remains of the former magnificence of the lords of Zindorf. The rare hangings and costly furniture were, however, fast decaying for want of proper care and attention. Dampness and dust were allowed to mingle together on the tapestry, dimming the rich colours and rotting the once highly-prized fabric whose beauty they now observed.

The rooms had a cold and damp smell from the long absence of any fires upon the ample hearths. The windows were, in many instances, broken, and for years the damp night air, loaded with vapours from the forest, had entered and deposited, like dew, a universal dampness upon everything, which had greatly accellerated the progress of decay.

It seemed as if the rooms had been lately visited, for the floors had evidently been recently swept clean, and there, was none of that black dust lying upon the boards which accumulate in apartments shut up for a length of time and entirely unvisited.

'These rooms,' aid Euphoric, observing that Claudio looked around him with an eye of curiosity, 'I am told were shut up for many years until recently, when they were opened and partially cleansed as a thoroughfare to the apartment which the Count Durlack chose to occupy.'

'They have,' answered Claudio, 'a dismal air of faded magnificence.'

'There is some story connected with them,' said Euphoric, 'in which the Baron of Zindorf is concerned, which caused them to be shut up, as well as other parts of the castle, for some years, and even now I am told that the baron, when he visits the count in his own chamber, always hurries through these apartments with fear and precipitation.'

'This castle,' said Claudio, ' is altogether an abode of horror and crime. How much misery has been created within its walls? How many have breathed their last sad sighs in its loathsome and gloomy dungeons? The time will come, and that I trust ere long, when Zindorf Castle will be levelled with the dust.'

'Hark!' cried Maurice, suddenly.

'What do you hear?' cried Claudio.

'I heard a sound from behind us,' answered Maurice, 'as of a door closing.'

'And so did I,' said Euphoric.

'Hush!' cried Maurice, again, 'do you not hear?'

'I do,' answered Claudio. 'It seems to me that some one is coming through the apartments by the very route we are ourselves taking. What say you, Euphoric? – You are quick of hearing.'

Euphoric threw himself on the floor, and laid his ear close to the boards. Then rising, he said:

'I have learned to distinguish the footstep of one person from that of all others. It is not the count who is approaching.'

'Who then?' said Claudio.

'Most probably the baron!'

'The baron!' cried Caroline; 'oh, Heavens, we are lost!'

Claudio mechanically placed his hand to his side, but there was no sword there. He groaned bitterly.

'In such a dilemma, and unarmed!' he said.

'For some reason,' said Euphoric, speaking rapidly to Claudio, 'the Baron Zindorf shrinks from you. I have heard so much in the castle. It is your likeness to some one else.'

'Ah!' cried Caroline, 'there is hope, then. It is your likeness, Claudio, to – to–'

'My poor brother,' said Claudio, mournfully, 'my poor brother!'

'Have we not time,' said Maurice, 'to escape yet, before the baron reaches us, Euphoric?'

'No,' said the page, quickly, 'the panel in the count's room is behind a heavy picture, to remove which will take some time, and still longer replace it. Indeed, the latter could not be done at all from the other side. Hark! he comes – he comes!'

'Hush!' said Claudio; 'not a word. Keep out of sight, all of you. I will try this last expedient. The baron is superstitious: these rooms prepare his mind for fear. Lend me your sword, Euphoric; if it come the worst I must slay him, although such an act would, most likely, cause so much search and enquiry in the castle that we might be discovered; and moreover, I would fain that the common executioner dealt with so black a villain and hardened a criminal.'

'I will stand here,' said Euphoric, 'out of sight of any one advancing, but close to you, and I can hand you the sword in a moment, should it be required; the baron might recognize it as mine, and the effect of your sudden appearance upon him would be spoiled.'

The door of the room opened inwards, and all but Claudio placed themselves so that when it should be opened they would be completely hidden from observation behind it.

Claudio stood in the very entrance and within one pace of the threshold, and there calmly with his arms folded across his breast, he awaited the Baron of Zindorf's appearance.

What Euphoric had heard among the domestics of the mansion was strictly true. The baron always did hurry with precipitation through those apartments which led to the chamber of Count Durlack.

Each room presented to his guilty imagination an aspect of fear. He trembled at the slightest breath of air that came through the broken windows. The very echo of his own footsteps in those apartments appalled his soul.

It was not surprising that the sight of those apartments should conjure up these awful feelings in the mind of the baron, when it is recollected that in that very apartment which the Count Durlack had chosen for his chamber, from its proximity to that of Caroline Mecklenburgh, the unfortunate Vileroy had breathed his last.

Through that long suite of chambers had his lifeless and half decomposed body been dragged by the baron and his vile associate in every species of guilt, the ruffian Roland.

Each room was thus to the soul of the Baron replete with horrors, and a cold perspiration of intense agony and fear broke upon his brow whenever he trod, which was rarely, their solitudes alone.

The page had been missed in the castle and sought for in vain, in order to accompany Roland to Caroline's apartment with provisions, for Euphoric had been by the count entrusted with the key of the ante-room.

The baron had became uneasy at the circumstance, an uneasiness which was much increased by being told that Roland had knocked at the door of the ante-room without receiving any answer.

He had resolved, therefore, to seek Count Durlack, who he imagined to be in his own apartment, and inform him of the sudden disappearance of his most trusty and highly-prized page, Euphoric.

Maurice had closed instinctively every door after the little party of fugitives as they passed through the apartments, and the delay that this occasioned the baron in his progress, had given them time to mature their plan of endeavouring to play upon his superstitious fears; at the same time, that his mind became better fitted to be so attacked each moment that he was detained in those much-dreaded rooms.

Claudio's anxiety on Caroline's account imparted to his countenance a pale and care-worn expression, which materially aided the effect he wished to produce upon the baron, and which no act could have equalled.

Caroline's heart beat more and more wildly as she heard this step approaching to the door at which Claudio stood.

There was not one of the little group in whose countenance intense and painful anxiety was not painted.

'He comes;' said Euphoric.

'Hush,' said Claudio, 'not a word – not a word! The spirit of my poor murdered brother, Alphonso Vileroy, would pardon me for thus attempting to personate it for the object I have in view.'

'It is to save the miscreant,' said Maurice.

'Hush! hush!' whispered Euphoric.

Now the step of the baron could be heard traversing the extent the next apartment. He approached the door – his hand touched the lock.

Calm and quiet stood Claudio, pale with excess of anxiety, not for himself, but for he whom he loved and those, who, to do him service had followed him into circumstances of so much risk and danger.

The baron opened the door without pausing, and his face before he could stop himself came within an inch of Claudio's.

Claudio stirred not a muscle.

For one moment the Baron Zindorf seemed bereft of the power of motion or speech, and with eyes starting from their sockets, mouth open, and every vein in his face distended with horror, he glanced at Claudio as if he was turned to stone at the sight of him.

With an effort which seemed awful he wrenched himself as it were from his fixed position and fell backwards.

The spell which chained his voice seemed broken, now that he had succeeded in withdrawing his eyes from Claudio's face.

He sprung to his feet, and shrieked till the deserted apartments rung again with the fearful sounds.

'Mercy! – mercy!' he cried. 'Oh, horror! horror! horror! 'Tis he – he – that pale face. Mercy! mercy!'

With his hand stretched out before him, and his head averted from Claudio, he retreated backwards step by step, through the room towards the opposite door.

Claudio was pleased with the success of his scheme, but, much as he had cause to hold the Baron of Zindorf in detestation, he could not help feeling a sensation of pity for the man whose fears could inflict upon him such intense and horrible agony.

'Advance, Claudio,' said the page, in a whisper.

Claudio now felt the necessity of carrying out his operations upon the baron's nerves sufficiently to ensure his absence from the whole suite of apartments immediately.

Slowly he now advanced from the door-way, with a solemn measured step. Although the baron's face was averted, yet he could not altogether withdraw his eyes from the figure before him, and when he saw it advancing, he burst into a scream of terror that made even Claudio involuntarily pause in his progress towards him.

'Oh, mercy! – mercy!' cried the baron. 'Follow me not – follow me not! – In mercy stay!'

Claudio advanced another step.

'You are,' cried the baron, 'the spirit of – of–'

'The murdered!' cried Claudio, in a solemn sepulchral voice.

'I – I – know it!' cried the baron. 'Too well I know that face! – That pale face, and those sunken eyes! Oh, hence, horrible vision, hence! Follow me not! – Oh, horror! horror! – You are–'

'Vileroy!' said Claudio.

'I – I – know it! – I know it!' gasped the baron, still retreating.

He had now nearly arrived at the door at the further end of the room. He dared not turn to open it, for then his back would have been towards Claudio, which he dreaded more than looking at him.

With his glaring eyes still fixed upon the supposed spirit of Vileroy, the baron stretched his arms behind him to feel for the door.

Claudio saw that this was the moment to give the climax to the fears of the baron, and with rapid strides he advanced.

'Repent!' he said; 'Baron Zindorf, repent!'

The baron had just succeeded in opening the door.

With a wild shriek he darted through it, and Claudio could hear him rush shrieking through the rooms, till his voice and footsteps became lost in the increasing distance.

VARNEY THE VAMPIRE

MIDNIGHT – THE HAIL-STORM – THE DREADFUL VISITOR – THE VAMPYRE

"How graves give up their dead.
And how the night air hideous grows
With shrieks!"

The solemn tones of an old cathedral clock have announced midnight – the air is thick and heavy – a strange, death like stillness pervades all nature. Like the ominous calm which precedes some more than usually terrific outbreak of the elements, they seem to have paused even in their ordinary fluctuations, to gather a terrific strength for the great effort. A faint peal of thunder now comes from far off. Like a signal gun for the battle of the winds to begin, it appeared to awaken them from their lethargy, and one awful, warring hurricane swept over a whole city, producing more devastation in the four or five minutes it lasted, than would a half century of ordinary phenomena.

It was as if some giant had blown upon some toy town, and scattered many of the buildings before the hot blast of his terrific breath; for as suddenly as that blast of wind had come did it cease, and all was as still and calm as before.

Sleepers awakened, and thought that what they had heard must be the confused chimera of a dream. They trembled and turned to sleep again.

All is still – still as the very grave. Not a sound breaks the magic of repose. What is that – a strange, pattering noise, as of a million of fairy feet? It is hail – yes, a hail-storm has burst over the city. Leaves are dashed from the trees, mingled with small boughs; windows that lie most opposed to the direct fury of the pelting particles of ice are broken, and the rapt repose that before was so remarkable in its intensity, is exchanged for a noise which, in its accumulation, drowns every cry of surprise or consternation which here and there arose from persons who found their houses invaded by the storm.

Now and then, too, there would come a sudden gust of wind that in its strength, as it blew laterally, would, for a moment, hold millions of the hailstones suspended in mid air, but it was only to dash them with redoubled force in some new direction, where more mischief was to be done.

Oh, how the storm raged! Hail – rain – wind. It was, in very truth, an awful night.

There is an antique chamber in an ancient house. Curious and quaint carvings adorn the walls, and the large chimney-piece is a curiosity of itself. The ceiling is low, and a large bay window, from roof to floor, looks to the west. The window is latticed, and filled with curiously painted glass and rich stained pieces, which send in a strange, yet beautiful light, when sun or moon shines into the apartment. There is but one portrait in that room, although the walls seem panelled for the express purpose of containing a series of pictures. That portrait is of a young man, with a pale face, a stately brow, and a strange expression about the eyes, which no one cared to look on twice.

There is a stately bed in that chamber, of carved walnut-wood is it made, rich in design and elaborate in execution; one of those works of art which owe their existence to the Elizabethan era. It is hung with heavy silken and damask furnishing; nodding feathers are at its corners – covered with dust are they, and they lend a funereal aspect to the room. The floor is of polished oak.

God! how the hail dashes on the old bay window! Like an occasional discharge of mimic musketry, it comes clashing, beating, and cracking upon the small panes; but they resist it – their small size saves them; the wind, the hail, the rain, expend their fury in vain.

The bed in that old chamber is occupied. A creature formed in all fashions of loveliness lies in a half sleep upon that ancient couch – a girl young and beautiful as a spring morning. Her long hair has escaped from its confinement and streams over the blackened coverings of the bedstead; she has been restless in her sleep, for the clothing of the bed is in much confusion. One arm is over her head, the other hangs nearly off the side of the bed near to which she lies. A neck and bosom that would have formed a study for the rarest sculptor that ever Providence gave genius to, were half disclosed. She moaned slightly in her sleep, and once or twice the lips moved as if in prayer – at least one might judge so, for the name of Him who suffered for all came once faintly from them.

She has endured much fatigue, and the storm does not awaken her; but it can disturb the slumbers it does not possess the power to destroy entirely. The turmoil of the elements wakes the senses, although it cannot entirely break the repose they have lapsed into.

Oh, what a world of witchery was in that mouth, slightly parted, and exhibiting within the pearly teeth that glistened even in the faint light that came from that bay window. How sweetly the long silken eyelashes lay upon the cheek. Now she moves, and one shoulder is entirely visible – whiter, fairer than the spotless clothing of the bed on which she lies, is the smooth skin of that fair creature, just budding into womanhood, and in that transition state which presents to us all the charms of the girl – almost of the child, with the more matured beauty and gentleness of advancing years.

Was that lightning? Yes – an awful, vivid, terrifying flash – then a roaring peal of thunder, as if a thousand mountains were rolling one over the other in the blue vault of Heaven! Who sleeps now in that ancient city? Not one living soul. The dread trumpet of eternity could not more effectually have awakened any one.

The hail continues. The wind continues. The uproar of the elements seems at its height. Now she awakens – that beautiful girl on the antique bed; she opens those eyes of celestial blue, and a faint cry of alarm bursts from her lips. At least it is a cry which, amid the noise and turmoil without, sounds but faint and weak. She sits upon the bed and presses her hands upon her eyes. Heavens! what a wild torrent of wind, and rain, and hail! The thunder likewise seems intent upon awakening sufficient echoes to last until the next flash of forked lightning should again produce the wild concussion of the air. She murmurs a prayer – a prayer for those she loves best; the names of those dear to her gentle heart come from her lips; she weeps and prays; she thinks then of what devastation the storm must surely produce, and to the great God of Heaven she prays for all living things. Another flash – a wild, blue, bewildering flash of lightning streams across that bay window, for an instant bringing out every colour in it with terrible distinctness. A shriek bursts from the lips of the young girl, and then, with eyes fixed upon that window, which, in another moment, is all darkness, and with such an expression of terror upon her face as it had never before known, she trembled, and the perspiration of intense fear stood upon her brow.

'What – what was it?' she gasped; 'real, or a delusion? Oh, God, what was it? A figure tall and gaunt, endeavouring from the outside to unclasp the window. I saw it. That flash of lightning revealed it to me. It stood the whole length of the window.'

There was a lull of the wind. The hail was not falling so thickly – moreover, it now fell, what there was of it, straight, and yet a strange clattering sound came upon the glass of that long window. It could not be a delusion – she is awake, and she hears it. What can produce it? Another flash of lightning – another shriek – there could be now no delusion.

A tall figure is standing on the ledge immediately outside the long window. It is its finger-nails upon the glass that produces the sound so like the hail, now that the hail has ceased. Intense fear paralysed the limbs of that beautiful girl. That one shriek is all she can utter – with hands clasped, a face of marble, a heart beating so wildly in her bosom, that each moment it seems as if it would break its confines, eyes distended and fixed upon the window, she waits, froze with horror. The pattering and clattering of the nails continue. No word is spoken, and now she fancies she can trace the darker form of that figure against the window, and she can see the long arms moving to and fro, feeling for some mode of entrance. What strange light is that which now gradually creeps up into the air? red and terrible – brighter and brighter it grows. The lightning has set fire to a mill, and the reflection of the rapidly consuming building falls upon that long window. There can be no mistake. The figure is there, still feeling for an entrance, and clattering against the glass with its long nails, that appear as if the growth of many years had been untouched. She tries to scream again but a choking sensation comes over her, and she cannot. It is too dreadful – she tries to move – each limb seems weighed down by tons of lead – she can but in a hoarse faint whisper cry–

'Help – help – help – help!'

And that one word she repeats like a person in a dream. The red glare of the fire continues. It throws up the tall gaunt figure in hideous relief against the long window. It shows, too, upon the one portrait that is in the chamber, and that portrait appears to fix its eyes upon the attempting intruder, while the flickering light from the fire makes it look fearfully lifelike. A small pane of glass is broken, and the form from without introduces a long gaunt hand, which seems utterly destitute of flesh. The fastening is removed, and one-half of the window, which opens like folding doors, is swung wide open upon its hinges.

And yet now she could not scream – she could not move. 'Help! – help! – help!' was all she could say. But, oh, that look of terror that sat upon her face, it was dreadful – a look to haunt the memory for a lifetime – a look to obtrude itself upon the happiest moments, and turn them to bitterness.

The figure turns half round, and the light falls upon the face. It is perfectly white – perfectly bloodless. The eyes look like polished tin; the lips are drawn back, and the principal feature next to those dreadful eyes is the teeth – the fearful looking teeth – projecting like those of some wild animal, hideously, glaringly white, and fang-like. It approaches the bed with a strange, gliding movement. It clashes together the long nails that literally appear to hang from the finger ends. No sound comes from its lips. Is she going mad – that young and beautiful girl exposed to so much terror? she has drawn up all her limbs; she cannot even now say help. The power of articulation is gone, but the power of movement has returned to her; she can draw herself slowly along to the other side of the bed from that towards which the hideous appearance is coming.

But her eyes are fascinated. The glance of a serpent could not have produced a greater effect upon her than did the fixed gaze of those awful, metallic-looking eyes that were bent on her face. Crouching down so that the gigantic height was lost, and the horrible, protruding, white face was the most prominent object, came on the figure. What was it? – what did it want there? – what made it look so hideous – so unlike an inhabitant of the earth, and yet to be on it?

Now she has got to the verge of the bed, and the figure pauses. It seemed as if when it paused she lost the power to proceed. The clothing of the bed was now clutched in her hands with unconscious power. She drew her breath short and thick. Her bosom heaves, and her limbs tremble, yet she cannot withdraw her eyes from that marble-looking face. He holds her with his glittering eye.

The storm has ceased – all is still. The winds are hushed; the church clock proclaims the hour of one: a hissing sound comes from the throat of the hideous being, and he raises his long, gaunt arms – the lips move. He advances. The girl places one small foot from the bed on to the floor. She is unconsciously dragging the clothing with her. The door of the room is in that direction – can she reach it? Has she power to walk? – can she withdraw her eyes from the face of the intruder, and so break the hideous charm? God of Heaven! is it real, or some dream so like reality as to nearly overturn the judgment for ever?

The figure has paused again, and half on the bed and half out of it that young girl lies trembling. Her long hair streams across the entire width of the bed. As she has slowly moved along she has left it streaming across the pillows. The pause lasted about a minute – oh, what an age of agony. That minute was, indeed, enough for madness to do its full work in.

With a sudden rush that could not be foreseen – with a strange howling cry that was enough to awaken terror in every breast, the figure seized the long tresses of her hair, and twining them round his bony hands he held her to the bed. Then she screamed – Heaven granted her then power to scream. Shriek followed shriek in rapid succession. The bed-clothes fell in a heap by the side of the bed – she was dragged by her long silken hair completely on to it again. Her beautifully rounded limbs quivered with the agony of her soul. The glassy, horrible eyes of the figure ran over that angelic form with a hideous satisfaction – horrible profanation. He drags her head to the bed's edge. He forces it back by the long hair still entwined in his grasp. With a plunge he seizes her neck in his fang-like teeth – a gush of blood, and a hideous sucking noise follows. The girl has swooned, and *the vampyre is at his hideous repast!*

THE STAKE AND THE DEAD BODY

The mob seemed from the first to have an impression that, as regarded the military force, no very serious results would arise from that quarter, for it was not to be supposed that, on an occasion which could not possibly arouse any ill blood on the part of the soldiery, or on which they could have the least personal feeling, they would like to get a bad name, which would stick to them for years to come.

It was no political riot, on which men might be supposed, in consequence of differing in opinion, to have their passions inflamed; so that, although the call of the civil authorities for military aid had been acceded to, yet it was hoped, and, indeed, almost understood by the officers, that their operations would lie confined more to a demonstration of power, than anything else.

Besides, some of the men had got talking to the townspeople, and had heard all about the vampyre story, and not being of the most refined or educated class themselves, they felt rather interested than otherwise in the affair.

Under these circumstances, then, we are inclined to think, that the disorderly mob of that inn had not so wholesome a fear as it was most certainly intended they should have of the redcoats. Then, again, they were not attacking the churchyard, which, in the first case, was the main point in dispute, and about which the authorities had felt so very sore, inasmuch as they felt that, if once the common people found out that the sanctity of such places could be outraged with impunity, they would lose their reverence for the church; that is to say, for the host of persons who live well and get fat in this country by the trade of religion.

Consequently, this churchyard was the main point of defence, and it was zealously looked to when it need not have been done so, while the public-house where there really reigned mischief was half unguarded.

There are always in all communities, whether large or small, a number of persons who really have, or fancy they have, something to gain by disturbance. These people, of course, care not for what pretext the public peace is violated; so long as there is a row, and something like an excuse for running into other people's houses, they are satisfied.

To get into a public-house under such circumstances is an unexpected treat; and thus, when the mob rushed into the inn with such symptoms of fury and excitement, there went with the leaders of the disturbance a number of persons who never thought of getting further than the bar, where they attacked the spirit-taps with an alacrity which showed how great was their love for ardent compounds.

Leaving these persons behind, however, we will follow those who, with a real superstition, and a furious interest in the affair of the vampyre, made their way towards the upper chamber, determining to satisfy themselves if there were truth in the statement so alarmingly made by the woman who had created such an emotion.

It is astonishing what people will do in crowds, in comparison with the acts that they would be able to commit individually. There is usually a calmness, a sanctity, a sublimity about death, which irresistibly induces a respect for its presence, alike from the educated or from the illiterate; and let the object of the fell-destroyer's presence be whom it may, the very consciousness that death has claimed it for its own, invests it with a halo of respect, that, in life, the individual could never aspire to probably.

Let us precede these furious rioters for a few moments, and look upon the chamber of the dead – that chamber, which for a whole week, had been looked upon with a kind of shuddering terror – that chamber which had been darkened by having its sources of light closed, as if it were a kind of disrespect to the dead to allow the pleasant sunshine to fall upon the faded form.

And every inhabitant of that house, upon ascending and descending its intricate and ancient staircases, had walked with a quiet and subdued step past that one particular door.

Even the tones of voice in which they spoke to each other, while they knew that that sad remnant of mortality was in the house, was quiet and subdued, as if the repose of death was but a mortal sleep, and could be broken by rude sounds.

Ay, even some of these very persons, who now with loud and boisterous clamour, had rushed into the place, had visited the house and talked in whispers; but then they were alone, and men will do in throngs acts which, individually, they would shrink from with compunction or cowardice, call it which we will.

The chamber of death is upon the second storey of the house. It is a back room, the windows of which command a view of that half garden, half farm-yard, which we find generally belonging to country inns.

But now the shutters were closed, with the exception of one small opening, that, in daylight, would have admitted a straggling ray of light to fall upon the corpse. Now, however, that the sombre shades of evening had wrapped everything in gloom, the room appeared in total darkness, so that the most of those adventurers who had ventured into the place shrunk back until lights were procured from the lower part of the house, with which to enter the room.

A dim oil lamp in a niche sufficiently lighted the staircase, and, by the friendly aid of its glimmering beams, they had found their way up to the landing tolerably well, and had not thought of the necessity of having lights with which to enter the apartments, until they found them in utter darkness.

These requisites, however, were speedily procured from the kitchen of the inn. Indeed, anything that was wanted was laid hold of without the least word of remark to the people of the place, as if might, from that evening forthwith, was understood to constitute right, in that town.

Up to this point no one had taken a very prominent part in the attack upon the inn if attack it could be called; but now the man whom chance, or his own nimbleness, made the first of the throng, assumed to himself a sort of control over his companions and, turning to them, he said,–

'Hark ye, my friends; we'll do everything quietly and properly; so I think we'd better three or four of us go in at once, arm-in-arm.'

'Psha!' cried one who had just arrived with a light; 'it's your cowardice that speaks. I'll go in first; let those follow me who like, and those who are afraid may remain where they are.'

He at once dashed into the room, and this immediately broke the spell of fear which was beginning to creep over the others in consequence of the timid suggestion of the man who, up to that moment, had been first and foremost in the enterprise.

In an instant the chamber was half filled with persons, four or five of whom carried lights; so that, as it was not of very large dimensions, it was sufficiently illuminated for every object in it to be clearly visible.

There was the bed, smooth and unruffled, as if waiting for some expected guest; while close by its side a coffin, supported upon tressles, over which a sheet was partially thrown, contained the sad remains of him who little expected in life that, after death, he should be stigmatised as an example of one of the ghastliest superstitions that ever found a home in the human imagination.

It was evident that some one had been in the room; and that this was the woman whose excited fancy had led her to look upon the face of the corpse there could be no doubt, for the sheet was drawn aside just sufficiently to discover the countenance.

The fact was that the stranger was unknown at the inn, or probably ere this the coffin lid would have been screwed on; but it was hoped, up to the last moment, as advertisements had been put into the county papers, that some one would come forward to identify and claim him.

Such, however, had not been the case, and so his funeral had been determined upon.

The presence of so many persons at once effectually prevented any individual from exhibiting, even if he felt any superstitious fears about approaching the coffin; and so, with one accord, they surrounded it, and looked upon the face of the dead.

There was nothing repulsive in that countenance. The fact was that decomposition had sufficiently advanced to induce a relaxation of the muscles, and a softening of the fibres, so that an appearance of calmness and repose had crept over the face which it did not wear immediately after death.

It happened, too, that the face was full of flesh – for the death had been sudden, and there had not been that wasting away of the muscles and integuments which makes the skin cling, as it were, to the bone, when the ravages of long disease have exhausted the physical frame.

There was, unquestionably, a plumpness, a freshness, and a sort of vitality about the countenance that was remarkable.

For a few moments there was a death-like stillness in the

apartment, and then one voice broke the silence by exclaiming–

'He's a vampyre, and has come here to die. Well he knows he'd be taken up by Sir Francis Varney, and become one of the crew.'

'Yes, yes,' cried several voices at once; 'a vampyre! a vampyre!'

'Hold a moment,' cried one; 'let us find somebody in the house who has seen him some days ago, and then we can ascertain if there's any difference in his looks.'

This suggestion was agreed to, and a couple of stout men ran down stairs, and returned in a few moments with a trembling waiter, whom they had caught in the passage, and forced to accompany them.

This man seemed to think that he was to be made a dreadful example of in some sort of way; and, as he was dragged into the room, he trembled, and looked as pale as death.

'What have I done, gentlemen?' he said; 'I ain't a vampyre. Don't be driving a stake through me. I assure you, gentlemen, I'm only a waiter, and have been for a matter of five-and-twenty years.'

'You'll be done no harm to,' said one of his captors; 'you've only got to answer a question that will be put to you.'

'Oh, well, certainly, gentlemen; anything you please. Coming – coming, as I always say; give your orders, the waiter's in the room.'

'Look upon the fare of that corpse.'

'Certainly, certainly – directly.'

'Have you ever seen it before?'

'Seen it before! Lord bless you! yes, a dozen of times. I seed him afore he died, and I seed him arter; and when the undertaker's men came, I came up with them and I seed 'em put him in his coffin. You see I kept an eye on 'em, gentlemen, 'cos knows well enough what they is. A cousin of mine was in the trade, and he assures me as one of 'em always brings a tooth-drawing concern in his pocket, and looks in the mouth of the blessed corpse to see if there's a blessed tooth worth pulling out.'

'Hold your tongue,' said one; 'we want none of your nonsense. Do you see any difference now in the face of the corpse to what it was some days since?'

'Well, I don't know; somehow, it don't look so rum.'

'Does it look fresher?'

'Well, somehow or another, now you mention it, it's very odd, but it does.'

'Enough,' cried the man who had questioned him, with considerable excitement of manner. 'Neighbours, are we to have our wives and our children scared to death by vampyres?'

'No – no!' cried everybody.

'Is not this, then, one of that dreadful order of beings?'

'Yes – yes; what's to be done?'

'Drive a stake through the body, and so prevent the possibility of anything in the shape of a restoration.'

This was a terrific proposition; and even those who felt most strongly upon the subject, and had their fears most awakened, shrank from carrying it into effect. Others, again, applauded it, although they determined, in their own minds, to keep far enough off from the execution of the job, which they hoped would devolve upon others, so that they might have all the security of feeling that such a process had been gone through with the supposed vampyre, without being in any way committed by the dreadful act.

Nothing was easier than to procure a stake from the garden in the rear of the premises; but it was one thing to have the means at hand of carrying into effect so dreadful a proposition, and another actually to do it.

For the credit of human nature, we regret that even then, when civilisation and popular education had by no means made such rapid strides as in our times they have, such a proposition should be entertained for a moment: but so it was; and just as an alarm was given that a party of the soldiers had reached the inn and had taken possession of the doorway with a determination to arrest the rioters, a strong hedge-stake had been procured, and everything was in readiness for the perpetration of the horrible deed.

Even then those in the room, for they were tolerably sober, would have revolted, probably, from the execution of so fearful an act; but the entrance of a party of the military into the lower portion of the tavern, induced those who had been making free with the strong liquors below, to make a rush up-stairs to their companions with the hope of escaping detection of the petty larceny, if they got into trouble on account of the riot.

These persons, infuriated by drink, were capable of anything, and to them, accordingly, the more sober parties gladly surrendered the disagreeable job of rendering the supposed vampyre perfectly innoxious, by driving a hedge-stake through his body – a proceeding which, it was currently believed, inflicted so much physical injury to the frame, as to render his resuscitation out of the question.

The cries of alarm from below, joined now to the shouts of those mad rioters, produced a scene of dreadful confusion.

We cannot, for we revolt at the office, describe particularly the dreadful outrage which was committed upon the corpse; suffice it that two or three, maddened by drink, and incited by the others, plunged the hedge-stake through the body, and there left it, a sickening and horrible spectacle to any one who might cast his eyes upon it.

With such violence had the frightful and inhuman deed been committed, that the bottom of the coffin was perforated by the stake so that the corpse was actually nailed to its last earthly tenement.

Some asserted, that at that moment an audible groan came from the dead man, and that this arose from the extinguishment of that remnant of life which remained in him, on account of his being a vampyre, and which would have been brought into full existence, if the body had been placed in the rays of the moon, when at its full, according to the popular superstition upon that subject.

Others, again, were quite ready to swear that at the moment the stake was used there was a visible convulsion of all the limbs, and that the countenance, before so placid and so calm, became immediately distorted, as if with agony.

But we have done with these horrible surmises; the dreadful deed has been committed, and wild, ungovernable superstition has had, for a time, its sway over the ignorant and debased.

THE RESUSCITATION OF A VAMPIRE

It is nearly half an hour to midnight. The sky is still cloudy. but glimpses of the moon can be got as occasionally the clouds slip from before her disc, and then what a glorious flood of silver light spreads itself over the landscape.

And a landscape in every respect more calculated to look beautiful and romantic under the chaste moon's ray, than that to which we would now invite attention, certainly could not have been found elsewhere, within many a mile of London. It is Hampstead Heath, that favoured spot where upon a small scale are collected some of the rarest landscape beauties that the most romantic mountainous counties of England can present to the gratified eye of the tourist.

Those who are familiar with London and its environs, of course, are well acquainted with every nook, glade, tree, and dell in that beautiful heath, where, at all and every time and season, there is much to recommend that semi-wild spot to notice. Indeed, if it were, as it ought to be, divested of its donkey-drivers and laundresses, a more delightful place of residence could scarcely be found than some of those suburban villas, that are dotted round the margin of this picturesque waste.

But it is midnight, nearly. That time is forthcoming, at which popular superstition trembles-that time, at which the voice of ignorance and of cant lowers to whispers, and when the poor of heart and timid of spirit imagine worlds of unknown terrors. On this occasion, though, it will be seen that there would have been some excuse if even the most bold had shrunk back appalled at what was taking place.

But we will not anticipate for truly in this instance might we say sufficient for the time are the horrors thereof.

If any one had stood on that portion of the high road which leads right over the heath and so on to Hendon or to Highgate, according as the left hand or the right hand route is taken, and after reaching the Castle Tavern, had looked across the wide expanse of heath to the west, they would have seen nothing for a while but the clustering bushes of heath blossom, and the picturesque fir trees, that there are to be beheld in great luxuriance. But, after a time, something of a more noticeable character would have presented itself.

At a quarter to twelve there rose up from a tangled mass of brushwood, which had partially concealed a deep cavernous place where sand had been dug, a human form, and there it stood in the calm still hour of night so motionless that it scarcely seemed to possess life, but presently another rose at a short distance.

And then there was a third, so that these three strangelooking beings stood like landmarks against the sky, and when the moon shone out from some clouds which had for a short time obscured her rays, they looked strange and tall, and superhuman.

One spoke.

"'Tis time,' he said, in a deep, hollow voice, that sounded as if it came from the tomb.

'Yes, time,' said another.

'Time has come,' said the third.

Then they moved, and by the gestures they used, it seemed as if an animated discussion was taking place among them, after which they moved along in perfect silence, and in a most stately manner, towards the village of Hampstead.

Before reaching it, however, they turned down some narrow shaded walks among garden walls, and the backs of stables, until they emerged close to the old churchyard, which stands on high ground, and which was not then – at least, the western portion of it – overlooked by any buildings. Those villas which now skirt it, are of recent elevation.

A dense mass of clouds had now been brought up by a south wind, and had swept over the face of the moon, so that at this juncture, and as twelve o'clock might be expected to strike, the night was darker than it had yet been since sunset. The circumstance was probably considered by the mysterious beings who sought the churchyard as favourable to them, and they got without difficulty within those sacred precincts devoted to the dead.

Scarcely had they found the way a dozen feet among the old

tomb-stones, when from behind a large square monument, there appeared two more persons; and if the attorney, Mr Miller, had been there, he would probably have thought they bore such a strong resemblance to those whom he had seen in the park, he would have had but little hesitation in declaring that they were the same.

These two persons joined the other three, who manifested no surprise at seeing them, and then the whole five stood close to the wall of the church, so that they were quite secure from observation, and one of them spoke.

'Brothers,' he said, 'you who prey upon human nature by the law of your being, we have work to do tonight – that work which we never leave undone, and which we dare not neglect when we know that it is to do. One of our fraternity lies here.'

'Yes,' said the others, with the exception of one, and he spoke passionately.

'Why,' he said, 'when there were enough. and mure than enough, to do the work, summon me?'

'Not more than enough, there are but five.'

'And why should you not be summoned,' said another, 'you are one of us. You ought to do your part with us in setting a brother free from the clay that presses on his breast.'

'I was engaged in my vocation. If the moon shines out all her lustre again, you will see that I am wan and wasted, and have need of–'

'Blood,' said one.

'Blood, blood, blood,' repeated the others. And then the first speaker said, to him who complained:

'You are one whom we are glad to have with us on a service of danger. You are strong and bold, your deeds are known, you have lived long, and are not yet crushed.'

'I do not know our brother's name,' said one of the others with an air of curiosity.

'I go by many.'

'So do we all. But by what name may we know you best?'

'Slieghton, I was named in the reign of the third Edward. But many have known me as Varney, the Vampire!'

There was a visible sensation among those wretched beings as these words were uttered, and one was about to say something, when Varney interrupted him.

'Come,' he said, 'I have been summoned here, and I have come to assist in the exhumation of a brother. It is one of the conditions of our being that we do so. Let the work be proceeded with then, at once, I have no time to spare. Let it be done with. Where lies the vampire? Who was he?'

'A man of good repute, Varney,' said the first speaker. 'A smooth, fair-spoken man, a religious man, so far as cant went, a proud, cowardly, haughty, worldly follower of religion. Ha, ha, ha!'

'And what made him one of us?'

'He dipped his hands in blood. There was a poor boy, a brother's only child, 'twas left an orphan. He slew the boy, and he is one of us.'

'With a weapon.'

'Yes, and a sharp one; the weapon of unkindness. The child was young and gentle, and harsh words, blows, and revilings placed him in his grave. He is in heaven, while the man will be a vampire.'

''Tis well – dig him up.'

They each produced from under the dark cloaks they wore, a short double-edged, broad, flat-bladed weapon, not unlike the swords worn by the Romans, and he who assumed the office of guide, led the way to a newly-made grave, and diligently, and with amazing rapidity and power, they commenced removing the earth.

It was something amazing to see the systematic manner in which they worked, and in ten minutes one of them struck the blade of his weapon upon the lid of a coffin, and said:

'It is here.'

The lid was then partially raised in the direction of the moon, which, although now hidden, they could see would in a very short time show itself in some gaps of the clouds, that were rapidly approaching at great speed across the heavens.

They then desisted from their labour, and stood around the grave in silence for a time, until, as the moon was no longer showing her fair face, they began to discourse in whispers.

'What shall become of him,' said one, pointing to the grave. 'Shall we aid him?'

'No,' said Varney, 'I have heard that of him which shall not induce me to lift hand or voice in his behalf. Let him fly, shrieking like a frightened ghost where he lists.'

'Did you not once know some people named Bannerworth?'

'I did. You came to see me, I think, at an inn. They are all dead.'

'Hush,' said another, 'look, the moon will soon be free from the vapours that sail between it and the green earth. Behold, she shines out fresh once more; there will be life in the coffin soon, and our work will be done.'

It was so. The dark clouds passed over the face of the moon, and with a sudden burst of splendour, it shone out again as before.

* * * * *

A death-like stillness now was over the whole scene, and those who had partially exhumed the body stood as still as statues, waiting the event which they looked forward to as certain to ensue.

The clear beauty and intensity of the moonbeams increased each moment, and the whole surrounding landscape was lit up with a perfect flood of soft silvery light. The old church stood out in fine relief, and every tree, and every wild flower, and every blade of grass in the churchyard, could be seen in its finest and most delicate proportions and construction.

The lid of the coffin was wrenched up on one side to about six inches in height, and that side faced the moon, so that some rays, it was quite clearly to be seen, found their way into that sad receptacle for the dead. A quarter of an hour, however, passed away, and nothing happened.

'Are you certain he is one of us?' whispered Varney.

'Quite, I have known it years past. He had the mark upon him.'

'Enough. Behold.'

A deep and dreadful groan came from the grave, and yet it could hardly be called a groan; it was more like a howl, and the lid which was partially open, was visibly agitatcd.

'He comes,' whispered one.

'Hush,' said another, 'hush; our duty will be done when he stands upon the level ground. Hush, let him near nothing, let him know nothing, since we will not aid him. Behold, behold.'

They all looked down into the grave, but they betrayed no

signs of emotion, and the sight they saw there was such as one would have supposed would have created emotion in the breast of any one at all capable of feeling. But then we must not reason upon these strange frightful existences as we reason upon human nature such as we usually know it.

The coffin lid was each moment more and more agitated. The deep frightful groans increased in number and sound, and then the corpse stretched out one ghastly hand from the open crevice and grasped despairingly and frantically at the damp earth that was around.

There was still towards one side of the coffin sufficient weight of mould that it would require some strength to turn it off, but as the dead man struggled within his narrow house it kept falling aside in lumps, so that his task of exhumation became each moment an easier one.

At length he uttered a strange wailing shriek, and by a great effort succeeded in throwing the coffin lid quite open, and then he sat up, looking so horrible and ghastly in the grave clothes, that even the vampires that were around the grave recoiled a little.

'Is it done?' said Varney.

'Not yet,' said he who had summoned them to the fearful rite, and so assumed a sort of direction over them, 'not yet; we will not assist him, but we may not leave him before telling him who and what he is.'

'Do so now.'

The corpse stood up in the coffin and the moonlight fell full upon him.

'Vampire arise,' said he who had just spoken to Varney. 'Vampire arise, and do your work in the world until your doom shall be accomplished. Vampire arise – arise. Pursue your victims in the mansion and in the cottage. Be a terror and a desolation, go you where you may, and if the hand of death strike you down, the cold beams of the moon shall restore you to new life. Vampire arise, arise!'

'I come, I come!' shrieked the corpse.

In another moment the five vampires who had dug him from the grave were gone.

Moaning, shrieking, and groaning he made some further attempts to get out of the deep grave. He clutched at it in vain, the earth crumbled beneath him, and it was only at last by dint of reaching up and dragging in the displaced material that lay in a heap at the sides, so that in a few minutes it formed a mound for him to stand upon in the grave, that he was at length able to get out.

Then, although he sighed, and now and then uttered a wailing shriek as he went about the work, he with a strange kind of instinct, began to carefully fill up the grave from which he had but just emerged, nor did he cease from his occupation until he had finished it, and so carefully shaped the mound of mould and turf over it that no one would have thought it had been disturbed.

When this work was done a kind of madness seemed to seize him, and he walked to the gate of the graveyard, which opens upon Church Street, and placing his hands upon the sides of his mouth he produced such an appalling shriek that it must have awakened everybody in Hampstead.

Then, turning, he fled like a hunted hare in the other direction, and taking the first turning to the right ran up a lane called Frognal Lane, and which is parallel to the town, for a town Hampstead may be fairly called now, although it was not then.

By pursuing this lane, he got upon the outskirts of the heath, and then turning to the right again, for, with a strange pertinacity, he always kept, as far as he could, his face towards the light of the moon, he rushed down a deep hollow, where there was a cluster of little cottages, enjoying such repose that one would have thought the flutter of an awakened bird upon the wing would have been heard.

It was quite clear that the new vampyre had as yet no notion of what he was about, or where he was going, and that he was with mere frantic haste speeding along, from the first impulse of his frightful nature.

The place into which he had now plunged, is called the Vale of Health: now a place of very favourite resort, but then a mere collection of white faced cottages, with a couple of places that might be called villas. A watchman went his nightly rounds in that place. And it so happened that the guardian of the Vale had just roused himself up at this juncture, and made up his mind to make his walk of observation, when he saw the terrific figure of a man attired in grave clothes coming along with dreadful speed towards him, as if to take the Vale of Health by storm.

The watchman was so paralysed by fear that he could not find strength enough to spring his rattle, although he made the attempt, and held it out at arm's length, while his eyes glared with perfect ferocity, and his mouth was wide enough open to nourish the idea, that after all he had a hope of being able to swallow the spectre.

But, nothing heeding him, the vampire came wildly on.

Fain now would the petrified watchman have got out of the way, but he could not, and in another moment he was dashed down to the earth, and trodden on by the horrible existence that knew not what it did.

A cloud came over the moon, and the vampire sunk down, exhausted, by a garden-wall, and there lay as if dead, while the watchman, who had fairly fainted away, lay in a picturesque attitude on his back, not very far off.

Half an hour passed, and a slight mist-like rain began to fall.

The vampire slowly rose to his feet, and commenced wringing his hands and moaning, but his former violence of demeanour had passed away. That was but the first flush of new life, and now he seemed to be more fully aware of who and what he was.

He shivered as he tottered slowly on, until he came to where the watchman lay, and then he divested that guardian of the Vale of his greatcoat, his hat, and some other portions of his apparel, all of which he put on himself, still slightly moaning as he did so, and ever and anon stopping to make a gesture of despair.

When this operation was completed, he slunk off into a narrow path which led on to the heath again, and there he seemed to waver a little, whether he would go towards London, or the country. At length it seemed that he decided upon the former course, and he walked on at a rapid pace right through Hampstead, and down the hill towards London, the lights of which could be seen gleaming in the distance.

When the watchman did recover himself, the first thing he did was, to be kind enough to rouse everybody up from their sleep in the Vale of Health, by springing his rattle at a prodigious rate, and by the time he had roused up the whole neighbourhood, he felt almost ready to faint again at the bare recollection of the terrible apparition that had knocked him down.

The story in the morning was told all over the place, with

many additions to it of course, and it was long afterwards before the inhabitants of the Vale could induce another watchman, for that one gave up the post, to run the risk of such a visitation.

And the oddest thing of all was, that the watchman declared that he caught a glance at the countenance, and that it was like that of a Mr Brooks, who had only been buried the day previous, that if he had not known that gentleman to be dead and buried, he should have thought it was he himself gone mad.

But there was the grave of Mr Brooks, with its circular mound of earth, all right enough; and then Mr B. was known to have been such a respectable man. He went to the city every day, and used to do so just for the purpose of granting audiences to ladies and gentlemen who might be labouring under any little pecuniary difficulties, and accommodating them. Kind Mr Brooks. He only took one hundred pounds per cent. Why should he be a Vampire? Bless him! Too severe, really!

There were people who called him a bloodsucker while he lived, and now he was one practically, and yet he had his own pew at church, and subscribed a whole guinea a year to a hospital – he did, although people did say it was in order that he might pack off any of his servants at once to it in case of illness. But then the world is so censorious.

And to this day the watchman's story of the apparition that visited the Vale of Health is still talked of by the old women who make what they call tea for Sunday parties at nine pence a head.

THE DISCOVERY OF THE BODY OF MARCHDALE IN THE RUINS BY THE MOB – THE BURNING OF THE CORPSE – THE MURDER OF THE HANGMAN

The mob reached the ruins of Bannerworth Hall, and crowded round it on all sides, with the view of ascertaining if a human creature, dead or alive, were there; various surmises were afloat, and some were for considering that everybody but themselves, or their friends, must be nothing less than vampyres. Indeed, a strange man, suddenly appearing among them, would have caused a sensation, and a ring would no doubt have been formed round him, and then a hasty council held, or, what was more probable, some shout, or word uttered by some one behind, who could not understand what was going on in front, would have determined them to commit some desperate outrage, and the sacrifice of life would have been the inevitable result of such an unfortunate concurrence of circumstances.

There was a pause before anyone ventured among the ruins; the walls were carefully looked to, and in more than one instance, but they were found dangerous, what were remaining; some parts had been so completely destroyed, that there were nothing but heaps of rubbish.

However, curiosity was exerted to such an extraordinary pitch that it overcame the fear of danger, in search of the horrible; for they believed that if there were any one in the ruins he must be a vampyre, of course, and they were somewhat cautious in going near such a creature, lest in so doing they should meet with some accident, and become vampyres too.

This was a dreadful reflection, and one that every now and then impressed itself upon the individuals composing the mob; but at the same time any new impulse, or a shout, and they immediately became insensible to all fear; the mere impulse is the dominant one, and then all is forgotten.

The scene was an impressive one; the beautiful house and grounds looked desolate and drear; many of the trees were stripped and broken down, and many scorched and burned, while the gardens and flower beds, the delight of the Bannerworth family, were rudely trodden under foot by the rabble, and all those little beauties so much admired and tended by the inhabitants, were now utterly destroyed, and in such a state that their site could not even be detected by the former owners.

It was a sad sight to see such a sacrilege committed, – such violence done to private feelings, as to have all these places thrown open to the scrutiny of the brutal and vulgar, who are incapable of appreciating or understanding the pleasures of a refined taste.

The ruins presented a remarkable contrast to what the place had been but a very short time before; and now the scene of desolation was complete, there was no one spot in which the most wretched could find shelter.

To be sure, under the lee of some broken and crumbling wall, that tottered, rather than stood, a huddled wretch might have found shelter from the wind, but it would have been at the risk of his life, and not there complete.

The mob became quiet for some moments, but was not so long; indeed, a mob of people, – which is, in fact, always composed of the most disorderly characters to be found in a place, is not exactly the assembly that is most calculated for quietness; somebody gave a shout, and then somebody else shouted, and the one wide throat of the whole concourse was opened, and sent forth a mighty yell.

After this exhibition of power, they began to run about like mad, – traverse the grounds from one end to the other, and then the ruins were in progress of being explored.

This was a tender affair, and had to be done with some care and caution by those who were so engaged; and they walked over crumbling and decayed masses.

In one or two places, they saw what appeared to be large holes, into which the building materials had been sunk, by their own weight, through the flooring, that seemed as roofs to some cellars or dungeons.

Seeing this, they knew not how soon some other part might sink in, and carry their precious bodies down with the mass of rubbish; this gave an interest to the scene – a little danger is a sort of salt to an adventure, and enables those who have taken part in it to talk of their exploits, and of their dangers, which is pleasant to do, and to hear in the ale-house, and by the inglenook in the winter.

However, when a few had gone some distance, others followed, when they saw them enter the place in safety: and at length the whole ruins were covered with living men, and not a few women, who seemed necessary to make up the elements of mischief in this case.

There were some shouting and hallooing from one to the other as they hurried about the ruins.

At length they had explored the ruins nearly all over, when one man, who had stood a few minutes upon a spot, gazing intently upon something, suddenly exclaimed–

'Hilloa! hurrah! here we are, altogether – come on – I've found him – I've found – recollect it's me, and nobody else has found, – hurrah!'

Then, with a wild kind of frenzy, he threw his hat up into the air, as if to attract attention, and call others round him, to see what it was he had found.

'What's the matter, Bill?' exclaimed one who came up to him, and who had been close at hand.

'The matter? why, I've found him; that's the matter, old man,' replied the first.

'What, a whale?'

'No, a wampyre; the blessed wampyre! there he is – don't you see him under them ere bricks?'

'Oh, that's not him; he got away.'

'I don't care,' replied the other, 'who got away, or who didn't; I know this much, that he's a wampyre – he wouldn't be there if he warn't.'

This was an unanswerable argument, and nobody could deny it; consequently, there was a cessation of talk, and the people then came up, as the two first were looking at the body.

'Whose is it?' inquired a dozen voices.

'Not Sir Francis Varney's!' said the second speaker; the clothes are not his–'

'No, no; not Sir Francis's.'

"But I tell you what, mates," said the first speaker; "that if it isn't Sir Francis Varney's, it is somebody else's as bad. I dare say, now, he's a wictim."

"A what!"

"A wictim to the wampyre; and, if he sees the blessed moonlight, he will be a wampyre hisself, and so shall we be, too, if he puts his teeth into us."

"So we shall – so we shall," said the mob, and their flesh begin to run cold, and there was a feeling of horror creeping over the whole body of persons within hearing.

"I tell you what it is; our only plan will be to get him out of the ruins, then', remarked another.

'What!' said one; 'who's going to handle such cattle? if you've a sore about you, and his blood touches you, who's to say you won't be a vampyre, too!'

'No, no you won't,' said an old woman.

'I won't try,' was the happy rejoinder; 'I ain't a-going to carry a wampyre on my two legs home to my wife and small family of seven children, and another a-coming.'

There was a pause for a few moments, and then one man more adventurous than the rest, exclaimed–

'Well, vampyre, or no vampyre, his dead body can harm no one; so here goes to get it out, help me who will; once have it out, and then we can prevent any evil, by burning it, and thus destroying the whole body.

'Hurrah!' shouted three or four more, as they jumped down into the hole formed by the falling in of the materials which had crushed Marchdale to death, for it was his body they had discovered.

They immediately set to work to displace such of the materials as lay on the body, and then, having cleared it of all superincumbent rubbish, they proceeded to lift it up, but found that it had got entangled, as they called it, with some chains: with some trouble they got them off, and the body was lifted out to a higher spot.

'Now, what's to be done?' inquired one.

'Burn it,' said another.

'Hurrah!' shouted a female voice; 'we've got the wampyre! run a stake through his body, and then place him upon some dry wood, – there's plenty to be had about here, I am sure, – and then burn him to a cinder.'

'That's right, old woman – that's right,' said a man; 'nothing better: the devil must be in him if he come to life after that, I should say.'

There might be something in that, and the mob shouted its approbation, as it was sure to do as anything stupid or senseless, and the proposal might be said to have been carried by acclamation, and it required only the execution.

This was soon done. There were plenty of laths and rafters, and the adjoining wood furnished an abundant supply of dry sticks, so there was no want of fuel.

There was a loud shout as each accession of sticks took place, and, as each individual threw his bundle into the heap, each man felt all the self-devotion to the task as the Scottish chieftain who sacrificed himself and seven sons in the battle for his superior; and, when one son was cut down, the man filled up his place with the exclamation – 'Another for Hector,' until he himself fell as the last of his race.

Soon now the heap became prodigious, and it required an effort to get the mangled corpse upon this funeral bier; but it was then a shout from the mob that rent the air announced, both the fact and their satisfaction.

The next thing to be done was to light the pile – this was no easy task; but like all others, it was accomplished, and the dead body of the vampyre's victim was thrown on to prevent that becoming a vampyre too, in its turn.

'There, boys,' said one, 'he'll not see the moonlight, that's certain, and the sooner we put a light to this the better; for it may be, the soldiers will be down upon us before we know anything of it; so now, who's got a light?'

This was a question that required a deal of searching; but, at length one was found by one of the mob coming forward, and after drawing his pipe vigorously for some moments, he collected some scraps of paper upon which he emptied the contents of the pipe, with the hope they would take fire.

In this, however, he was doomed to disappointment; for it produced nothing but a deal of smoke, and the paper burned without producing any flame.

This act of disinterestedness, however was not without its due consequences, for there were several who had pipes, and, fired with the hope of emulating the first projector of the scheme for raising the flame, they joined together, and potting the contents of their pipes together on some paper, straw, and chips, they produced, after some little trouble, a flame.

Then there was a shout, and the burning mass was then placed in a favourable position nearer the pile of materials collected for burning, and then, in a few moments, it began to take light; one piece communicated the fire to another, until the whole was in a blaze.

When the first flame fairly reached the top, a loud and tremendous shout arose from the mob, and the very welkin re-echoed with its fulness.

Then the forked flames rushed through the wood, and hissed and crackled as they flew, throwing up huge masses of black smoke, and casting a peculiar reflection around. Not a sound was heard save the hissing and roaring of the flames, which seemed like the approaching of a furious whirlwind.

At length there was nothing to be seen but the blackened mass; it was enveloped in one huge flame, that threw out a great heat, so much so, that those nearest to it felt induced to retire from before it.

'I reckon,' said one, 'that he's pretty well done by this time – he's had a warm berth of it up there.'

'Yes,' said another, 'farmer Walkings's sheep he roasted whole at last harvest-home hadn't such a fire as this, I'll warrant; there's no such fire in the county – why, it would prevent a frost, I do believe it would.'

'So it would, neighbour,' answered another.

'Yes,' replied a third, 'but you'd want such a one corner of each field though.'

There was much talk and joking going on among the men who stood around, in the midst of which, however, they were disturbed by a loud shout, and upon looking in the quarter whence it came, they saw stealing from among the ruins, the form of a man.

He was a strange, odd looking man, and at the time it was very doubtful among the mob as to whom it was – nobody could tell, and more than one looked at the burning pile, and then at the man who seemed to be so mysteriously present, as if they almost imagined that the body had got away.

'Who is it?' exclaimed one.

'Danged if I knows,' said another, looking very hard, and very white at the same time; 'I hope it ain't the chap what we've burned here jist now.'

'No,' said the female, 'that you may be sure of, for he's had a stake through his body, and as you said, he can never get over that, for as the stake is consumed, so are his vitals, and that's a sure sign he's done for.'

'Yes, yes, she's right – a vampyre may live upon blood, but cannot do without his inside.'

This was so obvious to them all, that it was at once conceded, and a general impression pervaded the mob that it might be Sir Francis Varney: a shout ensued.

'Hurrah! – After him – there's a vampyre – there he goes! – after him – catch him – burn him!'

And a variety of other exclamations were uttered, at the same time; the victim of popular wrath seemed to be aware that he was now discovered, and made off with all possible expedition, towards some wood.

Away went the mob in pursuit, hooting and hallooing like demons, and denouncing the unfortunate being with all the terrors that could be imagined, and which naturally added greater speed to the unfortunate man.

However, some among the mob, seeing that there was every probability of the stranger's escaping at a mere match of speed, brought a little cunning to bear upon matter, and took a circuit round, and thus intercepted him.

This was not accomplished without a desperate effort, and by the best runners, who thus reached the spot he made for, before he could get there.

When the stranger saw himself thus intercepted, he endeavoured to fly in a different direction; but was soon secured by the mob, who made somewhat free with his person, and commenced knocking him about.

'Have mercy on me,' said the stranger. 'What do you want? I am not rich; but take all I have.'

'What do you do here?' inquired twenty voices. 'Come, tell us that – what do you do here, and who are you?'

'A stranger, quite a stranger to these parts.'

'Oh, yes! he's a stranger; but that's all the worse for him – he's a vampyre – there's no doubt about that.'

'Good God,' said the man, 'I am a living and breathing man like yourselves. I have done no wrong, and injured no man – be merciful unto me; I intend no harm.'

'Of course not; send him to the fire – take him back to the ruins – to the fire.'

'Ay, and run a stake through his body, and then he's safe for life. I am sure he has something to do with the vampyre; and who knows, if he ain't a vampyre, how soon he may become one?'

'Ah! that's very true; bring him back to the fire, and we'll try the effects of the fire upon his constitution.'

'I tell you what, neighbour, it's my opinion, that as one fool makes many, so one vampyre makes many.'

'So it does, so it does; there's much truth and reason in that neighbour; I am decidedly of that opinion, too.'

'Come along then,' cried the mob, cuffing and pulling the unfortunate stranger with them.

'Mercy, mercy!'

But it was useless to call for mercy to men whose superstitious feelings urged them on; far when the demon of superstition is active, no matter what form it may take, it always results in cruelty and wickedness to all.

Various were the shouts and menaces of the mob, and the stranger saw no hope of life unless he could escape from the hands of the people who surrounded him.

They had now nearly reached the ruins, and the stranger, who was certainly a somewhat odd and remarkable looking man, and who appeared in their eyes the very impersonation of their notions of a vampyre, was thrust from one to the other, kicked by one, and then cuffed by the other, as if he was doomed to run the gauntlet.

'Down with the vampyre!' said the mob.

'I am no vampyre,' said the stranger; 'I am new to these parts, and I pray you have mercy upon me. I have done you no wrong. Hear me, – I know nothing of these people of whom you speak.'

'That won't do; you've come here to see what you can do, I dare say; and, though you may have been hurt by the vampyre, and may be only your misfortune, and not your fault, yet the mischief is as great as ever it was or can be, you become, in spite of yourself, a vampyre, and do the same injury to others that has been done to you

– there's no help for you.'

'No help – we can't help it,' shouted the mob; 'he must die – throw him on the pile.'

'Put a stake through him first, though,' exclaimed the humane female; 'put a stake through him, and then he's safe.'

This horrible advice had an electric effect on the stranger, who jumped up, and eluded the grasp of several hands that were stretched forth to seize him.

'Throw him upon the burning wood!' shouted one.

'And a stake through his body,' suggested the humane female again, who seemed to have this one idea in her heart, and no other, and, upon every available opportunity, she seemed to be anxious to give utterance to the comfortable notion.

'Seize him!' exclaimed one.

'Never let him go,' said another; 'we've gone too far to hang back now; and, if he escape, he will visit us in our sleep, were it only out of spite.'

The stranger made a dash among the ruins, and, for a moment, out-stripped his pursuers; but a few, more adventurous than the rest, succeeded in driving him into an angle formed by two walls, and the consequence was, he was compelled to come to a stand.

'Seize him – seize him!' exclaimed all those at a distance.

The stranger, seeing he was now nearly surrounded, and had no chance of escape, save by some great effort, seized a long piece of wood, and struck two of his assailants down at once, and then dashed through the opening.

He immediately made for another part of the ruins, and succeeded in making his escape for some short distance, but was unable to keep up the speed that was required, for his great exertion before had nearly exhausted him, and the fear of a cruel death before his eyes was not enough to give him strength, or lend speed to his flight. He had suffered too much from violence, and, though he ran with great speed, yet those who followed were uninjured, and fresher, – he had no chance.

They came very close upon him at the corner of a field, which he endeavoured to cross, and had succeeded in doing, and he made a desperate attempt to scramble up the bank that divided the field from the next, but he slipped back, almost exhausted, into the ditch, and the whole mob came up.

However, he got on the bank, and leaped into the next field, and then he was immediately surrounded by those who pursued him, and he was struck down.

'Down with the vampyre! – kill him – he's one of 'em, – run a stake through him!' were a few of the cries of the infuriated mob of people, who were only infuriated because he attempted to escape their murderous intentions.

It was strange to see how they collected in a ring as the unfortunate man lay on the ground, panting for breath, and hardly able to speak – their infuriated countenances plainly showing the mischief they were intent upon.

'Have mercy upon me!' he exclaimed, as he lay on the earth; 'I have no power to help myself.'

The mob returned no answer, but stood collecting their numbers as they came up.

'Have mercy on me! it cannot be any pleasure to you to spill my blood. I am unable to resist – I am one man among many, – you surely cannot wish to beat me to death?'

'We want to hurt no one, except in our own defence, and we won't be made vampyres of because you don't like to die.'

'No, no; we won't be vampyres,' exclaimed the mob, and there arose a great shout from the mob.

'Are you men – fathers? – have you families? if so, I have the same ties as you have; spare me for their sakes – do not murder me – you will leave one an orphan if you do; besides, what have I done? I have injured no one.'

'I tell you what, friends, if we listen to him we shall all be vampyres, and all our children will all be vampyres and orphans.'

'So we shall, so we shall; down with him!'

The man attempted to get up, but, in doing so, he received a heavy blow from a hedge-stake, wielded by the herculean arm of a peasant. The sound of the blow was heard by those immediately around, and the man fell dead. There was a pause, and those nearest, apparently fearful of the consequences, and hardly expecting the catastrophe, began to disperse, and the remainder did so very soon afterwards.

THE MYSTERIES OF LONDON

A DEN OF HORRORS

However filthy, unhealthy, and repulsive the entire neighbourhood of West Street (Smithfield), Field Lane, and Saffron Hill, may appear at the present day, it was far worse some years ago. There were then but few cesspools; and scarcely any of those which did exist possessed any drains. The knackers' yards of Cow Cross, and the establishments in Castle Street where horses' flesh is boiled down to supply food for the dogs and cats of the metropolis, send forth now, as they did then, a foetid and sickening odour which could not possibly be borne by a delicate stomach. At the windows of those establishments the bones of the animals are hung to bleach, and offend the eye as much as the horrible stench of the flesh acts repugnantly to the nerves. Upwards of sixty horses a day are frequently slaughtered in each yard; and many of them are in the last stage of disease when sent to their "long home." Should there not be a rapid demand for the meat on the part of the itinerant purveyors of that article for canine and feline favourites, it speedily becomes putrid; and a smell, which would alone appear sufficient to create a pestilence, pervades the neighbourhood.

As if nothing should be wanting to render that district as filthy and unhealthy as possible, water is scarce. There is in this absence of a plentiful supply of that wholesome article, an actual apology for dirt. Some of the houses have small back yards, in which the inhabitants keep pigs. A short time ago, an infant belonging to a poor widow, who occupied a back room on the ground-floor of one of these hovels, died, and was laid upon the sacking of the bed while the mother went out to make arrangements for its interment. During her absence a pig entered the room from the yard, and feasted upon the dead child's face!

In that densely populated neighbourhood that we are describing hundreds of families each live and sleep in one room. When a member of one of these families happens to die, the corpse is kept in the close room where the rest still continue to live and sleep. Poverty frequently compels the unhappy relatives to keep the body for days –

aye, and weeks. Rapid decomposition takes place; animal life generates quickly; and in four-and-twenty hours myriads of loathsome animalculae are seen crawling about. The very undertakers' men fall sick at these disgusting – these revolting spectacles.

The wealthy classes of society are far too ready to reproach the miserable poor for things which are really misfortunes and not faults. The habit of whole families sleeping together in one room destroys all sense of shame in the daughters: and what guardian then remains for their virtue? But, alas! a horrible – an odious crime often results from that poverty which thus huddles brothers and sisters, aunts and nephews, all together in one narrow room – the crime of incest!

When a disease – such as the small-pox or scarlatina – breaks out in one of those crowded houses, and in a densely populated neighbourhood; the consequences are frightful: the mortality is as rapid as that which follows the footsteps of the plague!

These are the fearful mysteries of that hideous district which exists in the very heart of this great metropolis. From St. John-street to Saffron Hill – from West-street to Clerkenwell Green, is a maze of narrow lanes, choked up with dirt, pestiferous with nauseous odours, and swarming with a population that is born, lives, and dies, amidst squalor, penury, wretchedness, and crime.

Leading out of Holborn, between Field Lane and Ely Place, is Upper Union Court – a narrow lane forming a thoroughfare for only foot passengers. The houses in this court are dingy and gloomy: the sunbeams never linger long there; and should an Italian-boy pass through the place, he does not atop to waste his music upon the inhabitants. The dwellings are chiefly let out in lodgings; and through the open windows upon the ground-floor may occasionly be seen the half-starved families of mechanics crowding round the scantily-supplied table. A few of the lower casements are filled with children's book, pictures of actors and highwaymen glaringly coloured, and lucifer-matches, twine, sweet-stuff, cotton, etc. At one door there stands an oyster-stall, when the comestible itself is in season: over another hangs a small board with a mangle painted upon it. Most of the windows on the ground-floors announce rooms to let, or lodgings for single men; and perhaps notice may be seen better written than the rest, that artificial-flower makers are required at that address.

It was about nine o'clock in the evening when two little

children – a boy of seven and a girl of five – walked slowly up this court, hand in hand, and crying bitterly. They were both clothed in rags, and had neither shoes nor stockings upon their feet. Every now and then they stopped, and the boy turned towards his little sister, and endeavoured to console her with kind words and kisses.

'Don't cry so, dear,' he said: 'I'll tell mother that it was all my fault that we couldn't bring home any more money; and so she'll beat me worst. Don't cry – there's a good girl – pray don't!'

And the poor little fellow endeavoured to calm his own grief in order to appease the fears of his sister.

Those children had now reached the door of the house in which their mother occupied an attic; but they paused upon the step, evincing a mortal repugnance to proceed any farther. At length the little boy contrived by promises and caresses to hush the violence of his sister's grief; and they entered the house, the door of which stood open for the accommodation of the lodgers.

Hand in hand these poor children ascended the dark and steep staircase, the boy whispering consolation in the girl's ears. At length they reached the door of the attic: and there they stood for a few moments.

'Now, Fanny dear, don't cry, there's a good girl; pray don't now – and I'll buy you some nice pears to-morrow with the first halfpenny I get, even if I shouldn't get another, and if mother beats me till I'm dead when we come home.'

The boy kissed his sister once more, and then opened the attic-door.

A man in a shabby black coat, and with an immense profusion of hair about his hang-dog countenance, was sitting on one side of a good fire, smoking a pipe. A thin, emaciated, but vixenish looking woman was arranging some food upon the table for supper. The entire furniture of the room consisted of that table, three broken chairs, and a filthy mattress in one corner.

As soon as the boy opened the door, he seemed for a moment quite surprised to behold that man at the fireside: then, in another instant, he clapped his little hands joyously together, and exclaimed, 'Oh! how glad I am: here's father come home again!'

'Father's come home again!' echoed the girl; and the two children rushed up to their parent with the most pure – the most unfeigned delight.

'Curse your stupidity, you fools,' cried the man, brutally repulsing his children; 'you've nearly broke my pipe.'

The boy fall back, abashed and dismayed: the little girl burst into tears.

'Come, none of this humbug,' resumed the man; 'let's know what luck you've had to-day, since your mother says that she's been obliged to send you out on the tramp since I've been laid up for this last six months in the jug.'

'Yes, and speak out pretty plain, too, Master Harry,' said the mother in a shrill menacing tone; 'and none of your excuses, or you'll know what you have got to expect.'

'Please, mother,' said the boy, slowly taking some halfpence from his pocket, 'poor little Fanny got all this. I was so cold and hungry I couldn't ask a soul; so if it ain't enough, mother, you must beat me – and not poor little Fanny.'

As the boy uttered these words in a tremulous tone, and with tears trickling down his face, he got before his sister, in order to shield her, as it were from his mother's wrath.

'Give it here, you fool!' cried the woman, darting forward, and seizing hold of the boy's hand containing the halfpence: then, having hastily glanced over the amount, she exclaimed, 'You vile young dog! I'll teach you to come home here with your excuses! I'll cut your liver out of ye, I will!'

'How much has he brought?' demanded the man.

'How much! Why not more than enough to pay for the beer,' answered the woman indignantly. 'Eightpence-halfpenny – and that's every farthing! But won't I take it out in his hide, that's all?'

The woman caught hold of the boy, and dealt him a tremendous blow upon the back with her thin bony fist. He fell upon his knees, and begged for mercy His unnatural parent levelled a volley of abuse at him, mingled with oaths and filthy expressions. and then beat him – dashed him upon the floor – kicked him – all but stamped upon his poor body as he writhed at her feet.

His screams were appalling.

Then came the turn of the girl. The difference in the years of the children did not cause any with regard to their chastisement; but while the unnatural mother dealt her heavy blows upon the head, neck, breast, and back of the poor little creature, the boy clasped his hands together, exclaiming, 'O mother! it was all my fault – pray don't beat little Fanny – pray don't!' Then forgetting his own pain, he threw himself before his sister to protect her – a noble act of self-devotion in so young a boy, and for which he only received additional punishment.

At length the mother sate down exhausted; and the poor lad drew his little sister into a corner, and endeavoured to soothe her.

The husband of that vile woman had remained on moved in his seat, quietly smoking his pipe, while this horrible scene took place; and if he did not actually enjoy it, he was very far from disapproving of it.

'There,' said the woman, gasping for breath 'that'll teach them to mind how they came home another time with less than eighteenpence in their pockets. One would actually think it was the people's fault, and not the children's: but it ain't – for people grows more charitable every day. The more humbug, the more charity.'

'Right enough there,' growled the man. 'A reg'lar knowing beggar can make his five bob a day. He can walk through a matter of sixty streets; and in each street he can get a penny. He's sure a' that. Well, there's his five bob.'

'To be sure,' cried the woman: 'and therefore such nice-looking little children as our'n couldn't help getting eighteen-pence if they was to try, the lazy vagabonds! What would ha' become of me all the time that you was in the Jug this last bout, if they hadn't have worked better than they do now? As it is, every thing's up the spout – all made away with–'

'Well, we'll devilish soon have 'em all down again,' interrupted the man. 'Dick will be here presently; and he and I shall soon settle some job or another. But hadn't you better give them kids a their supper, and make 'em leave off snivellin' afore Dick comes?'

'So I will, Bill,' answered the woman; and throwing the children each a piece of bread, she added, in a cross tone, 'And now tumble into bed, and make haste about it; and if you don't hold that blubbering row I'll take the poker to you this time.'

The little boy gave the larger piece of bread to his sister; and, having divested her of her rags, he made her as comfortable as he could on the filthy mattress, covering her over not only with her clothes but also with his own. He kissed her affectionately, but without making any noise with his lips, for fear that that should irritate his mother; and then lay down beside her.

Clasped in each other's arms, those two children of poverty – the victims of horrible and daily cruelties – repulsed by a father whose neck they had a longed to encircle with their little arms, and whose hand they had vainly sought to cover with kisses; trembling even at the looks of a mother whom they loved in spite of all her harshness towards them, and a from whose lips one word – one single word of kindness would have gladdened their poor hearts; under such circumstances, we say, did these persecuted but affectionate infants, still smarting with the pain of cruel blows, and with tears upon their cheeks, thus did they sink into slumber in each other's arms!

Merciful God! it makes the blood boil to think that this is no over-drawn picture – that there is no exaggeration in these details; but that there really exist monsters in a human form – wearing often, too, the female shape – who make the infancy and early youth of their offspring one continued hell – one perpetual scene of blows, curses, and cruelties! Oh! for how many of our fellow-creatures have we to blush – how many demons are there who have assumed our mortal appearance, who dwell amongst us, and who set us examples the most hideous – the most appalling!

As soon as the children were in bed, the woman went out, and returned in a few minutes with two pots of strong beer-purchased with the alms that day bestowed by the charitable upon her suffering offspring.

She and her husband then partook of some cold meat, of which there was a plentiful provision – enough to have allowed the boy and the girl each a good slice of bread.

And the bread which this man and this woman ate was new and good; but the morsels thrown to the children were stale and mouldy.

'I tell you what,' said the woman, whispering in a mysterious tone to her husband, 'I have thought of an excellent plan to make Fanny useful.'

'Well, Polly, and what's that?' demanded the man.

'Why,' resumed his wife, her countenance wearing an expression of demoniac cruelty and cunning 'I've been thinking that Harry will soon be of use to you in your line. He'll be so handy to shove through a window, or to sneak down a area and hide himself all day in a cellar to open the door at night, or a thousand things.'

'In course he will,' said Bill, with an approving nod.

'Well, but then there's Fanny. What good can she do for us for years and years to come. She won't beg – I know she won't. It's all that boy's lies when he says she does: he is very fond of her and only tells us that to screen her. Now I've a very great mind to do someot that will make her beg – aye, and be glad to beg – and beg too in spite of herself.'

'What the hell do you mean?'

'Why, doing that to her which will put her entirely at our mercy, and at the same time render her an object of such interest that the people must give her money. I'd wager that with my plan she'd get her five bob a day; and what a blessin' that would be.'

'But how?' said Bill impatiently.

'And then,' continued the woman, without heeding this question, 'she wouldn't want Henry with her; and you might begin to make him useful some how or another. All we should have to do would be to take Fanny every day to some good thoroughfare, put her down there of a mornin', and go and fetch her agen at night; and I'll warrant she'd keep us in beer – aye, and in brandy too.'

'What the devil are you driving at?' demanded the man.

'Can't you guess?'

'No – blow me if I can.'

'Do you fancy the scheme?'

'Am I a fool? Why, of course I do: but how the deuce is all this to be done? You never could learn Fanny to be so fly as that?'

'I don't want to learn her anything at all. What I propose is to force it on her.'

'And how is that?' asked the man.

'By putting her eyes out,' returned the woman.

Her husband was a robber – yes, and a murderer: but he started when this proposal met his ear.

'There's nothin' like a blind child to excite compassion,' added the woman coolly. 'I know it for a fact,' she continued, after a pause, seeing that her husband did not answer her. 'There's old Kate Betts, who got all her money by travelling about the country with two blind girls; and she made 'em blind herself too – she's often told me how she did it; and that has put the idea into my head.'

'And how did she do it?' asked the man, lighting his pipe, but not glancing towards his wife; for although her words had made a deep impression upon him, he was yet struggling with the remnant of a parental feeling, which remained in his heart in spite of himself.

'She covered the eyes over with cockle shells, the eye-lids, recollect, being wide open; and in each shell there was a large black beetle. A bandage tied tight round the head, kept the shells in their place; and the shells kept the eyelids open. In a few days the eyes got quite blind, and the pupils had a dull white appearance.'

'And you're serious, are you?' demanded the man.

'Quite,' returned the woman, boldly: 'why not?'

'Why not indeed?' echoed Bill, who approved of the horrible scheme, but shuddered at the cruelty of it, villain as he was.

'Ah! why not?' pursued the female: 'one must make one's children useful somehow or another. So, if you don't mind, I'll send Harry out alone tomorrow morning and keep Fanny at home. The moment the boy's out of the way, I'll try my hand at Kate Betts's plan.'

The conversation was interrupted by a low knock at the attic-door.

THE EXECUTION

From the moment that Bill Bolter had been removed from the condemned cell, after his trial at the Old Bailey for the murder of his wife, he preserved a sullen and moody silence.

Two turnkeys sat up with him constantly, according to the rules of the prison; but be never made the slightest advances towards entering into conversation with them. The Chaplain was frequent in his attendance upon the convict; but no regard was paid to his religious consolations and exhortations of the reverend gentleman.

The murderer ate his meals heartily, and enjoyed sound physical health: he was hale and strong, and might, in the common course of nature, have lived until a good old age.

By day he sate, with folded arms, meditating upon his condition He scarcely repented of the numerous evil deeds of which he had been guilty: but he trembled at the idea of a future state!

One night he had a horrid dream. He thought that the moment had arrived for his execution, and that he was standing upon the drop. Suddenly the board gave way beneath his feet – and he fell. An agonising feeling of the blood rushing with the the fury of a torrent and with a heat of molten lead up into his brain, seized upon him: his eyes shot sparks of fire; and in his ears there was a loud droning sound, like the moan of the ocean on a winter's night. This satiation, be fancied, lasted about two minutes – a short and insignificant space to those who feel no pain, but an age when passed in the endurance of agony the most intense. Then he died: and he thought that his spirit left his body with the last pulsation of the lungs, and was suddenly whirled downwards, with tearful rapidity, upon the wings of a hurricane. He felt himself in total darkness; and yet he had an idea that he was plunging precipitately into a fearful gulf, around the sides of which hideous monsters, immense serpents, formidable bats, and all kinds of slimy reptiles were climbing. At length he reached the bottom of the gulf; and then the faculty of sight was suddenly restored to him. At the same moment, he felt fires encircling him all around; and a horrible snake coiled itself about him. He was in the midst of a boundless lake of flame; and far as his eyes could reach, he beheld myriads of spirits all undergoing the same punishment – writhing in quenchless fire, and girt by hideous serpents And he thought that neither himself nor those spirits which he beheld around, wore any shape which he could define; and yet he saw them plainly – palpably. They had no heads – no limbs; and yet they were something more than shapeless trunks – all naked and flesh-coloured, and unconsumed and indestructible amidst that burning lake, which had no end. In a few moments this dread scene changed, and all was again dark. The murderer fancied that he was now groping about in convulsive agonies upon the bank of a river, the stream of which was tepid and thick like blood. The bank was slimy and moist, and overgrown with huge osiers and dark weeds amidst which loathsome reptiles and enormous alligators were crowded together. And it was in this frightful place that the murderer was now spiritually groping his way, in total and coal-black darkness. At length he slipped down the slimy bank – and his feet touched the river, which he now knew to be of blood. He grasped convulsively at the osiers to save himself from falling into that horrible stream; a huge serpent sprang from the thicket, and coiled itself about his arms and neck; and at the same moment an enormous alligator rose from the river of blood, and seized him in the middle between its tremendous jaws. He uttered a fearful cry – and awoke.

This dream made a deep impression upon him. He believed that he had experienced a foretaste of Hell – of that hell, with all its horrors, in which he would he doomed for ever and ever – without hope, without end.

And yet, by a strange idiosyncracy of conduct, he did not court the consolation if the clergyman: he breathed no prayer, gave no outward and visible sign of repentance: but continued in the same sullen state of reserve before noticed.

Still after that dream, he dreaded to seek his bed at night. He was afraid of sleep; for when he closed his eyes in slumber, visions of hell, varied in a thousand horrible ways presented themselves to his mind.

He never thought of his children: and once when the clergyman asked him if he would like to see them, he shook his bead impatiently.

Death! he shuddered at the idea – and yet he never sought to escape from its presence by conversation or books. He sat moodily brooding upon death and what would probably occur hereafter, until he conjured up to his imagination all the phantasmagorical displays of demons, spectres, and posthumous horrors ever conceived by human mind.

On another occasion – the Friday before the Monday in which he was executed – he dreamt of heaven. He thought that the moment the drop had fallen from beneath his feet, a brilliant light, such as he had never seen on earth, shone all around him – the entire atmosphere was illuminated as with gold-dust in the rays of a powerful sun. And the sun and moon and stars all appeared of amazing size – immense orbs of lustrous and shining metal. He fancied that he winged his way upwards with a slow and steady motion, a genial warmth prevailing all around, and sweet odours delighting his senses. In this manner he soared on high until at length he passed sun, moon and stars, and beheld them all shining far, far beneath his feet. Presently the sounds of the most ravishing sacred music, accompanied by choral voices hymning to the praise of the Highest, fell upon his ear. His soul was enchanted by these notes of promise, of hope, and of love; and, raising his eyes, he beheld the shining palaces of heaven towering above vast and awe-inspiring piles of clouds. He reached a luminous avenue amidst those clouds, which led to the gates of paradise. He was about to enter upon that glorious and radiant path, when a sudden change came over the entire spirit of his dream; and in a moment he found himself dashing precipitately downwards, amidst darkness increasing in intensity, but through which the sun, moon, end planets might be seen, at immense distances, if a lurid and ominous red. Down – down be continued falling, until he was pitched with violence upon the moist and slimy bank of that river of tepid blood, whose margin was crowded with hideous reptiles, and whose depths swarmed with wide-mouthed alligators.

Thus passed the murderer's time – dread meditations by day, and appalling dreams by night.

Once he thought of committing suicide, and thus avoiding the ignominy of the scaffold. He had no shame; but he dreaded hanging on account of the pain – whereof he had experienced the dread sensations in his dreams. Besides, death is not quite so terrible when inflicted by one's own hand, as it is when dealt by another. He was, however, closely watched; and the only way in which he could have killed himself was by dashing the back of his head violently against the stone-wall. Then be reflected that he might not do this effectually; and so he abandoned the idea of self-destruction.

On the last Sunday of his life he attended the Chapel. A condemned sermon was preached according to custom. The sacred fane was filled with elegantly dressed ladies – the wives, daughters and friends of the City authorities. The Clergyman enjoined the prisoner repentance, and concluded by assuring him that it was not even then too late to acknowledge his errors and save his soul. God would still forgive him!

If God could thus forgive him, why could not Man? Oh! wherefore did that preacher confine his observations to the mercy of the Almighty? why did be not address a terrible lecture to bloodthirsty and avenging mortals? Of what use was the death of that sinner? Surely there is no moral example in a public execution? 'There is,' says the Legislature. We will see presently.

Oh! why could not the life of that man – stained with crime and red with blood though it were – have been spared, and he himself allowed to live to see the horror of his ways, and learn to admire virtue? He might have been locked up for the remainder of his existence: bars and bolts in English gaols are very strong; there was enough air for him to be allowed to breathe it ; and there was enough bread to have spared him a morsel at the expense of the state!

We cannot give life : we have no right to take it away.

On the Sunday afternoon, the murderer's children were taken to see him in the condemned cell. He had not asked for them, but the authorities considered it proper that they should take leave of him.

The pour little innocents were dressed in the workhouse garb. The boy understood that his father was to be hanged on the following morning; and his grief was heart-rending. The little girl could not understand why her parent was in that gloomy place, nor what horrible fate awaited him ;- but she had an undefined and vague sense of peril and misfortune; and she cried also.

The murderer kissed them, and told them to be good children ; but he only thus conducted himself because he was ashamed to appear so unfeeling and brutal as he knew himself to be, in the presence of the Ordinary, the Governor, the Sheriffs, and the ladies who were admitted to have a glimpse of him in his dungeon.

* * * * *

The morning of the second Monday after the Sessions dawned.

This was the one fixed by the Sheriffs for the execution of William Bolter, the murderer.

At four o'clock on that fatal morning the huge black stage containing the drop, was wheeled out of a shed in the Press Yard, and stationed opposite the debtors' door of Newgate. A carpenter and his assistant then hastily fitted up the two perpendicular spars, and the one horizontal beam, which formed the gibbet.

There were already several hundreds of persons collected to witness these preliminary arrangement.; and from that hour until eight o'clock multitudes continued pouring from every direction towards that spot – the focus of an all-absorbing interest.

Man – that social, domestic, and intelligent animal, will leave his child crying in the cradle, his wife tossing upon a bed of pain and sickness, and his blind old parents to grope their way about in the dark, in order to be present at an exhibition of fellow creatures disgrace, agony, or death. And the law encourages this morbid taste in all countries termed civilised – whether it be opposite the debtors door of Newgate, or around the guillotine erected at the Barriere Sant Jacques of Paris – whether it be in the midst of ranks of soldiers, drawn up to witness the abominable infliction of the lash in the barracks of Charing Cross, or the buttons cut off a deserter's coat in the Place Vendome – whether it be to see a malefactor broken on the wheel in the dominion of the tyrant who is called "Europe's Protestant Sovereign", or to behold the military execution of a great general at Madrid – whether it be to hear an English judge in the nineteenth century, unblushingly condemn a man to be hanged, drawn, and quartered, and his dissected corpse disposed of according to the will of our Sovereign Lady the Queen; or to witness some miserable peasant expire beneath the knout in the territories of the Czar.

But the Law is vindictive, cowardly, mean, and ignorant. It is vindictive because its punishments are more severe than the offences, and because its officers descend to any dirtiness in order to obtain conviction. It is cowardly, because it cuts off from the world, with a rope or an axe, those men whose dispositions it fears to undertake to curb. It is mean, because it is all in favour of the wealthy, and reserves its thunders for the poor and obscure who have no powerful interest to protect them; and because itself originates nearly half the crimes which it punishes. And it is ignorant, because it erects the gibbet where it should rear the cross – because it makes no allowance for the cool calculating individual who commits a crime, but takes into its consideration the case of the passionate man who assassinates his neighbour in a momentary and uncontrollable burst of rage – thus forgetting that the former is the more likely one to be led by redaction to virtue, and that the latter is a demon subject to impulses which he can never subdue.

From an early hour a glittering light was seen through the small grated window above the debtors door; for the room to which that door belongs is now the kitchen.

These was something sinister and ominous in that oscillating glare, breaking through the mists of the cold December morning, and playing upon the black spars of the gibbet which stood high above the already dense but still increasing multitudes.

Towards eight o'clock the crowd had congregated to such an extent that it moved and undulated like the stormy ocean. And, oh! what characters were collected around that jibbet. Every hideous den, every revolting hole – every abode of vice, squalor, and low debauchery, had vomited forth their horrible population. Women, with young children in their arms – pickpockets of all ages – swell-mobsmen – prostitutes, thieves and villains of all degrees and descriptions, were gathered there on that fatal morning.

And amidst that multitude prevailed mirth, and laughter, and gaiety. Ribald language, obscene jokes, and filthy expressions, were heard around, even to the very foot of the gallows; and even at that early hour intoxication was depicted upon the countenances of several whom the law had invited thither to derive an example from the tragedy about to be enacted!

Example, indeed! Listen to those shouts of laughter: they emanate from a group collected round a pickpocket only twelve years old, who is giving an account of how he robbed an elderly lady on the preceding evening. But, ah! what are those moans, accompanied with horrible oaths and imprecations? Two women fighting: they are tearing each other to pieces – and their husbands are backing them. In another direction, a simple-looking countryman suddenly discovers that his handkerchief and purse are gone. In a moment his hat is knocked over his eyes; and he himself is cuffed, and kicked, and pushed about in a most brutal manner.

Near the scaffold the following conversation takes place:

'I wonder what the man who is going to be hanged is doing at this moment.'

'It is now half-past seven. He is about receiving sacrament.'

'Well – if I was he, I'd send the old parson to the devil, and pitch into the sheriff.'

'Yes – so would I. For my part, I should like to live such a life as Jack Sheppard or Dick Turpin did, even if I did get hanged at last.'

'There is something noble and exciting in the existence of a highwayman: and then – at last – what admiration on the part of the crowd – what applause when be appears upon the drop!'

'Yes. If this fellow Bolter bad contented himself with being a burglar, or had only murdered those who resisted him, I should have cheered him heartily; but to kill his wife – there's something cowardly in that; and so I shall hiss him.'

'And so shall I.'

'A quarter to eight! The poor devil's minutes are pretty well numbered.'

'I wonder what he is about now.'

'The pinioning will begin directly, I dare say.'

'That must be the worst part.'

'Oh! no – not a bit of it. You may depend upon it that he is not half so miserable as we are inclined to think him. A man makes up his mind to die as well as to anything else. But what the devil noise is that?'

'Oh! only some fool of a fellow singing a patter song about a man hanging, and imitating all the convulsions of the poor wretch. My eyes! how the people do laugh !'

'Five minutes to eight! They won't be long now.'

At this moment the bell of Saint Sepulchre's church began to toll the funeral knell – that same bell whose ominous sound had fallen upon the ears of the wretched murderer, where he lay concealed in the vault of the Old House.

The laughing – the joking – the singing – and the fighting now suddenly subsided; and every eye was turned towards the scaffold. The most breathless curiosity prevailed.

Suddenly the entrance of the debtor's door was darkened by a human form; the executioner hastily ascended the steps, and appeared upon the scaffold.

He was followed by the Ordinary in his black-gown, walking with slow and measured pace along, and reading the funeral service – while the bell of Saint Sepulchre continued its deep, solemn, and foreboding death-note.

The criminal came next.

His elbows were bound to his sides, and his wrists fastened together with thin cord. He had on a decent suit of clothes, supplied by the generosity of Tom the Cracksman; and on his head was a white night-cap.

The moment be appeared upon the scaffold, a tremendous shout arose from the thousands and thousands of spectators assembled to witness his punishment.

He cast a hurried and anxious glance around him.

The large open space opposite the northern wing of Newgate seemed literally paved with human faces, which were continued down the Old Bailey and Giltspur Street, as far as he could see. The houses facing the prison were crammed with life – roof and window.

It seemed as if he were posted upon a rock in the midst of an ocean of people.

Ten thousand pairs of eyes were concentrated in him. All was animation and interest, as if a grand national spectacle was about to take place.

'Hats off!' was the universal cry: the multitudes were determined to lose nothing! The cheapness of an amusement augments the pleasure derived from it. We wonder that the government has never attempted to realise funds by charging a penny a-piece for admission to behold the execution at Newgate In such a country as England, where even religion is made a compulsory matter of taxation, the dues collected at executions would form a fund calculated to thrive bravely.

While the executioner was occupied in fixing the halter round the convict's neck, the Ordinary commenced that portion of the Burial Service, which begins thus:

'Man that is born of a woman hath but a short time to live, and and is full of misery. He cometh up, and is cut down like a flower: he fleeth as it were a shadow, and never continueth in one stay.'

The executioner having attached the rope, and drawn the nightcap over the criminal's face, disappeared from the scaffold, and went beneath the platform to draw the bolt that sustained the drop.

'In the midst of life we are in death; of whom may we seek for succour, but of thee, O Lord who–'

Here the drop fell.

A dreadful convulsion appeared to pass through the murderer's frame; and for nearly a minute his hands moved nervously up and down. Perhaps during those fifty seconds, the horrors of his dream were realised, and he felt the blood rushing with the fury of a torrent and with the heat of molten lead up into his brain; perhaps his eyes shot sparks of fire; and in his ears was a loud droning sound like the moan of the ocean on a winter's night!

But the convulsive movement of the hands soon ceased, and the murderer hung a lifeless corpse.

The crowd retained its post till nine o'clock, when the body was cut down: then did that vast assemblage of persons, of both sexes and all ages, begin to disperse.

The public-houses in the Old Bailey and the immediate neighbourhood drove a roaring trade throughout that day.

THE BODY-SNATCHERS

The Resurrection Man, the Cracksman, and the Buffer hastened rapidly along the narrow lanes and filthy alleys leading towards Shoreditch Church. They threaded their way in silence, through the jet-black darkness of the night, and without once hesitating as to the particular turnings which they were to follow. Those men were as familiar with that neighbourhood as a person can be with the rooms and passages in his own house.

At length the body-snatchers reached the low wall surmounted with a high railing which encloses Shoreditch churchyard. They were now at the back part of that burial ground, in a narrow and deserted street, whose dark and lonely appearance tended to aid their designs upon an edifice situated in one of the most populous districts in all London.

For some minutes before their arrival an individual, enveloped in a long cloak, was walking up and down beneath the shadow of the wall.

This was the surgeon, whose thirst after science had called into action the energies of the body-snatchers that night.

The Cracksman advanced first, and ascertained that the surgeon had already arrived, and that the coast was otherwise clear.

He then whistled in a low and peculiar manner; and his two confederates came up.

'You have got all your tools?' said the surgeon in a hasty whisper.

'Every one that we require,' answered the Resurrection Man.

'For opening a vault inside the church, mind?' added the surgeon. interrogatively.

'You show us the vault, sir, and we'll soon have out the body,' said the Resurrection Man.

'All right,' whispered the surgeon; ' and my own carriage will be in this street at three precisely. We shall have plenty of time -there's no one stirring till five, and its dark till seven.'

The surgeon and the body-snatchers then scaled the railing, and in a few moments stood in the churchyard.

The Resurrection Man addressed himself to his two confederates and the surgeon, and said, 'Do you lie snug under the wall here while I go forward and see how we must manage the door.' With these words he crept stealthily along, amidst the tomb-stones, towards the church.

The surgeon and the Cracksman seated themselves upon a grave close to the wall; and the Buffer threw himself flat upon his stomach, with his ear towards the ground. He remained in this position for some minutes, and then uttered a species of low growl as if he were answering some signal which caught his ears alone.

'The skeleton-keys won't open the side-door, the Resurrection Man says,' whispered the Buffer, raising his head towards the surgeon and the Cracksman.

He then laid his ear close to the ground once score, and resumed his listening posture.

In a few minutes he again replied to a signal; and this time his answer was conveyed by means of a short sharp whistle.

'It appears there is a bolt; and it will take a quarter of an hour to saw through the padlock that holds it,' observed the Buffer in a whisper.

Nearly twenty minutes elapsed after this announcement. The surgeon's teeth chattered with the intense cold; and he could not altogether subdue certain feelings of horror at the idea of the business which had brought him thither. The almost mute correspondence which those two men were enabled to carry on together – the methodical precision with which they performed their avocations – and the coolness they exhibited in undertaking a sacrilegious task, made a powerful impression upon his mind. He shuddered from head to foot:- his feelings of aversion were the same as he would have experienced had a loathsome reptile crawled over his naked flesh.

'It's all right now!' suddenly exclaimed the Buffer, rising from the ground. 'Come along.'

The surgeon and the Cracksman followed the Buffer to the southern side of the church where there was a flight of steps leading up to a side-door in a species of lobby, or lodge. This door was open; and the Resurrection Man was standing inside the lodge.

As soon as they had all entered the sacred edifice, the door was carefully closed once more.

We have before said that the night was cold: but the interior of the church was of a chill so intense, that an icy feeling appeared to penetrate to the very back-bone. The wind murmured down the aisle; and every footstep echoed, like a hollow sound in the distance, throughout the spacious pile.

'Now, sir,' said the Resurrection Man to the surgeon, 'it is for you to tell us whereabouts we are to begin.'

The surgeon groped his way towards the communion-table, and at the northern side or the railings which surrounded it he stopped short.

'I must now be standing,' he said, 'upon the very stone which you are to remove. You can, however, soon ascertain; for the funeral only took place yesterday morning, and the mortar must be quite soft.'

The Resurrection Man stooped down, felt with his hand for the joints of the pavement in that particular spot, and thrust his knife between them.

'Yes,' he said, after a few minutes' silence 'this stone has only been put down a day or two. But do you wish, sir, that all traces of our work should disappear?'

'Certainly! I would not for the world that the family of the deceased should learn that this tomb has been violated. Suspicion would immediately fall upon me; for it would be remembered how earnestly I desired to open the body, and how resolutely my request was refused.'

'We must use a candle, then, presently,' said the Resurrection Man; 'and that is the most dangerous part of the whole proceeding.'

'It cannot be helped, returned the surgeon,' in a decided tone. 'The fact that the side-door has been opened by unfair means must transpire in a day or two; and search will then be made inside the church to ascertain whether those who have been guilty of the sacrilege were thieves or resurrection-men. You see, then, how necessary it is that there should remain no proofs of the violation of a tomb.'

'Well and good, sir,' said the Resurrection Man. 'You command – we obey. Now, then, my mates, to work.'

In a moment the Resurrection Man lighted a piece of candle,

and placed it in the tin shade before alluded to. The glare which it shed was thereby thrown almost entirely downwards. He then carefully, and with surprising rapidity, examined the joints of the large flag-stone whirls was to be removed, and on which no inscription had yet been engraved. He observed the manner in which the mortar was laid down, and noticed even the places where it spread a little over the adjoining stones or where it was slightly deficient. This inspection being completed, he extinguished the light, and set to work in company with the Cracksman and the Buffer.

The eyes of the surgeon gradually became accustomed to the obscurity; and be was enabled to observe to some extent the proceedings of the body-snatchers.

These men commenced by pouring vinegar over the mortar round the stone which they were to raise. They then took long clasp-knives, with very thin and flexible blades, from their pockets; and inserted them between the joints of the stones. They moved these knives rapidly backwards and forwards for a few seconds, so as effectually to loosen the mortar, and moistened the interstices several times with the vinegar.

This operation being finished, they introduced the thin and pointed end of a lever between the end of the stone which they were to raise and the one adjoining it. The Resurrection Man, who held the lever, only worked it very gently; but at every fresh effort on his part, the Cracksman and the Buffer introduced each a wedge of wood into the space which thus grew larger and larger. By these means, had the lever suddenly given way, the stone would not have fallen back into its setting. At length it was raised to a sufficient height to admit of its being supported by a thick log about three feet in length.

While these three men were thus proceeding as expeditiously as possible with their task, the surgeon, although a man of a naturally strong mind, could not control the strange feelings which crept upon him, it suddenly appeared to him as if he beheld those men for the first time. That continuation of regular and systematic movements – that silent perseverance, faintly shadowed forth amidst the obscurity of the night, at length assumed so singular a character, that the surgeon felt as if he beheld three demons disinterring a doomed one to carry him off to hell!

He was aroused from this painful reverie by the Resurrection

Man, who said to him, 'Come and help us remove the stone.'

The surgeon applied all his strength to this task; and the huge flag-stone was speedily moved upon two wooden rollers away from the mouth of the grave.

'You are certain that this is the place?' said the Resurrection Man.

'As certain as one can be who stood by the grave for a quarter of an hour in day-light, and who has to recognise it again in total darkness,' answered the surgeon. 'Besides, the mortar was soft–'

'There might have been another burial close by,' interrupted the Resurrection Man; 'but we will soon find out whether you are right or not, sir. Was the coffin a wooden one?'

'Yes! an elm coffin, covered with black cloth,' replied the surgeon. 'I gave the instructions for the funeral myself, being the oldest friend of the family.'

The Resurrection Man took one of the long flexible rods which we have before noticed, and thrust it down into the vault. The point penetrated into the lid of a coffin. He drew it back, put the point to his tongue, and tasted it.

'Yes,' he said, smacking his lips, 'the coffin in this vault is an elm one, and is covered with black cloth.'

'I thought I could not be wrong,' observed the surgeon.

The body-snatchers then proceeded to raise the coffin, by means of ropes passed underneath it. This was a comparatively easy portion of their task; and in a few moments it was placed upon the flag-stones of the church.

The Resurrection Man took a chisel and opened the lid with considerable care. He then lighted his candle a second time; and the glare fell upon the pale features of the corpse in its narrow shell.

'This is the right one,' said the surgeon, casting a hasty glance upon the face of the dead body, which was that of a young girl of about sixteen.

The Resurrection Man extinguished the light ; and he and his companions proceeded to lift the corpse out of the coffin.

The polished marble limbs of the deceased were rudely grasped by the sacrilegious hands of the body-snatchers; and, having stripped the corpse stark asked, they tied its neck and heels together by means of a strong cord. They then thrust it into a large sack made for the purpose.

The body-snatchers then applied themselves to the restoration of the vault to its original appearance.

The lid of the coffin was carefully fastened down; and that now tenantless bed was lowered into the tomb. The stone was rolled over the mouth of the vault; and one of the small square boxes previously alluded to, furnished mortar wherewith to fill up the joints. The Resurrection Man lighted his candle a third time, and applied the cement in such a way that even the very workman who laid the stone down after the funeral would not have known that it had been disturbed. Then, as this mortar was a shade fresher and lighter than that originally used, the Resurrection Man scattered over it a thin brown powder, which was furnished by the second box brought away from his house on this occasion. Lastly, a light brush was swept over the scene of these operations, and the necessary precautions were complete.

The clock struck three as the surgeon and the body-snatchers issued from the church, carrying the sack containing the corpse between them.

They reached the wall at the back of the churchyard, and there deposited their burden, while the Cracksman hastened to see if the surgeon's carriage had arrived.

In a few minutes he returned to the railing, and said in a low tone, 'All right!'

The body was lifted over the iron barrier and conveyed to the vehicle. The surgeon counted ten sovereigns into the hands of each of the body-snatchers; and, having taken his seat inside the vehicle, close by his strange freight, was whirled rapidly away towards his own abode.

The three body-snatchers retraced their steps to the house in the vicinity of the Bird-cage Walk and the Cracksman and Buffer, having deposited the implements of their avocation in the corner of the front room, took their departure.

The moment the Resurrection Man was thus relieved from the observation of his companions, he seized the candle and hastened into the back room, where be expected to find the corpse of Richard Markham stripped and washed.

To his surprise the room was empty.

'What the devil has the old fool been up to?' he exclaimed; then, hastening to the foot of the stairs, he cried, 'Mummy, are you awake?'

In a few moments a door on the first floor opened, and the old woman appeared in her night gear at the head of the stairs.

'Is that you, Tony?' she exclaimed.

'Yes! who the hell do you think it could be? But what have you done with the fresh 'un?'

'The fresh 'un came alive again–'

'Gammon! Where is the money? how much was there? and is his skull fractured?' demanded the Resurrection Man.

'I tell you that he came to his senses,' returned the old hag: 'and that he sprung upon me like a tiger when I went into the back room after you was gone.'

'Damnation! what a fool I was not to stick three inches of cold steel into him!' ejaculated the Resurrection Man, stamping his foot. 'So I suppose he got clear away – money and all ? – Gone, may be, to fetch the traps!'

'Don't alarm yourself, Tony,' said the old hag, with a horrible cackling laugh; 'he's safe enough, I'll warrant it!'

'Safe! where – where?'

'Where his betters have been afore him,' answered the Mummy.

'What! – in the well in the yard?' exclaimed the Resurrection Man, in a state of horrible suspense.

'No – in the hole under the stairs.'

'Wretch! – drivelling fool! – idiot that you are!' cried the Resurrection Man in a voice of thunder: 'you decoyed him into the very place from which he was sure to escape!'

'Escape!' exclaimed the Mummy, in a tone of profound alarm.

'Yes – escape!' repeated the Resurrection Man. 'Did I not tell you a month or more ago that the wall between the hole and the saw-pit in the empty house next door had given way!'

'No – you never told me! I'll swear you never told me!' cried the old hag, now furious in her turn. 'You only say so to throw all the blame on me: it's just like you.'

'Don't provoke me, mother!' said the Resurrection Man, grinding his teeth. 'You know that I told you about the wall falling

134

down; and you know that I spoke to you about not using the place any more!'

'It's false!' exclaimed the Mummy.

'It's true; for I said to you at the time that I must brick up the wall myself some night, before any new people take the carpenter's yard, or they might wonder what the devil we could want with a place under ground like that; and it would be the means of blowing us!'

'It's a lie! you never told me a word about it,' persisted the old harridan doggedly.

'Perdition take you!' cried the man. 'The affair of this cursed Markham will be the ruin of us both!'

The Resurrection Man still had a hope left: the subterranean pit beneath the stairs was deep, and Markham might have been stunned by the fall.

He hastened to the trap-door, and raised it. The vivid light of his candle was thrown to the very bottom of the pit by means of the bright reflector of tin.

The hole was empty.

Maddened by disappointment – a prey to the most terrible apprehensions – and uncertain whether to flee or remain in his den, the Resurrection Man paced the passage in a state of mind which would not have been envied by even a criminal on his way to execution.

THE EXHUMATION

The night was fine – frosty – and bright with the lustre of a lovely moon.

Even the chimneys and gables of the squalid houses of Globe Town appeared to bathe their heads in that flood of silver light.

The Resurrection Man and the Buffer pursued their way towards the cemetery.

For some minutes they preserved a profound silence: at length the Buffer exclaimed, 'I only hope, Tony, that this business won't turn out as bad as the job with young Markham three nights ago.'

'Why should it?' demanded the Resurrection Man, in a gruff tone.

'Well, I don't know why,' answered the Buffer. 'P'rhaps, after all, it was just as well that feller escaped as he did. We might have swung for it.'

'Escape!' muttered the Resurrection Man, grinding his teeth savagely. 'Yes – he did escape them; but I haven't done with him yet. He shall not get off so easy another time.'

'I wonder who those chaps was that come up so sudden?' observed the Buffer, after a pause.

'Friends of his, no doubt,' answered Tidkins. 'Most likely he suspected a trap, or thought he would be on the right side. But the night was to plaguy dark, and the whole thing was too sudden, it was impossible to form an idea of who the two strangers might be.'

'One on 'em was precious strong, I know,' said the Buffer. 'But, for my part, I think you'd better leave the young feller alone in future. It's no good standing the chance of getting scragged for mere wengeance. I can't, understand that sort of thing. If you like to crack his crib for him and hive the swag, I'm your man; but I'll have no more of a business that's all danger and no profit.'

'Well, well, as you like,' said the Resurrection Man, impatiently. 'Here we are; so look alive.'

They were now under the wall of the cemetery.

The Buffer clambered to the top of the wall, which was not very high; and the Resurrection Man handed him the implements and tools, which he dropped cautiously upon the ground inside the enclosure.

He then helped hit companion upon the wall; and in another moment they stood together within the cemetery.

'Are you sure you can find the way to the right grave?' demanded the Buffer in a whisper.

'Don't be afraid,' was the reply: 'I could go straight up to it blindfold.'

They then shouldered their implements, and the Resurrection Man led the way to the spot where Mrs. Smith's anonymous lodger had been buried.

'I'm afeard the ground's precious hard,' observed the Buffer, when he and his companion had satisfied themselves by a cautious glance around that no one was watching their movements.

The eyes of these men had become so habituated to the obscurity of night, in consequence of the frequency with which they pursued their avocations during the darkness which cradled others to rest, that they were possessed of the visual acuteness generally ascribed to the cat.

'We'll soon turn it up, let it be as hard as it will,' said the Resurrection Man, in answer to his comrade's remark.

Then, suiting the action to the word, he began his operations hi the following manner.

He measured a distance of five paces from the head of the grave. At the point thus marked he took a long iron rod and drove it in an oblique direction through the ground towards one end of the coffin. So accurate were his calculations relative to the precise spot in which the coffin was embedded in the earth, that the iron rod struck against it the very first time he thus sounded the soil.

'All right,' he whispered to the Buffer.

He than took a spade and began to break up the earth just at that spot where the end of the iron rod peeped out of the ground.

'Not so hard as you thought,' he observed. 'The fact is, the whole burial-place is so mixed up with human remains, that the day is too greasy to freeze very easy.'

'I s'pose that's it,' said the Buffer.

The Resurrection Man worked for about ten minutes with a skill and an effect that would have astonished even Jones the grave-digger himself, had he been thereto see. He then resigned the spade to the Buffer, who took his turn with equal ardour and ability.

When his ten minutes elapsed, the resurrectionists regaled themselves each with a dram from Tidkins' flask; and this individual then applied himself once more to the work in hand. When he was wearied, the Buffer relieved him; and thus did they fairly divide the toil until the excavation of the ground was completed.

This portion of the task was finished in about forty minutes. An oblique channel, about ten feet long, and three feet square at the mouth, and decreasing only in length, as it verged towards the head of the coffin at the bottom, was not formed.

The Resurrection Man provided himself with a stout chisel the handle of which was covered with leather, and with a mallet, the ends of which were also protected with pieces of the same material. Thus the former instrument when struck by the latter emitted but little noise.

He then descended into the channel which terminated at the very head of the coffin.

Breaking away the soil that lay upon that end of the coffin, he inserted the chisel into the joints of the wood, and in a very few moments knocked off the board that closed the coffin at that extremity.

The wood-work of the head of the shell was also removed with ease – for Banks had purposely nailed those parts of the two cases very slightly together.

The Resurrection Man next handed up the tools to his companies, who threw him down a strong cord.

The end of this rope was then fastened under the armpits of the corpse as it lay in its coffin.

This being done, the Buffer helped the Resurrection Man out of the hole.

'So far, so good,' said Tidkins: 'it must be close upon one o'clock. We have got a quarter of an hour left – and that's plenty of time to do all that's yet to be done.'

The two men then took the rope between them, and drew the corpse gently out of its coffin – up the slope of the channel – and landed it safely on the ground at a little distance from the mouth of the excavation.

The moon fell upon the pale features of the dead – those features which were still as unchanged, save in colour, as if they had never come in contact with a shroud – nor belonged to a body that lead been swathed in a winding-sheet!

The contrast formed by the white figure and the black soil on which it was stretched, would have struck terror to the heart of any one save a resurrectionist.

Indeed, the moment the corpse was this, dragged forth from its grave, the Resurrection Man thrust his hand into its breast, and felt for the gold.

It was there – wrapped up as the undertaker has described..

'The blunt is all safe, Jack,' said the Resurrection Man; and he secured the coin about his person.

They then applied themselves vigorously to shovel back the earth; but, when they had filled up the excavation, a considerable quantity of the soil still remained to dispose of, it being impossible, in spite of stamping down, to condense the earth into the same space from which it was originally taken.

They therefore filled two sacks with the surplus soil, and proceeded to empty them in different parts of the ground.

Their task we so far accomplished, when they heard the low rumble of wheels in the lane outside the cemetery.

To bundle the corpse neck and heels into a sack, and gather to their implements, was the work of only a few moments. They then conveyed their burdens between them to the wall overlooking the lane, where the well-known voice of Mr. Banks greeted their ears, as he stood upright in his cart peering over the barrier into the cemetery.

'Got the blessed defunct?' said the undertaker interrogatively.

'Right and tight,' answered the Buffer; 'and the tin too. Now, then, look sharp – here's the tools.'

'I've got 'em,' returned Banks.

'Look out for the stiff 'un, then,' added the Buffer; and, aided by the Resurrection Man, he shoved the body up to the undertaker, who deposited it in the bottom of his cart.

The Resurrection Man and the Buffer then mounted the wall, and got into the vehicle, in which they laid themselves down, so that any person whom they might meet in the streets through which they were to pass would only see one individual in the cart – namely, the driver. Otherwise, the appearance of three men at that time of night, or rather at that hour in the morning, might have excited suspicion.

Banks lashed the sides of his horse; and the animal started offset a round pace.

Not a word was spoken during the short drive to the surgeon's residence in the Cambridge Road.

When they reached his house the road was quiet and deserted. A light glimmered through the fanlight over the door; and the door itself was opened the moment the cart stopped.

The Resurrection Man and the Buffer sprang and, seeing that the coast was clear, bundled the corpse out of the vehicle in an instant; then in less than half a minute the "blessed defunct", as the undertaker called it, was safely lodged in the passage of the surgeon's house.

Mr. Banks, as soon as the body was removed from his vehicle, drove rapidly away. His portion of the night's work was done; and he knew that his accomplices would give him his "reg'lars" when they should meet again.

The Resurrection Man and the Buffer conveyed the body into a species of out-house, which the surgeon, who was passionately attached to anatomical studies, devoted to purposes of dissection and physiological experiment.

In the middle of this room, which was shout ten feet long and six broad, stood a strong deal table, forming a slightly inclined plane. The stone pavement of the out-house was perforated with holes in the immediate vicinity of the table, so that the fluid which poured from subjects for dissection might escape into a drain communicating with the common sewer. To the ceiling, immediately above the head of the table, was attached a pulley with a strong cord, by means of which a body might be supported in any position that was most convenient to the anatomist.

The Resurrection Man and his companion carried the corpse into this dissecting-room, and placed it upon the table, the surgeon holding a candle to light their movements.

'Now, Jack,' said Tidkins to the Buffer, 'do you take the stiff 'un out of the sack, and lay him along decently on the table ready for business, while I retire a moment to this gentleman's study and settle accounts with him.'

'Well and good,' returned the Buffer. 'I'll stay here till you come back.'

The surgeon lighted another candle, which he placed on the window-sill, and then withdrew, accompanied by the Resurrection Man.

The Buffer shut the door of the dissecting-room, because the draught caused the candle to flicker, and menaced the light with extinction. He then proceeded to obey the directions which he had received from his accomplice.

The Buffer removed the sack from the body, which he then stretched out at length upon the inclined table, taking care to place its head on the higher extremity and immediately beneath the pulley.

'There, old feller,' he said, 'you're comfortable, at any rate. What a blessin' it would be to your friends, if they was ever to find out that you'd been had up again, to know into what skilful hands you'd happened to fall!'

Thus musing, the Buffer turned his back listlessly towards the corpse, and leant against the table on which it was lying.

'Let me see,' he said to himself, 'there's thirty-one pounds that was buried along with him, and then there's ten pounds that the sawbones is a paying now to Tony for the match; that makes forty-one pounds, and there's three to go shares. What does that make? Threes into four goes once – threes into eleven goes three and two over – that's thirteen pounds a-piece, and two pound to split–'

The Buffer started abruptly round, and became deadly pale. He thought he heard a slight movement of the corpse, and his whole frame trembled.

Almost at the same moment some object was hurled violently against the window; the glass was shivered to atoms; the candle was thrown down and extinguished; and total darkness reigned in the dissecting-room.

'Holloa!' cried the Buffer, turning sick at heart; 'what's that?'

Scarcely had these words escaped his lips when he felt his hand suddenly grasped by the cold fingers of the corpse.

'O God!' cried the miscreant; and he fell insensible across the body on the table.

THE STRING OF PEARLS

THE MADHOUSE CELL

When the porter of the madhouse went out to the coach, his first impression was that the boy, who was said to be insane, was dead; for not even the jolting ride to Peckham had been sufficient to arouse him to a consciousness of how he was situated; and there he lay still at the bottom of the coach alike insensible to joy or sorrow.

'Is he dead?' said the man to the coachman.

'How should I know?' was the reply; 'he may be or he may not, but I want to know how long I am to wait here for my fare.'

'There is your money, be off with you. I can see now that the boy is all right, for he breathes, although it's after an odd fashion that he does so. I should rather think he has had a knock on the head, or something of that kind.'

As he spoke, he conveyed Tobias within the building, and the coachman, since he had no further interest in the matter, drove away at once, and paid no more attention to it whatever.

When Sweeney Todd reached the door at the end of the passage, he tapped at it with his knuckles, and a voice cried–

'Who knocks – who knocks? Curses on you all, who knocks?'

Sweeney Todd did not make any verbal reply to this polite request, but opening the door he walked into the apartment, which is one that really deserves some description.

It was a large room with a vaulted roof, and in the centre was a superior oaken table, at which sat a man considerably advanced in years, as was proclaimed by his grizzled locks that graced the sides of his head, but whose herculean frame and robust constitution had otherwise successfully resisted the assaults of time.

A lamp swung from the ceiling, which had a shade over the top of it, so that it kept a tolerably bright glow upon the table below, which was covered with books and papers, as well as glasses and bottles of different kinds, which showed that the madhouse keeper was, at all events, as far as he himself was concerned, not at all indifferent to personal comfort.

The walls, however, presented the most curious aspect, for they were hung with a variety of tools and implements, which would have puzzled anyone not initiated into the matter even to guess at their nature.

These were, however, in point of fact, specimens of the different kinds of machinery which were used for the purpose of coercing the unhappy persons whose evil destiny made them members of that establishment.

Those were what is called the good old times, when all sorts of abuses flourished in perfection, and when the unhappy insane were actually punished, as if they were guilty of some great offence. Yes, and worse than that were they punished, for a criminal who might have injustice done to him by any who were in authority over him, could complain, and if he got hold of a person of higher power, his complaints might be listened to, but no one heeded what was said by the poor maniac, whose bitterest accusations of his keepers, let their conduct have been to him what it might, was only listened to and set down as a further proof of his mental disorder.

This was indeed a most awful and sad state of things, and, to the disgrace of this country, it was a social evil allowed until very late years to continue in full force.

Mr Fogg, the madhouse keeper, fixed his keen eyes, from beneath his shaggy brows, upon Sweeney Todd, as the latter entered his apartment, and then he said,-

'Mr Todd, I think, unless my memory deceives me.'

The same,' said the barber, making a hideous face. 'I believe I am not easily forgotten.'

'True,' said Mr Fogg, as he reached for a book, the edges of which were cut into a lot of little slips, on each of which was a capital letter, in the order of the alphabet, 'true, you are not easily forgotten, Mr Todd.'

He then opened the book at the letter T, and read from it:

'Mr Sweeney Todd, Fleet-street, London, paid one year's keep and burial of Thomas Simkins, aged 13, found dead in his bed after a residence in the asylum of 14 months and 4 days. I think, Mr Todd, that was our last little transaction: what can I do now for you, sir?'

'I am rather unfortunate,' said Todd, 'with my boys. I have got another here, who has shown such decided symptoms of insanity, that it has become absolutely necessary to place him under your care.'

'Indeed! does he rave?'

'Why, yes, he does, and it's the most absurd nonsense in the world he raves about; for, to hear him, one would really think that, instead of being one of the most humane of men, I was in point of fact an absolute murderer.'

'A murderer, Mr Todd!'

'Yes, a murderer – a murderer to all intents and purposes; could anything be more absurd than such an accusation? – I, that have the milk of human kindness flowing in every vein, and whose very appearance ought to be sufficient to convince anybody at once of my kindness of disposition.'

Sweeney Todd finished his speech by making such a hideous face, that the madhouse keeper could not for the life of him tell what to say to it; and then there came one of those short, disagreeable laughs which Todd was such an adept in, and which, somehow or another, never appeared exactly to come from his mouth, but always made people look up at the walls and ceiling of the apartment in which they were, in great doubt as to whence the remarkable sound came.

'For how long,' said the madhouse keeper, 'do you think this malady will continue?'

'I will pay,' said Sweeney Todd, as he leaned over the table, and looked into the face of his questioner, 'I will pay for twelve months; but I don't think, between you and I, that the case will last anything like so long – I think he will die suddenly.'

'I shouldn't wonder if he did. Some of our patients do die very suddenly, and somehow or another, we never know exactly how it happens; but it must be some sort of fit, for they are found dead in the morning in their beds, and then we bury them privately and quietly, without troubling anybody about it at all, which is decidedly the best way, because it saves a great annoyance to friends and relations, as well as prevents any extra expenses which otherwise might be foolishly gone to.'

'You are wonderfully correct and considerate,' said Todd, 'and it's no more than what I expected from you, or what anyone might expect from a person of your great experience, knowledge, and acquirements. I must confess I am quite delighted to hear you talk in

145

so elevated a strain.'

'Why,' said Mr Fogg, with a strange leer upon his face, 'we are forced to make ourselves useful, like the rest of the community; and we could not expect people to send their mad friends and relatives here, unless we took good care that their ends and views were answered by so doing. We make no remarks, and we ask no questions. Those are the principles upon which we have conducted business so successfully and so long; those are the principles upon which we shall continue to conduct it, and to merit, we hope, the patronage of the British public.'

'Unquestionably, most unquestionably.'

'You may as well introduce me to your patient at once, Mr Todd, for I suppose, by this time, he has been brought into this house.'

'Certainly, certainly, I shall have great pleasure in showing him to you.'

The madhouse keeper rose, and so did Mr Todd, and the former, pointing to the bottles and glasses on the table, said, 'When this business is settled, we can have a friendly glass together.'

To this proposition Sweeney Todd assented with a nod, and then they both proceeded to what was called a reception-room in the asylum, and where poor Tobias had been conveyed and laid upon a table, when he showed slight symptoms of recovering from the state of insensibility into which he had fallen, and a man was sluicing water on his face by the assistance of a hearth broom, occasionally dipped into a pailful of that fluid.

'Quite young,' said the madhouse keeper, as he looked upon the pale and interesting face of Tobias.

'Yes,' said Sweeney Todd, 'he is young – more's the pity – and, of course, we deeply regret his present situation.'

'Oh, of course, of course; but see, he opens his eyes, and will speak directly.'

'Rave, you mean, rave!' said Todd; 'don't call it speaking, it is not entitled to the name. Hush, listen to him.'

'Where am I?' said Tobias, 'where am I – Todd is a murderer. I denounce him.'

'You hear – you hear,' said Todd.

'Mad indeed,' said the keeper.

'Oh, save me from him, save me from him,' said Tobias, fixing his eyes upon Mr Fogg. 'Save me from him, it is my life he seeks, because I know his secrets – he is a murderer – and many a person comes into his shop who never leaves it again in life, if at all.'

'You hear him,' said Todd, 'was there anybody so mad?'

'Desperately mad,' said the keeper. 'Come, come, young fellow, we shall be under the necessity of putting you in a straight waistcoat, if you go on in that way. We must do it, for there is no help in such cases if we don't.'

Todd slunk back into the darkness of the apartment, so that he was not seen, and Tobias continued, in an imploring tone.

'I do not know who you are, sir, or where I am; but let me beg of you to cause the house of Sweeney Todd, the barber, in Fleet-street, near St Dunstan's church, to be searched, and there you will find that he is a murderer. There are at least a hundred hats, quantities of walking-sticks, umbrellas, watches and rings, all belonging to unfortunate persons who, from time to time, have met with their deaths through him.'

'How uncommonly mad!' said Fogg.

'No, no,' said Tobias, 'I am not mad; why call me mad, when the truth or falsehood of what I say can be ascertained so easily? Search his house, and if those things be not found there, say that I am mad, and have but dreamed of them. I do not know how he kills the people. That is a great mystery to me yet, but that he does kill them I have no doubt – I cannot have a doubt.'

'Watson,' cried the madhouse keeper, 'hilloa! here, Watson.'

'I am here, sir,' said the man, who had been dashing water upon poor Tobias's face.

'You will take this lad, Watson, as he seems extremely feverish and unsettled. You will take him, and shave his head, Watson, and put a straight waistcoat upon him, and let him be put in one of the dark, damp cells. We must be careful of him, and too much light encourages delirium and fever.'

'Oh! no, no!' cried Tobias; 'what have I done that I should be subjected to such cruel treatment? What have I done that I should be placed in a cell? If this be a madhouse, I am not mad. Oh, have mercy upon me, have mercy upon me!'

'You will give him nothing but bread and water, Watson, and the first symptoms of his recovery, which will produce better treatment, will be his exonerating his master from what he has said about him, for he must be mad so long as he continues to accuse such a gentleman as Mr Todd of such things; nobody but a mad man or a mad boy would think of it.'

'Then,' said Tobias, 'I shall continue mad, for if it be madness to know and to aver that Sweeney Todd, the barber, of Fleet-street, is a murderer, mad am I, for I know it, and aver it. It is true, it is true.'

'Take him away, Watson, and do as I desired you. I begin to find that the boy is a very dangerous character, and more viciously mad than anybody we have had here for a considerable time.'

The man named Watson seized upon Tobias, who again uttered a shriek something similar to the one which had come from his lips when Sweeney Todd clutched hold of him in his mother's room. But they were used to such things at that madhouse, and cared little for them, so no one heeded the cry in the least, but poor Tobias was carried to the door half maddened in reality by the horrors that surrounded him.

Just as he was being conveyed out, Sweeney Todd stepped up to him, and putting his mouth close to his ear, he whispered, 'Ha! ha! Tobias! how do you feel now? Do you think Sweeney Todd will be hung, or will you die in the cell of a madhouse?'

THE LAST BATCH OF THE DELICIOUS PIES

It would have been clear to anyone, who looked at Sweeney Todd as he took his route from his own shop in Fleet-street to Bell-yard, Temple Bar, that it was not to eat pies he went there.

No; he was on very different thoughts indeed intent, and as he neared the shop of Mrs Lovett, where those delicacies were vended, there was such a diabolical expression upon his face that, had he not stooped like grim War to 'Smooth his wrinkled form', ere he made his way into the shop, he would, most unquestionably, have excited the violent suspicions of Mrs Lovett, that all was not exactly as it should be, and that the mysterious bond of union that held her and the barber together was not in that blooming state that it had been.

When he actually did enter the shop, he was all sweetness and placidity.

Mrs Lovett was behind the counter, for it seldom happened that the shop was free of customers, for when the batches of hot pies were all over, there usually remained some which were devoured cold with avidity by the lawyers' clerks, from the offices and chambers in the neighbourhood.

But at nine o'clock, there was a batch of hot pies coming up, for of late Mrs Lovett had fancied that between half-past eight and nine, there was a great turn-out of clerks from Lincoln's Inn, and a pie became a very desirable and comfortable prelude to half-price at the theatre, or any other amusements of the three hours before midnight.

Many people, too, liked them as a relish for supper, and took them home quite carefully. Indeed, in Lincoln's Inn, it may be said, that the affections of the clerks oscillated between Lovett's pies and sheep's heads; and it frequently so nicely balanced in their minds, that the two attractions depended upon the toss-up of a halfpenny, whether to choose 'sang amary Jameses' from Clare Market, or pies from Lovett's.

Half-and-half washed both down equally well.

Mrs Lovett, then, may be supposed to be waiting for the nine o'clock batch of pies, when Sweeney Todd, on this most eventful evening, made his appearance.

Todd and Mrs Lovett met now with all the familiarity of old acquaintance.

'Ah, Mr Todd,' said the lady, 'how do you do? Why, we have not seen you for a long time.'

'It has been some time; and how are you, Mrs Lovett?'

'Quite well, thank you. Of course, you will take a pie?'

Todd made a horrible face, as he replied, 'No, thank you; it's very foolish, when I knew I was going to make a call here, but I have just had a pork chop.'

'Had it the kidney in it, sir?' asked one of the lads who were eating cold pies.

'Yes, it had.'

'Oh, that's what I like! Lor' bless you, I'd eat my mother, if she was a pork chop, done brown and crisp, and the kidney in it; just fancy it, grilling hot, you know, and just popped on a slice of bread, when you are cold and hungry.'

Will you walk in, Mr Todd?' said Mrs Lovett, raising a portion of the counter, by which an opening was made, that enabled Mr Todd to pass into the sacred precincts of the parlour.

The invitation was complied with by Todd, who remarked that he hadn't above a minute to spare, but that he would sit down while he could stay, since Mrs Lovett was so kind as to ask him.

This extreme suavity of manner, however, left Sweeney Todd when he was in the parlour, and there was nobody to take notice of him but Mrs Lovett; nor did she think it necessary to wreathe her face in smiles, but with something of both anger and agitation in her manner, she said, 'And when is all this to have an end, Sweeney Todd? you have been now for these six months providing me such a division of spoil as shall enable me, with an ample independence, once again to appear in the salons of Paris. I ask you now when is this to be?'

'You are very impatient!'

'Impatient, impatient? May I not well be impatient? Do I not run a frightful risk, while you must have the best of the profits? It is useless your pretending to tell me that you do not get much. I know you better, Sweeney Todd; you never strike, unless for profit or revenge.

'Well?'

'Is it well, then, that I should have no account? Oh God! if you had the dreams I sometimes have!'

'Dreams?'

She did not answer him, but sank into a chair, and trembled so violently that he became alarmed, thinking she was very, very unwell. His hand was upon a bell rope, when she motioned him to be still, and then she managed to say in a very faint and nearly inarticulate voice, 'You will go to that cupboard. You will see a bottle. I am forced to drink, or I should kill myself, or go mad, or denounce you; give it to me quick – quick, give it to me: it is brandy. Give it to me, I say: do not stand gazing at it there, I must, and I will have it. Yes, yes, I am better now, much better now. It is horrible, very horrible, but I am better; and I say, I must, and I will have an account at once. Oh. Todd, what an enemy you have been to me!'

'You wrong me. The worst enemy you ever had is in your head.'

'No, no, no! I must have that to drown thought!'

'Indeed! can you be so superstitious? I presume you are afraid of your reception in another world.'

'No, no – oh no! you and I do not believe in a hereafter, Sweeney Todd; if we did, we should go raving mad, to think what we had sacrificed. Oh, no – no, we dare not, we dare not!'

'Enough of this,' said Todd, somewhat violently, 'enough of this; you shall have an account tomorrow evening; and when you find yourself in possession of £20,000, you will not accuse me of having been unmindful of your interests; but now, there is someone in the shop who seems to be enquiring for you.'

Mrs Lovett rose, and went into the shop. The moment her back was turned, Todd produced the little bottle of poison he had got from the chemist's boy, and emptied it into the brandy decanter. He had just succeeded in this manoeuvre, and concealed the bottle again, when she returned, and flung herself into a chair.

'Did I hear you aright,' she said, 'or is this promise but a mere mockery; £20,000 – is it possible that you have so much? oh, why was not all this dreadful trade left off sooner? Much less would have been done. But when shall I have it – when shall I be enabled to fly from here for ever? Todd, we must live in different countries; I could never bear the chance of seeing you.'

'As you please. It don't matter to me at all; you may be off tomorrow night, if you like. I tell you your share of the last eight years' work shall be £20,000. You shall have the sum tomorrow, and then you are free to go where you please; it matters not to me one straw where you spend your money. But tell me now, what immediate danger do you apprehend from your new cook?'

'Great and immediate; he has refused to work – a sign that he has got desperate, hopeless and impatient; and then only a few hours ago, I heard him call to me, and he said he had thought better of it, and would bake the nine o'clock batch, which, to my mind, was saying, that he had made up his mind to some course which gave him hope, and made it worth his while to temporise with me for a time, to lull suspicion.'

'You are a clever woman. Something must and shall be done. I will be here at midnight, and we shall see if a vacancy cannot be made in your establishment.

'It will be necessary, and it is but one more.'

'That's all – that's all, and I must say you have a very perfect and philosophic mode of settling the question; avoid the brandy as much as you can, but I suppose you are sure to take some between now and the morning.'

'Quite sure. It is not in this house that I can wean myself of such a habit. I may do so abroad, but not here.'

'Oh, well, it can't matter; but, as regards the fellow downstairs, I will, of course, come and rid you of him. You must keep a good lookout now for the short time you will be here, and a good countenance. There, you are wanted again, and I may as well go likewise.'

Mrs Lovett and Todd walked from the parlour to the shop together, and when they got there, they found a respectable-looking woman and a boy, the latter of whom carried a bundle of printed papers with him; the woman was evidently in great distress of mind.

'Cold pie, marm?' said Mrs Lovett.

'Oh dear no, Mrs Lovett,' said the woman; 'I know you by sight, mom, though you don't know me. I am Mrs Wrankley, mom, the wife of Mr Wrankley, the tobacconist, and I've come to ask a favour of you, Mrs Lovett, to allow one of these bills to be put in your window?'

'Dear me,' said Mrs Lovett, 'what's it about?'

Mrs Wrankley handed her one of the bills and then seemed so overcome with grief, that she was forced to sink into a chair while it was read, which was done aloud by Mrs Lovett, who, as she did so, now and then stole a glance at Sweeney Todd, who looked as impenetrable and destitute of all emotion as a block of wood.

'Missing! – Mr John Wranldey, tobacconist, of 92 Fleet-street. The above gentleman left his home to go over the water, on business, and has not since been heard of. He is supposed to have had some valuable property with him, in the shape of a string of pearls. The said Mr John Wrankley is five feet four inches high, full face, short thick nose, black whiskers, and what is commonly called a bullet-head; thickset and skittle-made, not very well upon his feet; and whoever will give any information of him at 92 Fleet-street, shall be amply rewarded.'

'Yes, yes,' said Mrs Wrankley, when the reading of the bill was finished, 'that's him to a T, my poor, dear, handsome Wrankley! oh, I shall never be myself again; I have not eaten anything since he went out.'

'Then buy a pie, madam,' said Todd, as he held one close to her. 'Look up, Mrs Wrankley, lift off the top crust, madam, and you may take my word for it you will soon see something of Mr Wrankley.'

The hideous face that Todd made during the utterance of these words quite alarmed the disconsolate widow, but she did partake of the pie for all that. It was very tempting – a veal one, full of coagulated gravy – who could resist it? Not she, certainly, and besides, did not Todd say she would see something of Wrankley? There was hope in his words, at all events, if nothing else.

'Well,' she said, 'I will hope for the best; he may have been taken ill, and not have had his address in his pocket, poor dear soul! at the time.'

'And at all events, madam,' said Todd, 'you need not be cut up about it, you know; I dare say you will know what has become of him someday, soon.'

NEWGATE. A ROMANCE

THE OFFAL CELLAR

Newgate! What crowds of strange associations rush across the mind at the very pronunciation of that melancholy name! Stern, unpitiful, and terrific rises the massive structure before the mind's eye. Of all the crowds that hurry past its portals, who is there that now pauses to reflect for one moment upon the mass of human misery which those rough hewn walls have enclosed?

I had mused upon Newgate from the archway of the ancient inn in the broad light of day, and many strange thoughts and feelings had swept across me; but I longed to look at it in a quieter and more solemn hour – I wished to experience what would be the feelings that it would give to me at midnight, or at some short time beyond that hour, when the great city would be in its most composed and calm state. It was at such an hour that I longed to contemplate the gloomy structure.

It is not easy in London to find an hour for quiet contemplation, but observation had induced me to believe that the one which precedes day-break was that in which the greatest repose existed: the honest, pains-taking citizen is of course in his house and at rest; the theatres, and various places of amusement, have disgorged their multitudes; the latest visitors of the public-houses have reeled homeward, and those who were too far gone in inebriety to do so have probably fallen into the paternal arms of the police; the night robber has done his work, and, like some hideous phantom of humanity, begins to scent the morning air, and goes skulking home to the dismal haunt which conceals him from the eye of day; exhaustion has compelled the night-wanderer, be he whom or what he may, to lie down somewhere : and so for about an hour before the slant rays of the morning sun falls upon the city, we may find the greatest amount of quietude and repose that so vast a hive of humanity can know.

It was at such a time that I stood alone, opposite to Newgate, musing upon its chronicles and conjuring up ghostly visions of beings over whom the grave had long since closed, and whose faults, follies, crimes, and virtues, had rolled alike down the stream of time, alike unheeded and forgotten.

I noticed not a remarkable and sudden change in the aspect of the weather. The night had been serene, but now the wind blew in short puffy gusts around the melancholy building; the sky became of a pitchy darkness, and occasionally a strange moaning sound pervaded the air, as if the sighs of some of the unhappy beings, imprisoned in that terrible building, had escaped, and were borne on the wings of the night air, to some sympathising bosom.

At times, too, a dashing gust of rain would fly laterally before the wind, dashing against the houses for a moment, and then as rapidly disappearing as if it had ha no existence. The eastern sky ought to have been getting bright with the early tints of morn, but huge masses of black clouds interposed themselves, and all around was dark, dreary, and desolate.

But dimly did the grim outline of the ancient prison now present itself to my eyes. I could see it, and that was all; but yet the very dimness of its aspect seemed to conjure up with more distinctness to my mind's eye the visions of the past.

"Innocent hearts," I said, "have felt the painful throb of causeless agony within thy walls; the guiltless have even been heralded to death by thy sad ceremonies; and the blood of the judicially murdered cries aloud for vengeance against thee, Newgate! Oh, what a catalogue of woe would a brief chronicle of but a few of the scenes enacted within thy massive walls afford r

Something at this moment touched me, and I started on one side, for truly I thought I had been alone in the archway of that ancient inn.

" Are you deaf?" said a querulous voice. "Are you deaf? I have spoken twice, and had no answer."

I looked to where the voice came from, and I saw a miserable-looking object. It was a little old beggarman. As the Duke of Gloucester says, he was made up "unfashionably", and so much to one side had nature or accident inclined him, that he was compelled to use a crutch for support, and it was with that he had touched me, and made me start so suddenly.

"Well," he said, when he saw me by the very dim light there

was, regarding him minutely. "Well, what do you think of me now? I am a cripple and a beggar. Can you add anything else to the description?"

"I had no intention of offending you," I said, "if I have done so. I thought I was alone."

"Humph! did you come here to look at Newgate? I wonder how many times I have come to look at it by night and by day – in sunshine and in gloom – in serenity and in storms. What do you know of Newgate?"

"It is to me full of reflection."

"It is full of facts. You spoke of the guiltless suffering unknown pangs within those walls. I like the tone in which you spoke. Look at me again. I am hideously ugly. I am wretchedly poor. L am somewhat crabbed, too, in disposition. I don't seem to be fashioned by God. Perhaps I am a little mad. Will you come home with me and pass an hour, if you are at all curious about Newgate ?"

"Willingly."

"'Tis well. I say I like your voice. When I see your face, I will decide upon what more I can do. Perhaps I may give you an admission to Newgate.'

"You give me an admission? I thought that only the city dignitaries had such a power?"

"The city dignitaries!' cried the little old man, with scorn in his tone. "The city dignitaries show you Newgate?" Here he knocked his crutch against the ground furiously, as he added, " They never saw it themselves."

"Indeed! You much surprise me."

"You will be more surprised. If I please I can show you Newgate. Look there," and he raised his crutch towards the building. "You have been moralising upon what you see, upon what those walls may have enclosed; but it is below the level of the moving mass of humanity that throng the city, you will find there is something to see."

"Subterraneous places?"

"Ay; beneath Newgate are its sights. Who will show you the old dungeons, and the dusky passages long since deserted to noisome reptiles? Who will guide you through the curiosities of that part of Newgate which lies far below the level of all that those walls you now see before you enclose? There is not a cell, not a dungeon, but has its romance. If I chose to tell that which I know – but I have not seen your face. Will you sup with me?"

"I will accompany you with pleasure; but I think it is nearer the hour of breakfast than of supper."

"Call it what you will. Come on."

Curiosity, interest, and great expectation that I should really learn from the little old man something highly entertaining, urged me on, and I followed him willingly, saying, as I did so,

"I feel greatly obliged to you, indeed, for the offer, and will gladly follow you to your home, be it where it may."

"You don't know that," he said, sharply. "Probably you was never in such a home as mine before. Do you know what an offal cellar is?"

"A what?" I said.

"An offal cellar. You have talked largely or accompanying me wheresoever I shall please to lead you; that is my only home, and therefore it is that to such a place I must conduct you. Now, I presume, you shrink, and the romance of accompanying the old cripple is lost in the reality of his wretched home. Ah, ah! is it not so?"

"No," I replied, "you judge me wrongly. It matters not to me whether it be a cellar, or a saloon, to which you would conduct me. I admit with you, the hour is a strange one, and that probably I am wanting in worldly wisdom in accompanying you at all."

"That speech," said the curious little creature, "would be insulting, were it not for its candour. But, come on, follow me quickly, I am wearied, and would be at home."

It amazed me to see the dexterity and quickness with which he darted across the Street; cripple as he was, and using a crutch, I had enough to do to follow him closely. I think he saw that such was the case, and, with the pardonable vanity of one so afflicted, he put on an extra vigour, to show how well he could compete with the man fashioned according to the mass of mankind, and with all his physical energies fresh and young about him.

I made sure of this by his laugh of satisfaction, when, as we reached the corner of Newgate-street, I requested him to go at an easier pace.

"Ah, indeed!" he said; "and how much nearer Heaven you are than I. Strong, too, and your limbs well knit, and yet the old cripple with his crutch can beat you. Come on, come on. This way lies our route."

In a few moments he darted down one of the narrow avenues leading to Newgate-market, and now I trod closely upon his heels, for I was much afraid of losing him in the intricacies of that, to me, maze-like place.

The wind had dropped, or else it was so cut up among the narrow thoroughfares which we now were threading, that I heard it not; but the rain fell more heavily than before, and I began to think that any shelter would be desirable, until some more advanced hour of the morning should enable me to procure some easy means of transit homewards through the moist streets.

And yet now that I was out of the shadow of that huge building, which seemed to have thrown a halo of romance across my spirit. I began to revolve in my mind the imprudence I was guilty of in promising to accompany a total stranger to his home, It was true that the poor deformed little creature who was flitting before me through the miry, kennel-looking thoroughfares could have but little powers of mischief; but Heaven knows what more sinewy confederates he might have.

All that I had heard of midnight murders – of assassinations of unwary passengers – of heedless people decoyed into dens of crime, and then slaughtered perhaps for the mere value of their apparel, or because it would be dangerous, even when disappointed of booty, to let them go again, flashed across my imagination so that when the little old man suddenly paused in an extremely dark corner of the market, I felt half inclined to give up the idea of accompanying him further.

"This is my home," he cried.

I glanced at the place, and saw that it was a butcher's shop, for there were all the insignia of the trade, in the shape of huge hooks and benches for the meat to rest upon.

"How!" I said; "Are you in this trade?"

"No," he cried; but this is one of the oldest shops in the market. When business was not near so great as now it is, and London not the leviathan it has become, the butchers would cast the offal from their slaughter-houses into the cellars beneath these places. It is a practice long since abandoned, and the wealthy man who owns this place, out of the abundance of his benevolence, allows the poor crippled beggar a refuge in the deserted offal cellar, which otherwise were tenantless. Follow me!"

He seemed now to have no manner of hesitation whatever, but to consider the point as quite settled regarding my accompanying him. Had he doubted, I should have held back, but somehow or another, by his own confidence, he hurried me on, and I found myself following him down a most unpleasant flight of steps, for each one had a prodigious slope downwards, before I had time to think again of what I was about. Indeed these stairs were so ingeniously constructed, that when you commenced descending them, you were in a manner compelled to go all the way, from the impetus which the first two or three gave you.

"Stop!" cried the old cripple, in a shrill voice, "I'll get you a light; there's a deep hole somewhere about here; the remains of some old well, I think."

"Good God!" I said, "Why did you not mention that before?"

"Time enough! time enough!" he muttered, and presently I heard him striking a light, and as the showers of sparks fell upon the tinder, I caught strange, spectral-looking glances at his face. I dared not move, for I had a wholesome fear of the old well before my eyes, and right glad I was when I saw that he had procured a light, and the strange cavernous-looking place in which I was became unfolded to my gaze.

I don't know why I should have thought so, but I had got a notion in my head that the offal cellar was small and mean in its proportions. This was a great mistake. I found its roof massively arched, and the feeble rays of the candle which the old cripple held above his head, were all insufficient to penetrate into its deepest recesses.

"You can come in safety now," he said. "You are welcome. Is it not a splendid place? Saw you ever the like? Well suited either for the quick or the dead! A word or two in your ear. See you yon walls, partly of flints, and partly of bricks?"

"I do not yet," I said, "for my eyes are not sufficiently accustomed to the place to enable me to see so far."

"Come closer, come closer," he said, and hopping along by the assistance of his crutch in the peculiar mode of progress which belonged to him, he led the way to the further end of the offal cellar.

I followed him very quickly, for I got over my fears upon finding that we were alone, so that when he suddenly turned, which he did, and held up the light, I nearly fell over him, and the rays dazzled my eyes for a moment.

"Ah! ah!" he said, "I thought I should not be deceived! I don't like every one; but you have my kind of face."

"Thank'ee," I said, and I thought the compliment a dubious one at the moment he uttered it.

"Look!" he said, as he swung round on his crutch, and held the light towards the wall. "Look! we share that between us."

"Share what?' I said.

"That wall, and the low, arched door-way you see, once built up, but which I have rescued, and brought again to human observance; we share it between us.°

"Very good," I said; "but I am very willing to give up my moiety."

"Bah! bah!" he cried, with a fretfulness incidental to such creatures. "I meant not you; Newgate and I share it between us. This is my offal cellar – my home – my palace of thought. It will be my tomb! On the other side is Newgate, for we are exactly at the back of that mansion of despair. Think you the secrets of that prison-house lie upon its surface to meet the gaze of any casual visitant? Think you you have seen Newgate when you have strolled through its whitened, ventilated walls, preceded by an obsequious official? Do you know one of its secrets – one of its mysteries? Is there aught to carry you back to the past, and make you familiar with the human hearts that from time to time have beat within its walls? No the romance of the old prison has departed. It may be better – perchance it is – but time was when within those walls truth, far stranger than those wildest fictions which imagination pictures to the most discursive thinker, could be found. Oppression has there raised its gigantic head, remorse has shrieked its shriek of agony, the suicide has taken his last shuddering look upon that stony fragment of the world, to which he was to bid adieu for ever! Innocent hearts have broken with the worse than agony of hopelessness! The audacious, bold libertine – the cringing, shrieking wretch – the beautiful – the brave – the true – the callous – vicious – and the selfish, have alike aroused the melancholy echoes of the ancient pile! Look at me! Old, wretched, and despised! Yet am I the living chronicle of those things which have been! Newgate, I know you – I knew you in your pride of power! I knew you in your inquisitorial moods! I knew you when the voice of sweet humanity has not appealed to you in vain! Through the vista of years long past have I viewed you! In your social relations to the vast herd of humanity, among which you are centred. Yes, I – even I – the cripple – the beggar – the felon's father – he who has taken the hangman's cord from the neck of his own child – a ghastly relic –"

He paused abruptly, and the crutch dropped from his hold. Before I could catch him, for I had to stoop to do so, he had fallen to the earth, and it was a rare chance the candle was not extinguished.

"You are ill," I said ; "you have worked yourself into a state of excitement. Let me pray you to be calm; this is a subject which affects you too strongly to talk upon."

"Newgate! Newgate!" he gasped. "It is my destiny!"

There was a strange pallid hue upon his face. I began to get seriously alarmed, and anxiously asked of him if he had no restorative in the place which would aid in his recovery.

He merely shook his head, and then, in a faint voice, requested me to raise him from the ground. I did so; and he said languidly that he was better, and forbade me to leave him.

"I have said," he added, "that Newgate is my destiny. I never set foot within what may be called its public walls. That low arched doorway conducts to all its subterraneous cells and gloomiest passages. Places long since hidden from the public gaze, and forgotten even by those who, if they would, might visit them. A wiser, better policy prevails; the criminal now is believed to be human; and men will not, as once they did, cast off their erring fellow because his iniquity has assumed, perchance, a more troublesome shape than theirs. The time is coming when human nature will shrink from the perpetration of a great crime to be revenged for a lesser. In the dreary future I can see so much. It is not religion that will work the miracle, but pure and holy humanity, that origin of the heart which knows no dogmas and laughs at creeds. Man will know man better, and will judge his fellows more by motives than by acts! and so, Charles, some glimpses of happiness may yet be ours, and when you see your mother, tell her – Hush! hush I who speaks? Where are we now?"

A feeling at the moment came over me that he was dying. His

strange and abrupt transition from the present to some picture of the past which was traced upon his imagination, convinced me that delirium had seized upon him.

"You must permit me," I said, "to seek for aid."

"Hush, hush!" he cried, "Stir not, move not; like bloodhounds they're upon your path – they will drag you to a scaffold, but I must first be killed. You see the door that leads to the vaults of Newgate. A strange hiding-place for a convicted felon. It is the blessed sun that blinds my eyes. A fleecy mist is spread between me and the murmuring trees. The wallet! the wallet! This way, this way; support me better."

He indicated with his finger a particular corner of the cellar; and, as he struggled to reach it, I hesitated not to support him in his progress.

"Now unhand me," he said; "with a blessing and a forgiveness, I bid farewell to all. Adieu! The night of death has come."

He turned slowly, and faced me. How he stood without assistance I know not. It was, however, but for a moment, and then he swung slowly backward, and disappeared, as if by magic, from my sight. I made a spring forward to save him. God of Heaven! How near I was to destruction. It was the well he had spoken of. For one instant I trembled on the very brink; some loose earth slipped from beneath my feet; with a cry of horror I flung myself back, and then lay for some minutes half fainting on the edge of that abyss, down which my feet still hung. A cold perspiration bedewed my limbs; it was some moments before I believed in the fact of my own safety. I drew my breath shortly and with difficulty; and then I began to see objects a little clearer, and along with regret and much excitement at the scene I had gone through, came the blissful feeling that, although for a moment I had shivered upon the confines of mortal existence, I had been as if by a miracle, snatched back again to the world and its inhabitants.

THE ARCH DOOR

I know not how long I lay, for I was not in a state of mind to be able to appreciate time's progress; but, upon after recollection, I think nearly half an hour must have elapsed before I staggered to my feet, and removed myself as far as possible from the verge of the well. I found as I walked what a shock the mind had given to the physical powers; the muscles of my body had lost their tension, and I shook like one first attempting after a long and serious illness to move as he was wont to do.

And then arose the anxious question of what steps It behoved me to take under the circumstances in which I was placed. My thoughts were naturally confused and various; and, although I felt that I ought to do so, it was some time before I could muster courage sufficient to take the light and advance to the brink of the well.

It was then only by lying on the floor, and looking over it, that I could trust myself to try to see into its depths; but it was all in vain, it mocked investigation. The rays of the candle shot a sickly stream of light for a few feet below the surface, and beyond that all was mystery and gloom.

I strained my attention in a vain effort to listen for a faint sound of human agony that might come from the profound depths below – all was still and motionless. I felt the conviction that he was dead; and that with some strange insane resolve that the awful cellar, should be the resting-place of his remains, he had willfully cast himself into the well.

I had a duty to perform unto myself. To all appearance this poor creature was friendless; but still the usages of society compelled me to make known the manner of his death.

"I will leave this place at once, and those who have proper authority to do so shall again seek it with me. The very atmosphere here is close and strange. Where are the steps?"

With some difficulty I found them, for I was faint and weak. I left the candle still burning on the earthen floor and then I crawled from the frightful vault into the light of day.

I found upon reaching the top of the stairs that it was a swing trap hanging upon hinges, exactly beneath the window of the meat salesman's shop, which led to that subterranean region. It yielded to my touch, and I was once again in the free open air, feeling like a man awakened from some fearful dream, which has affected his imagination to an extent that makes it seem too real.

There are some facts of so startling and untoward a nature that we can scarce believe them real; while, again, there are some unreal pictures presented to the mind, which, in their semblance to that which is, come so near to reality, that we tremble to call them visions as much a we feel bewildered to conceive the possibility of the reality of the former.

In some such strange and unsettled state of mind I walked from the spot, and reached my own home without taking one single step to carry out what I had just proclaimed to myself to be a duty.

It was morning, and early passengers were already breaking the stillness of the giant city. The sunlight was gilding the church steeples, and lending beauty to the roughest and most uncouth objects, and as I inhaled the pure morning air, purer at such at an hour in London than it can be at any other time, I felt my strength return, and that, along with the noisome effluvium from the offal cellar, I was beginning to shake off much of the shuddering fear which the singular events that had there taken place had inspired me with.

And then I began to doubt, and, with a hesitation that each moment was answering itself, to ask myself what good I should accomplish by dragging the miserable body of the crippled beggar from the resting-place he had himself chosen for it.

There was no deed of crime to divulge – there was no retribution to come. I might dilate the eye of vulgar curiosity, or feed the ear of greedy gossip, and that was all. "Wherefore, then," I asked myself, "should I impose upon myself the task of detailing those events which just as well might he known to me alone as to all the world, so far as regarded any practical result arising from the knowledge ?"

This might be false reasoning, but it sufficed; and, moreover, it soon enabled me to add a more cogent argument than all the rest, which was, that because I had not at first communicated to the authorities what I knew, I should be blamed instead of commended; and, therefore, it was better left alone altogether.

Probably we oftener deceive ourselves mentally than we succeed in deceiving any one else. It is strange, but true, that we often want the candour to fish up from the bottom of our thoughts our real motives of action; but as I consider myself, in a manner of speaking, on my confession, I do not hesitate to say, that the romantic thought of another visit to the awful cellar, and, perhaps, an exploration alone of what wonders might lie beyond the low arched doorway, materially aided me in my resolution of reserving to myself the secret of the beggar's death.

He had spoken of a wallet, too; what if it contained some of those records of the past with which he professed himself to he so familiar? The very thought was a delicious one, and it grew upon me hour by hour, and day by day.

If anything could have been more charming to my imagination than another, it was certainly the capacity to view society accurately through some strange and new medium. What, I asked myself, can be more likely to present to me the conflict of human passions in all its various phases than the history of Newgate? Not the dull record of its walls, by whom they were erected, or in what year; by whom or under what circumstances they were destroyed, and in what era raised again to be a terror to evil doers. This was not what my imagination pictured to me as the history of Newgate. It was an acquaintance with what I might call its personal and domestic records that I panted for. I cared not for the building as a building; but for the living forms it had immured, with all their passions and propensities, their feelings, and their hopes, and their actions, of good or of evil, I cared much; for those were records of humanity, and such as had ever been deeply interesting to me.

I was not one ever inclined to look upon those who had outraged man's ordinances as absolute outcasts from the great human family. I had ever seen much concerning them set down in malice, and but very little extenuated.

Hence, through the medium of that cold and pitiless building, I hoped to obtain glimpses of human nature, such as through no other medium could I have any chance or expectation of beholding.

What pictures, too, of the manners, and the habits, and the

modes of thought of times gone by, would the veritable records of criminals present. They must to the mind's eye, show the very age and body of the times. For, in the contemplation of such people, and such scenes, we should see humanity in its most unaffected state.

The audacious criminal who spurns the law's control, and mocks morality, has thrown off all that affectation which might cast a veil over his real character and impulses. Those who love him and who pity him for the consequences of his crimes, as if he were the victim rather of misfortune than willfulness, will shine forth in the unaffected lustre of their real characters. Those, too, who may have suffered from his depredations, and of whom he may have exacted that support which he considered society owed him from other sources than honest industry, will show themselves in their true colours, and we shall be enabled to judge of them better, probably, than under any other circumstances under which we might have an opportunity of viewing them.

With these feelings and thoughts a week had passed away, and then, with rather a sudden impulse, than from a determination to do so, I, one dark and cloudy evening, started from my home to pay another visit to the offal cellar in Newgate-market.

When once I had commenced proceeding in that direction, I seemed to entertain no doubts of the propriety of my doing so, and I wondered to myself that I had remained so long inactive.

That no discovery whatever had taken place with regard either to the mortal remains of the crippled beggar, or any matter which he might have left behind him in his dungeon-like home, I was well convinced, because, if such had been the case, popular rumour would soon have brought it to my ears.

I chose the hour of my visit when the business of the market was completely over, with the exception of those few salesmen who make a practice of disposing of the refuse of the general stock. None of these men, however, inhabited the quarter where the offal cellar was situated, so that when I reached the exterior of the shop beneath which it was, I found myself alone, and at liberty, without observation, to take what steps I pleased.

I noticed now what had before escaped my observation; namely, that the shop above was to let, so that the chances of anything like interruption were much less under ordinary circumstances than they would have been, and being provided with the means of procuring light in abundance, I hesitated not. By pushing aside the swing-trap, I slowly descended the staircase until I completely removed myself from the street, and then procured a light to guide me on the remainder of my way.

Being thus enabled to proceed fearlessly, I was soon on the earthen floor of the cellar, and then it is not to be wondered at that my eye should wander restlessly towards the well wherein I had nearly found my grave.

I could picture to myself the body of the cripple slowly mouldering away, and, sad and pale as he looked in life, how much more ghastly and terrific must be his appearance now.

I was not, and I am not superstitious; but I trod softly on the floor of that place, for I felt that I was alone with the dead.

I went then to make a more narrow inspection of the small door he had shown to me, and it presented to my eyes a curious and antique appearance. There were all the remains about it of massiveness and huge strength. It was cased with iron, and there was a lock upon it, of such dimensions, that had the door itself, stripped of its accessories, been placed in one scale, and that ponderous lock in another, it is a doubtful point which would have turned the balance.

"And can it be possible," I asked myself, "Newgate, terrible, gigantic Newgate, is on the other side of this door-way? Am I separated only from its long hidden and gloomiest recesses by these few inches of wood and iron, and shall I not make some effort to pass them?. He spoke of a wallet and a key. I see no wallet."

I now narrowly searched throughout the entire vault, but was bitterly disappointed, for wallet found I none. My disappointment, too, was the more acute, because I had a vivid recollection of the cripple pointing in a particular direction, as though it were there to be found.

It was a great pang to me to think that, after all, notwithstanding my supposition to the contrary, some one had been beforehand with me.

But of what use was it now to remain within the gloomy place? I could not pass the door which communicated with Newgate, for I had no means with me then to force aside so serious an obstacle, and so sorrowfully, and with a bitter feeling of disappointment. I commenced reascending the steps.

Something possessed me to return and look into the vault, when I had got about three parts of the way from its floor, and then I saw what I had entirely overlooked before; namely, a leathern valise hanging from the ceilings and under which I must have passed many times in my fruitless search.

I think scarcely a minute must have elapsed ere I possessed myself of the prize. It felt weighty, and with it firmly clasped beneath my arm, I left the place.

To proceed home at a rapid pace was the work of a very short period of time, and with what trembling fingers of anticipation did I unfold the wallet.

The first object which presented itself to say eyes was a bunch of keys of massive weight and structure. I hastily glanced at them, and then placed them aside, for beneath them lay a dense heap of papers, closely written, and apparently got up most systematically.

I found them to consist of different packets, and each tied with cord; slipped within the cordage of the topmost one was a scrap of paper, on which I read the following words:

"The labour of years will be rewarded if the following chronicles of Newgate fall into congenial hands. Do not doubt their truthfulness, for they are either drawn from the life Itself, or from such oral or documentary tradition as ought to stamp them with integrity."

I eagerly opened the first of the papers, and, written largely at the top, was the date – 1720 – and immediately beneath that was a paragraph to the following effect:

"Look kindly on the errors of those who now sleep the sleep of death. Let their vices suffice, if they may, to point a moral; but in the records which the following pages present, let there be found some excuse for the errors of one who might have been, under better auspices, far other than that which he became, in the self-denial, the virtue, and the noble generosity of another; who, perchance, but for such a stimulant as love for one who little deserved such devotion of tenderness, might have glided more calmly through life, certainly adorning its domestic privacy, but not exhibiting to the world's wonder so exquisite a lesson of fortitude, of utter abandonment of self, and of enduring affection through all trials, and all privations, as these pages will portray.

"And if it be not the humour of the reader to look for morals, let him not look for food to feed a censure which we may now spare to those who are no more. Let the pages then amuse if they take no higher flight; but yet that those who read them may rise from their perusal wiser and better, and with a kindlier feeling to their fellows, has ever been the wish of him who will take care that these records never see the light of day while the breath of life is in him."

Immediately beneath this was the following title:

THE SHADOW OF DEATH; OR, THE COFFIN CELL.

WAGNER THE WEHR-WOLF

PROLOGUE

It was the month of January, 1516.

The night was dark and tempestuous; the thunder growled around; the lightning flashed at short intervals: and the wind swept furiously along in sudden and fitful gusts.

The streams of the great Black Forest of Germany babbled in playful melody no more, but rushed on with deafening din, mingling their torrent roar with the wild creaking of the huge oaks, the rustling of the firs, the howling of the affrighted wolves, and the hollow voices of the storm.

The dense black clouds were driving restlessly athwart the sky; and when the vivid lightning gleamed forth with rapid and eccentric glare, it seemed as if the dark jaws of some hideous monster, floating high above, opened to vomit flame.

And as the abrupt but furious gusts of wind swept through the forest, they raised strange echoes – as if the impervious mazes of that mighty wood were the abode of hideous fiends and evil spirits, who responded in shrieks, moans, and lamentations to the fearful din of the tempest.

It was, indeed, an appalling night!

An old – old man sat in his cottage on the verge of the Black Forest.

He had numbered ninety years; his head was completely bald – his mouth was toothless – his long beard was white as snow, and his limbs were feeble and trembling.

He was alone in the world; his wife, his children, his grandchildren, all his relations, in fine, save one, had preceded him on that long, last voyage, from which no traveler returns.

And that one was a grand-daughter, a beauteous girl of sixteen, who had hitherto been his solace and his comfort, but who had suddenly disappeared – he knew not how – a few days previously to the time when we discover him seated thus lonely in his poor cottage.

But perhaps she also was dead! An accident might have snatched her away from him, and sent her spirit to join those of her father and mother, her sisters and her brothers, whom a terrible pestilence – the Black Death – hurried to the tomb a few years before.

No: the old man could not believe that his darling granddaughter was no more – for he had sought her throughout the neighboring district of the Black Forest, and not a trace of her was to be seen. Had she fallen down a precipice, or perished by the ruthless murderer's hand, he would have discovered her mangled corpse: had she become the prey of the ravenous wolves, certain signs of her fate would have doubtless somewhere appeared.

The sad – the chilling conviction therefore, went to the old man's heart, that the only being left to solace him on earth, had deserted him; and his spirit was bowed down in despair.

Who now would prepare his food, while he tended his little flock? who was there to collect the dry branches in the forest, for the winter's fuel, while the aged shepherd watched a few sheep that he possessed? who would now spin him warm clothing to protect his weak and trembling limbs?

'Oh! Agnes,' he murmured, in a tone indicative of a breaking heart, 'why couldst thou have thus abandoned me? Didst thou quit the old man to follow some youthful lover, who will buoy thee up with bright hopes, and then deceive thee? O Agnes – my darling! hast thou left me to perish without a soul to close my eyes?'

It was painful how that ancient shepherd wept.

Suddenly a loud knock at the door of the cottage aroused him from his painful reverie; and he hastened, as fast as his trembling limbs would permit him, to answer the summons.

He opened the door; and a tall man, apparently about forty years of age, entered the humble dwelling. His light hair would have been magnificent indeed, were it not sorely neglected; his blue eyes were naturally fine and intelligent, but fearful now to meet, so wild and wandering were their glances: his form was tall and admirably symmetrical, but prematurely bowed by the weight of sorrow, and his attire was of costly material, but indicative of inattention even more than it was travel-soiled.

The old man closed the door, and courteously drew a stool near the fire for the stranger who had sought in his cottage a refuge against the fury of the storm.

He also placed food before him; but the stranger touched it not – horror and dismay appearing to have taken possession of his soul.

Suddenly the thunder which had hitherto growled at a distance, burst above the humble abode; and the wind swept by with so violent a gust, that it shook the little tenement to its foundation, and filled the neighboring forest with strange, unearthly noises.

Then the countenance of the stranger expressed such ineffable horror, amounting to a fearful agony, that the old man was alarmed, and stretched out his hand to grasp a crucifix that hung over the chimney-piece; but his mysterious guest made a forbidding sign of so much earnestness mingled with such proud authority, that the aged shepherd sank back into his seat without touching the sacred symbol.

The roar of the thunder past – the shrieking, whistling, gushing wind became temporarily lulled into low moans and subdued lamentations, amid the mazes of the Black Forest; and the stranger grew more composed.

'Dost thou tremble at the storm?' inquired the old man.

'I am unhappy,' was the evasive and somewhat impatient reply. 'Seek not to know more of me – beware how you question me. But you, old man, are not happy! The traces of care seem to mingle with the wrinkles of age upon your brow!'

The shepherd narrated, in brief and touching terms, the unaccountable disappearance of his much-beloved granddaughter Agnes.

The stranger listened abstractedly at first; but afterward he appeared to reflect profoundly for several minutes.

'Your lot is wretched, old man,' said he at length: 'if you live a few years longer, that period must be passed in solitude and cheerlessness: if you suddenly fall ill you must die the lingering death of famine, without a soul to place a morsel of food, or the cooling cup to your lips; and when you shall be no more, who will follow you to the grave? There are no habitations nigh; the nearest village is half-a-day's journey distant; and ere the peasants of that hamlet, or some passing traveler, might discover that the inmate of this hut had breathed his last, the wolves from the forest would have entered and mangled your corpse.'

'Talk not thus!' cried the old man, with a visible shudder; then darting a half-terrified, half-curious glance at his guest, he said, 'but who are you that speak in this awful strain – this warning voice?'

Again the thunder rolled, with crashing sound, above the cottage; and once more the wind swept by, laden, as it seemed, with the shrieks and groans of human beings in the agonies of death.

The stranger maintained a certain degree of composure only by means of a desperate effort, but he could not altogether subdue a wild flashing of the eyes and a ghastly change of the countenance – signs of a profoundly felt terror.

'Again I say, ask me not who I am!' he exclaimed, when the thunder and the gust had passed. 'My soul recoils from the bare idea of pronouncing my own accursed name! But – unhappy as you see me – crushed, overwhelmed with deep affliction as you behold me – anxious, but unable to repent for the past as I am, and filled with appalling dread for the future as I now proclaim myself to be, still is my power far, far beyond that limit which hems mortal energies within so small a sphere. Speak, old man – wouldst thou change thy condition? For to me – and to me alone of all human beings – belongs the means of giving thee new life – of bestowing upon thee the vigor of youth, of rendering that stooping form upright and strong, of restoring fire to those glazing eyes, and beauty to that wrinkled, sunken, withered countenance – of endowing thee, in a word, with a fresh tenure of existence and making that existence sweet by the aid of treasures so vast that no extravagance can dissipate them!'

A strong though indefinite dread assailed the old man as this astounding proffer was rapidly opened, in all its alluring details, to his mind, and various images of terror presented themselves to his imagination; but these feelings were almost immediately dominated by a wild and ardent hope, which became the more attractive and exciting in proportion as a rapid glance at his helpless, wretched, deserted condition led him to survey the contrast between what he then was, and what, if the stranger spoke truly, he might so soon become.

The stranger saw that he had made the desired impression; and he continued thus:

'Give but your assent, old man, and not only will I render thee young, handsome, and wealthy; but I will endow thy mind with an intelligence to match that proud position. Thou shalt go forth into the world to enjoy all those pleasures, those delights, and those luxuries, the names of which are even now scarcely known to thee!'

'And what is the price of this glorious boon?' asked the old man, trembling with mingled joy and terror through every limb.

'There are two conditions,' answered the stranger, in a low, mysterious tone. 'The first is, that you become the companion of my wanderings for one year and a half from the present time, until the hour of sunset, on the 30th of July, 1517, when we must part forever, you to go whithersoever your inclinations may guide you, and I – but of that, no matter!' he added, hastily, with a sudden motion as if of deep mental agony, and with wildly flashing eyes.

The old man shrank back in dismay from his mysterious guest: the thunder rolled again, the rude gust swept fiercely by, the dark forest rustled awfully, and the stranger's torturing feelings were evidently prolonged by the voices of the storm.

A pause ensued; and the silence was at length broken by the old man, who said, in a hollow and tremulous tone, 'To the first condition I would willingly accede. But the second?'

'That you prey upon the human race, whom I hate; because of all the world I alone am so deeply, so terribly accurst!' was the ominously fearful yet only dimly significant reply.

The old man shook his head, scarcely comprehending the words of his guest, and yet daring not to ask to be more enlightened.

'Listen!' said the stranger, in a hasty but impressive voice: 'I require a companion, one who has no human ties, and who still ministers to my caprices – who will devote himself wholly and solely to watch me in my dark hours, and endeavor to recall me back to enjoyment and pleasure, who, when he shall be acquainted with my power, will devise new means in which to exercise it, for the purpose of conjuring up those scenes of enchantment and delight that may for a season win me away from thought. Such a companion do I need for a period of one year and a half; and you are, of all men, the best suited to my design. But the Spirit whom I must invoke to effect the promised change in thee, and by whose aid you can be given back to youth and comeliness, will demand some fearful sacrifice at your hands. And the nature of that sacrifice – the nature of the condition to be imposed – I can well divine!'

'Name the sacrifice – name the condition!' cried the old man, eagerly. 'I am so miserable – so spirit-broken – so totally without hope in this world, that I greedily long to enter upon that new existence which you promised me! Say, then, what is the condition?'

'That you prey upon the human race, whom he hates as well as I,' answered the stranger.

'Again those awful words!' ejaculated the old man, casting trembling glances around him.

'Yes – again those words,' echoed the mysterious guest, looking with his fierce burning eyes into the glazed orbs of the aged shepherd. 'And now learn their import!' he continued, in a solemn tone. 'Knowest thou not that there is a belief in many parts of our native land that at particular seasons certain doomed men throw off the human shape and take that of ravenous wolves?'

'Oh, yes – yes – I have indeed heard of those strange legends in which the Wehr-Wolf is represented in such appalling colours!' exclaimed the old man, a terrible suspicion crossing his mind.

''Tis said that at sunset on the last day of every month the mortal, to whom belongs the destiny of the Wehr-Wolf, must exchange his natural form for that of the savage animal; in which horrible shape he must remain until the moment when the morrow's sun dawns upon the earth.'

'The legend that told thee this spoke truly,' said the stranger. 'And now dost thou comprehend the condition which must be imposed upon thee?'

'I do – I do!' murmured the old man with a fearful shudder. 'But he who accepts that condition makes a compact with the evil one, and thereby endangers his immortal soul!'

'Not so,' was the reply. 'There is naught involved in this condition which – but hesitate not,' added the stranger, hastily: 'I have no time to waste in bandying words. Consider all I offer you: in another hour you shall be another man!'

'I accept the boon – and on the conditions stipulated!' exclaimed the shepherd.

''Tis well, Wagner–'

'What! you know my name!' cried the old man. 'And yet, meseems, I did not mention it to thee.'

'Canst thou not already perceive that I am no common mortal?' demanded the stranger, bitterly. 'And who I am, and whence

I derive my power, all shall be revealed to thee so soon as the bond is formed that must link us for eighteen months together! In the meantime, await me here!'

And the mysterious stranger quitted the cottage abruptly, and plunged into the depths of the Black Forest.

One hour elapsed ere he returned – one mortal hour, during which Wagner sat bowed over his miserably scanty fire, dreaming of pleasure, youth, riches, and enjoyment; converting, in imagination, the myriad sparks which shone upon the extinguishing embers into piles of gold, and allowing his now uncurbed fancy to change the one single room of the wretched hovel into a splendid saloon, surrounded by resplendent mirrors and costly hangings, while the untasted fare for the stranger on the rude fir-table, became transformed, in his idea, into a magnificent banquet laid out, on a board glittering with plate, lustrous with innumerable lamps, and surrounded by an atmosphere fragrant with the most exquisite perfumes.

The return of the stranger awoke the old man from his charming dream, during which he had never once thought of the conditions whereby he was to purchase the complete realization of the vision.

'Oh! what a glorious reverie you have dissipated!' exclaimed Wagner. 'Fulfill but one tenth part of that delightful dream–'

'I will fulfill it all!' interrupted the stranger: then, producing a small vial from the bosom of his doublet, he said, 'Drink!'

The old man seized the bottle, and speedily drained it to the dregs.

He immediately fell back upon the seat, in a state of complete lethargy.

But it lasted not for many minutes; and when he awoke again, he experienced new and extraordinary sensations. His limbs were vigorous, his form was upright as an arrow; his eyes, for many years dim and failing, seemed gifted with the sight of an eagle, his head was warm with a natural covering; not a wrinkle remained upon his brow nor on his cheeks; and, as he smiled with mingled wonderment and delight, the parting lips revealed a set of brilliant teeth. And it seemed, too, as if by one magic touch the long fading tree of his intellect had suddenly burst into full foliage, and every cell of his brain was instantaneously stored with an amount of knowledge, the accumulation of which stunned him for an instant, and in the next appeared as familiar to him as if he had never been without it.

'Oh! great and powerful being, whomsoever thou art,' exclaimed Wagner, in the full, melodious voice of a young man of twenty-one, 'how can I manifest to thee my deep, my boundless gratitude for this boon which thou hast conferred upon me!'

'By thinking no more of thy lost grand-child Agnes, but by preparing to follow me whither I shall now lead thee,' replied the stranger.

'Command me: I am ready to obey in all things,' cried Wagner. 'But one word ere we set forth – who art thou, wondrous man?'

'Henceforth I have no secrets from thee, Wagner,' was the answer, while the stranger's eyes gleamed with unearthly lustre; then, bending forward, he whispered a few words in the other's ear.

Wagner started with a cold and fearful shudder as if at some appalling announcement; but he uttered not a word of reply – for his master beckoned him imperiously away from the humble cottage.

THE WEHR-WOLF

'Twas the hour of sunset.

The eastern horizon, with its gloomy and somber twilight, offered a strange contrast to the glorious glowing hues of vermilion, and purple, and gold, that blended in long streaks athwart the western sky.

For even the winter sunset of Italy is accompanied with resplendent tints – as if an emperor, decked with a refulgent diadem, were repairing to his imperial couch.

The declining rays of the orb of light bathed in molten gold the pinnacles, steeples, and lofty palaces of proud Florence, and toyed with the limpid waves of the Arno, on whose banks innumerable villas and casinos already sent forth delicious strains of music, broken only by the mirth of joyous revelers.

And by degrees as the sun went down, the palaces of the superb city began to shed light from their lattices, set in rich sculptured masonry; and here and there, where festivity prevailed, grand illuminations sprung up with magical quickness, the reflection from each separate galaxy rendering it bright as day far, far around.

Vocal and instrumental melody floated through the still air; and the perfume of exotics, decorating the halls of the Florentine nobles, poured from the widely-opened portals, and rendered the air delicious.

For Florence was gay that evening – the last day of each month being the one which the wealthy lords and high-born ladies set apart for the reception of their friends.

The sun sank behind the western hills; and even the hothouse flowers closed up their buds – as if they were eyelids weighed down by slumber, and not to wake until the morning should arouse them again to welcome the return of their lover – that glorious sun!

Darkness seemed to dilate upon the sky like an image in the midst of a mirage, expanding into superhuman dimensions – then rapidly losing its shapeliness, and covering the vault above densely and confusedly.

But, by degrees, countless stars began to stud the colorless canopy of heaven, like gems of orient splendor; for the last – last flickering ray of the twilight in the west had expired in the increasing obscurity.

But, hark! what is that wild and fearful cry?

In the midst of a wood of evergreens on the banks of the Arno, a man – young, handsome, and splendidly attired – has thrown himself upon the ground, where he writhes like a stricken serpent, in horrible convulsions.

He is the prey of a demoniac excitement: an appalling consternation is on him – madness is in his brain – his mind is on fire.

Lightnings appear to gleam from his eyes, as if his soul were dismayed, and withering within his breast.

'Oh! no – no!' he cries with a piercing shriek, as if wrestling madly, furiously, but vainly against some unseen fiend that holds him in his grasp.

And the wood echoes to that terrible wail; and the startled bird flies fluttering from its bough.

But, lo! what awful change is taking place in the form of that doomed being? His handsome countenance elongates into one of savage and brute-like shape; the rich garments which he wears become a rough, shaggy, and wiry skin; his body loses its human contours, his arms and limbs take another form; and, with a frantic howl of misery, to which the woods give horribly faithful reverberations, and, with a rush like a hurling wind, the wretch starts wildly away, no longer a man, but a monstrous wolf!

On, on he goes: the wood is cleared – the open country is gained. Tree, hedge, and isolated cottage appear but dim points in the landscape – a moment seen, the next left behind; the very hills appear to leap after each other.

A cemetery stands in the monster's way, but he turns not aside – through the sacred inclosure – on, on he goes. There are situated many tombs, stretching up the slope of a gentle acclivity, from the dark soil of which the white monuments stand forth with white and ghastly gleaming, and on the summit of the hill is the church of St. Benedict the Blessed.

From the summit of the ivy-grown tower the very rooks, in the midst of their cawing, are scared away by the furious rush and the wild howl with which the Wehr-Wolf thunders over the hallowed ground.

At the same instant a train of monks appear round the angle of the church – for there is a funeral at that hour; and their torches flaring with the breeze that is now springing up, cast an awful and almost magical light on the dark gray walls of the edifice, the strange effect being enhanced by the prismatic reflection of the lurid blaze from the stained glass of the oriel window.

The solemn spectacle seemed to madden the Wehr-Wolf. His speed increased – he dashed through the funeral train – appalling cries of terror and alarm burst from the lips of the holy fathers – and the solemn procession was thrown into confusion. The coffin-bearers dropped their burden, and the corpse rolled out upon the ground, its decomposing countenance seeming horrible by the glare of the torch-light.

The monk who walked nearest the head of the coffin was thrown down by the violence with which the ferocious monster cleared its passage; and the venerable father – on whose brow sat the snow of eighty winters – fell with his head against a monument, and his brains were dashed out.

On, on fled the Wehr-Wolf, over mead and hill, through valley and dale. The very wind seemed to make way: he clove the air – he appeared to skim the ground – to fly.

Through the romantic glades and rural scenes of Etruria the monster sped – sounds, resembling shrieking howls, bursting ever and anon from his foaming mouth – his red eyes glaring in the dusk of the evening like ominous meteors – and his whole aspect so full of appalling ferocity, that never was seen so monstrous, so terrific a spectacle!

A village is gained; he turns not aside, but dashes madly through the little street formed by the huts and cottages of the Tuscan vine-dressers.

A little child is in his path – a sweet, blooming, ruddy, noble boy; with violet-colored eyes and flaxen hair – disporting merrily at a short distance from his parents, who are seated at the threshold of their dwelling.

Suddenly a strange and ominous rush – an unknown trampling

of rapid feet falls upon their ears; then, with a savage cry, a monster sweeps past.

'My child! my child!' screams the affrighted mother; and simultaneously the shrill cry of an infant in the sudden agony of death carries desolation to the ear!

'Tis done – 'twas but the work of a moment; the wolf has swept by, the quick rustling of his feet is no longer heard in the village. But those sounds are succeeded by awful wails and heart-rending lamentations: for the child – the blooming, violet-eyed, flaxen-haired boy – the darling of his poor but tender parents, is weltering in his blood!

On, on speeds the destroyer, urged by an infernal influence which maddens the more intensely because its victim strives vainly to struggle against it: on, on, over the beaten road – over the fallow field – over the cottager's garden – over the grounds of the rich one's rural villa.

And now, to add to the horrors of the scene, a pack of dogs have started in pursuit of the wolf – dashing – hurrying – pushing – pressing upon one another in all the anxious ardor of the chase.

The silence and shade of the open country, in the mild starlight, seem eloquently to proclaim the peace and happiness of a rural life; but now that silence is broken by the mingled howling of the wolf, and the deep baying of the hounds – and this shade is crossed and darkened by the forms of the animals as they scour so fleetly – oh! with such whirlwind speed along.

But that Wehr-Wolf bears a charmed life; for though the hounds overtake him – fall upon him – and attack him with all the courage of their nature, yet does he hurl them from him, toss them aside, spurn them away, and at length free himself from their pursuit altogether!

And now the moon rises with unclouded splendor, like a maiden looking from her lattice screened with purple curtains; and still the monster hurries madly on with unrelaxing speed.

For hours has he pursued his way thus madly; and, on a sudden, as he passes the outskirts of a sleeping town, the church-bell is struck by the watcher's hand to proclaim midnight.

Over the town, over the neighboring fields – through the far-off forest, clanged that iron tongue: and the Wehr-Wolf sped all the faster, as if he were running a race with that Time whose voice had just spoken.

On, on went the Wehr-Wolf; but now his course began to deviate from the right line which he had hitherto pursued, and to assume a curved direction.

From a field a poor man was turning an ox into the main road, that he might drive the animal to his master's residence by daylight; the wolf swept by, and snapped furiously at the ox as he passed: and the beast, affrighted by the sudden appearance, gushing sound, and abrupt though evanescent attack of the infuriate monster, turned on the herdsman and gored him to death.

On went the terrific wolf, with wilder and more frequent howlings, which were answered in a thousand tones from the rocks and caverns overlooking the valley through whose bosom he was now careering with whirlwind speed along.

It was now two o'clock in the morning, and he had already described an immense circuit from the point where he had begun to deviate from a direct course.

At a turning of the road, as he emerged from the valley, the monster encountered a party of village girls repairing with the produce of their dairies, and of their poultry-yards, to some still far distant town, which they had hoped to reach shortly after daybreak.

Fair, gay, and smiling was the foremost maiden, as the bright moon and the silver starlight shone upon her countenance; but that sweet face, clad in the richest hues of health, was suddenly convulsed with horror, as the terrible Wehr-Wolf thundered by with appalling howls.

For a few moments the foremost village maiden stood rooted to the spot in speechless horror: then, uttering a wild cry, she fell backward, rolled down a steep bank, and was ingulfed in the rapid stream that chafed and fretted along the side of the path.

Her companions shrieked in agony of mind – the wail was echoed by a despairing cry from the drowning girl – a cry that swept frantically over the rippling waters; and, in another moment, she sank to rise no more!

The breeze had by this time increased to a sharp wind, icy and cold, as it usually is, even in southern climes, when the dawn is approaching; and the gale now whistled through the branches of the evergreen wood in the neighborhood of Florence – that vicinity to which the Wehr-Wolf was at length returning!

Still was his pace of arrow-like velocity – for some terrible power appeared to urge him on; and though his limbs failed not, though he staggered not in his lightning speed, yet did the foam at his mouth, the thick flakes of perspiration on his body, and the steam that enveloped him as in a dense vapor, denote how distressed the unhappy being in reality was.

At last – at last a faint tinge was visible above the eastern horizon; gradually the light increased and put to flight the stars.

But now the Oriental sky was to some extent obscured with clouds; and the Wehr-Wolf gnashed his teeth with rage, and uttered a savage howl, as if impatient of the delay of dawn.

His speed began to relax; the infernal influence which had governed him for so many hours already grew less stern, less powerful, and as the twilight shone forth more plainly in proportion did the Wehr-Wolf's velocity diminish.

Suddenly a piercing chill darted through his frame, and he fell in strong convulsions upon the ground, in the midst of the same wood where his transformation had taken place on the preceding evening.

The sun rose angrily, imparting a lurid, reddened hue to the dark clouds that hung upon the Oriental heaven, as if the mantling curtains of a night's pavilion strove to repel the wooing kisses of the morn; and the cold chill breeze made the branches swing to and fro with ominous flapping, like the wings of the fabulous Simoorg.

But in the midst of the appalling spasmodic convulsions, with direful writhings on the soil, and with cries of bitter anguish, the Wehr-Wolf gradually threw off his monster-shape; and at the very moment when the first sunbeam penetrated the wood and glinted on his face he rose a handsome, young, and perfect man once more!

THE DESCENT – THE CHAMBER OF PENITENCE

Having bound Flora Francatelli to the chair in the manner just described, the three nuns fell back a few paces, and the wretched girl felt the floor giving way under her.

A dreadful scream burst from her lips, as slowly – slowly the chair sank down, while the working of hidden machinery in the roof, and the steady, monotonous revolution of wheels, sounded with ominous din upon her ears.

An icy stream appeared to pour over her soul; wildly she cast around her eyes, and then more piercing became her shrieks, as she found herself gradually descending into what seemed to be a pit or well – only that it was square instead of round.

The ropes creaked – the machinery continued its regular movement, and the lamp fixed in the skylight overhead became less and less brilliant.

And bending over the mouth of this pit into which she was descending were the three nuns – standing motionless and silent like hideous specters, on the brink of the aperture left by the square platform or trap, whereon the chair was fixed.

'Mercy! Mercy!' exclaimed Flora, in a voice expressive of the most acute anguish.

And stretching forth her snowy arms (for it was round the waist and by the feet that she was fastened to the chair), she convulsively placed her open palms against the wooden walls of the pit, as if she could by that spasmodic movement arrest the descent of the terrible apparatus that was bearing her down into that hideous, unknown gulf! But the walls were smooth and even, and presented nothing whereon she could fix her grasp.

Her brain reeled, and for a few minutes she sat motionless, in dumb, inert despair.

Then again, in obedience to some mechanical impulse, she glanced upward; the light of the lamp was now dimly seen, like the sun through a dense mist – but the dark figures were still bending over the brink of the abyss, thirty yards above.

The descent was still progressing and the noise of the machinery still reached her ears, with buzzing, humming, monotonous indistinctness.

She shrieked not now – she screamed not any more; but it was not resignation that sealed her lips – it was despair!

Suddenly she became aware of the gradual disappearance of the three nuns; as she descended, the wall seemed to rise slowly upward and cover them from her view.

Then, for an instant there was a slight shock given to the platform whereon the chair was placed – as if it rested on something beneath.

But no – the fearful descent still went on – for, when she again stretched forth her hand to touch the walls, they appeared to be slowly rising – rising!

She was now involved in almost total darkness; but far – far overhead the dim luster of the lamp was seen; and the four walls of the gulf now appeared to touch the ceiling of the room above, and to inclose that faint but still distinct orb within the narrow space thus shut in.

The noise of the machinery also reached her still – but merely with a humming sound that was only just audible.

For an instant she doubted whether she was still descending; but, alas! when her arms were a third time convulsively stretched forth, her fair hands felt the walls slipping away from her touch – gliding upward, as it were, with steady emotion.

Then she knew that the descent had not ceased.

But whither was she going? to what awful depth was she progressing?

Already she conjectured, was she at least sixty yards beneath that dim yellow orb which every instant appeared to shine as through a deeper, deepening mist.

For what fate was she reserved? and where was she?

Suddenly it struck her that she was an inmate of the Carmelite Convent; for the rumors alluded to in a preceding chapter had often met her ears; and her imagination naturally associated them with the occurrences of that dreadful night.

The piercing shrieks – the noise of machinery – the disappearance from time to time of some member of that monastic institution, all the incidents, in fine, to which those rumors had ever pointed, now seemed to apply to her own case.

These reflections flashed, with lightning rapidity, through her brain, and paralyzed her with horror.

Then she lost all further power of thought; and though not absolutely fainting, she was stunned and stupefied with the tremendous weight of overwhelming despair.

How long she remained in this condition she knew not; but she was suddenly aroused by the opening of a low door in the wall in front of her.

Starting as from a dreadful dream, she stretched forth her arms, and became aware that the descent had stopped; and at the same moment she beheld a nun, bearing a lamp, standing on the threshold of the door which had just opened.

'Sister, welcome to the chamber of penitence!' said the recluse, approaching the terrified Flora.

Then, placing the lamp in a niche near the door, the nun proceeded to remove the cords which fastened the young maiden to the chair.

Flora rose, but fell back again on the seat – for her limbs were stiff in consequence of the length of time they had been retained in one position. The nun disappeared by the little door for a few minutes; and, on her return, presented the wretched girl a cup of cold water. Flora swallowed the icy beverage, and felt refreshed.

Then, by the light of the lamp in the niche, she hastily examined the countenance of the nun; but its expression was cold – repulsive – stern: and Flora knew that it was useless to seek to make a friend of her.

A frightful sense of loneliness, as it were, struck her like an ice-shaft penetrating to her very soul; and clasping her hands together, she exclaimed: 'Holy Virgin! protect me!'

'No harm will befall you, daughter,' said the nun, 'if you manifest contrition for past errors and a resolution to devote your future years to the service of Heaven.'

'My past errors!' repeated Flora, with mingled indignation and astonishment. 'I am not aware that I ever injured a living soul by a word or deed – nor entertained a thought for which I need to blush! Neither have I neglected those duties which manifest the gratitude of mortals for the bounties bestowed upon them by Providence.'

'Ah! daughter,' exclaimed the nun, 'you interpret not your own heart rightly. Have you never abandoned yourself to those carnal notions – those hopes – those fears – those dreams of happiness – which constitute the passion which the world calls love?'

Flora started, and a blush mantled on her cheeks, before so pale!

'You see that I have touched a chord which vibrates to your heart's core, daughter,' continued the nun, on whom that sudden evidence of emotion was not lost. 'You have suffered yourself to be deluded by the whisperings of that feeling whose tendency was to wean your soul from Heaven.'

'And is it possible that a pure and virtuous love can be construed into a crime?' demanded the young maiden, her indignation overpowering her fears.

'A love that is founded on, and fostered by ambition is a sin,' replied the nun. 'Marriage is doubtless an institution ordained by Heaven; but it becomes a curse, and is repulsive to all pious feelings, when it unites those whose passion is made up of sensuality and selfishness.'

'You dare not impute such base considerations to me!' exclaimed Flora, her cheeks again flushing, but with the glow of conscious innocence shamefully outraged by the most injurious suspicions.

'Nay, daughter,' continued the nun, unmoved by the manner of the young maiden; 'you are unable to judge rightly of your own heart. You possess a confidence in integrity of purpose, which is but a mental blindness on your part.'

'Of what am I accused? and wherefore am I brought hither?' asked Flora, beginning to feel bewildered by the sophistry that characterized the nun's discourse.

'Those who are interested in your welfare,' replied the nun evasively, 'have consigned you to the care of persons devoted to the service of Heaven, that your eyes may be opened to the vanity of the path which you have been pursuing, but from which you are so happily rescued.'

'And where am I? is this the Convent of the Carmelites? why was I subjected to all the alarms – all the mental tortures through which I have just passed?' demanded the young maiden, wildly and rapidly.

'Think not that we have acted toward you in a spirit of persecution,' said the nun. 'The mysteries which have alarmed you will be explained at a future period, when your soul is prepared by penance, self-mortification, and prayer to receive the necessary revelation. In the meantime, ask no questions, forget the world, and resolve to embrace a life devoted to the service of Heaven.'

'To embrace a conventual existence!' almost shrieked the wretched girl. 'Oh! no, never!'

'Not many days will elapse ere your mind will undergo a salutary change,' said the nun, composedly. 'But if you will follow me – as you appear to be somewhat recovered – I will conduct you to your cell adjoining the Chamber of Penitence.'

Flora, perceiving that any further attempt to reason with the recluse would be fruitlessly made, rose and followed her into a narrow, dark passage, at the end of which was a door standing half open.

The nun extinguished her lamp, and led the way into a large apartment hung with black. At the further end there was an altar, surmounted by a crucifix of ebony, and lighted up with four wax candles, which only served to render the gloom of the entire scene more apparent.

At the foot of the altar knelt five women, half naked, and holding scourges in their hands.

'These are the penitents,' whispered the nun to Flora. 'Pause for a moment and contemplate them.'

A minute elapsed, during which the five penitents remained motionless as statues, with their heads bowed upon their bosoms, and their hands hanging down by their sides, as if those limbs were lifeless – save in respect to the hands that held the scourges. But, suddenly, one of them – a young and beautiful woman – exclaimed, in a tone of piercing anguish, 'It is my fault! it is my fault! it is my fault!' – and the others took up the wail in voices equally characteristic of heartfelt woe.

Then they lacerated their shoulders with the hard leathern thongs of their scourges; and a faintness came over Flora Francatelli when she observed the blood appear on the back of the young and beautiful penitent who had given the signal for this self-mortification.

The nun, perceiving the effect thus produced upon the maiden, touched her upon the shoulder as a signal to follow whither she was about to lead; and, opening one of the several doors communicating with the Chamber of Penitence, she said in a low whisper – 'This is your cell. May the Virgin bless you!'

Flora entered the little room allotted to her, and the nun retired, simply closing, but not bolting the door behind her.

A taper burnt before a crucifix suspended to the wall; and near it hung a scourge, from which last mentioned object Flora averted her eyes with horror.

A bed, a simple toilet-table, a praying-desk, and a single chair, completed the furniture of the cell, which was of very narrow dimensions.

Seating herself on the bed, Flora burst into an agony of tears.

What would her aunt think when she received the news of her disappearance? for she could not suppose that any friendly feeling on the part of her persecutors would induce them to adopt a course which might relieve that much-loved relative's mind concerning her. What would Francisco conjecture? Oh! these thoughts were maddening!

Anxious to escape from them, if possible, the almost heartbroken girl proceeded to lay aside her garments and retire to rest.

Physical and mental exhaustion cast her into a deep sleep; but the horrors of her condition pursued her even in her dreams; so that when she awoke she was not startled to find herself in that gloomy cell.

Casting her eyes around, she observed two circumstances which showed her that some one had visited her room during the hours she slept; for a new taper was burning before the crucifix, and her own garments had been removed – the coarse garb of a penitent now occupying their place on the chair.

'Oh! is it possible that I am doomed to bid farewell to the world forever?' exclaimed Flora, in a voice of despair, as she clasped her hands convulsively together.

PART III
SHORT TALES

THE DEMON OF THE HARTZ

The solitudes of the Hartz forest in Germany, but especially the mountains called Blockberg, or rather Blockenberg, are the chosen scene for tales of witches, demons, and apparitions. The occupation of the inhabitants, who are either miners or foresters, is of a kind that renders them peculiarly prone to superstition, and the natural phenomena which they witness in pursuit of their solitary or subterraneous profession, are often set down by them to the interference of goblins or the power of magic. Among the various legends current in that wild country, there is a favourite one which supposes the Hartz to be haunted by a sort of tutelar demon, in the shape of a wild man, of huge stature, his head wreathed with oak leaves, and his middle tinctured with the same, bearing in his hand a pine torn up by the root. It is certain that many persons profess to have seen such a man traversing, with huge strides, the opposite ridge of a mountain, when divided from it by a narrow glen; and indeed the fact of the apparition is so generally admitted, that modern scepticism has only found refuge by ascribing it to optical deception.

In elder times, the intercourse of the demon with the inhabitants was more familiar, and, according to the traditions of the Hartz, he was wont, with the caprice usually ascribed to these earthborn powers to interfere with the affairs of mortals, sometimes for their welfare. But it was observed, that even his gifts often turned out, in the long run, fatal to those on whom they were bestowed, and it was no uncommon thing for the pastors, in their care for their flock, to compose long sermons the burthen whereof was a warning against having any intercourse, direct or indirect, with the Hartz demon. The fortunes of Martin Waldeck have been often quoted by the aged to their giddy children, when they were heard to scoff at a danger which appeared visionary.

A travelling capuchin had possessed himself of the pulpit of the thatched church at a little hamlet called Morgenbrodt, lying in the Hartz district, from which he declaimed against the wickedness of the inhabitants, their communication with fiends, witches, and fairies, and particularly with the woodland goblin of the Hartz. The doctrines of Luther had already begun to spread among the peasantry, for the incident is placed under the reign of Charles V, and they laughed to scorn the zeal with which the venerable man insisted upon his topic. At length, as his vehemence increased with opposition, so their opposition rose in proportion to his vehemence. The inhabitants did not like to hear an accustomed demon, who had inhabited the Brockenberg for so many ages, summarily confounded with Baal-peor, Ashtaroth, and Beelzebub himself, and condemned without reprieve to the bottomless Tophet. The apprehensions that the spirit might avenge himself on them for listening to such an illiberal sentence, added to the national interest in his behalf. A travelling friar, they said, that is here today and away tomorrow, may say what he pleases, but it is we the ancient and constant inhabitants of the country, that are left at the mercy of the insulted demon, and must, of course, pay for all. Under the irritation occasioned by these reflections the peasants from injurious language betook themselves to stones, and having pebbled the priest most handsomely, they drove him out of the parish to preach against demons elsewhere.

Three young men, who had been present and assisting in the attack upon the priest, carried on the laborious and mean occupation of preparing charcoal for the smelting furnaces. On their return to their hut, their conversation naturally turned upon the demon of the Hartz and the doctrine of the capuchin. Maximilian and George Waldeck, the two elder brothers, although they allowed the language of the capuchin to have been indiscreet and worthy of censure, as presuming to determine upon the precise character and abode of the spirit, yet contended it was dangerous, in the highest degree, to accept his gifts, or hold any communication with him. He was powerful they allowed, but wayward and capricious, and those who had intercourse with him seldom came, to a good end. Did he not give the brave knight, Echert of Rabenwald, that famous black steed, by means of which he vanquished all the champions at the great tournament at Bremen? And did not the same steed afterwards precipitate itself wit its rider into an abyss so deep and fearful, that neither horse nor man was ever seen more? Had he not given to Dame Gertrude Trodden a curious spell for making butter come? and was she not burnt for a witch by the grand criminal judge of the Electorate, because she availed herself of his gift?

But these, and many other instances which they quoted, of mischance and ill-luck ultimately attending upon the apparent benefits conferred by the Hartz spirit, failed to make any impression on Martin Waldeck, the youngest of the brothers.

Martin was youthful, rash, and impetuous; excelling in all the exercises which distinguish a mountaineer, and brave and undaunted from the familiar intercourse with the dangers that attend them. He laughed at the timidity of his brothers. 'Tell me not of such folly,' he said; 'the demon is a good demon – he lives among us as if he were a peasant like ourselves – haunts the lonely crags or recesses of the mountains like a huntsman or goatherd – and he who loves the Hartz-forest and its wild scenes cannot be indifferent to the fate of the hardy children of the soil. But if the demon were as malicious as you make him, how should he derive power over mortals who barely avail themselves of his gifts, without binding themselves to submit to his pleasure? When you carry your charcoal to the furnace, is not the money as good that is paid you by blaspheming Blaize, the old reprobate overseer, as if you got it from the pastor himself? It is not the goblin's gifts which can endanger you then, but it is the use you shall make of them that you must account for. And were the demon to appear at this moment, and indicate to me a gold or silver mine, I would begin to dig away before his back were turned, and I would consider myself as under protection of a much Greater than he, while I made a good use of the wealth he pointed out to me.'

To this the elder brother replied, that wealth ill won was seldom well spent, while Martin presumptuously declared, that the possession of all the Hartz would not make the slightest alteration on his habits, morals, or character.

His brother entreated Martin to talk less wildly upon this subject, and with some difficulty contrived to withdraw his attention, by calling it to the consideration of an approaching boar chase, This talk brought them to their hut, a wretched wigwam, situated upon one side of a wild, narrow, and romantic dell in the recesses of the Brockenberg. They released their sister from attending upon the operation of charring the wood, which requires constant attention, and divided among themselves the duty of watching it by night, according to their custom, one always waking while his brothers slept.

Max Waldeck, the eldest, watched during the two first hours

of night, and was considerably alarmed, by observing upon the opposite bank of the glen, or valley a huge fire surrounded by some figures that appeared to wheel around it with antic gestures. Max at first bethought him of calling up his brothers; but recollecting the daring character of the youngest, and finding it impossible to wake the elder without also disturbing him – conceiving also what he saw to be an illusion of the demon, sent perhaps in consequence of the venturous expressions used by Martin on the preceding evening, he thought it best to betake himself to the safe-guard of such prayers as he could murmur over, and to watch in great terror and annoyance this strange and alarming apparition. After blazing for some time, the fire faded gradually away into darkness, and the rest of Max's watch was only disturbed by the remembrance of its terrors.

George now occupied the place of Max, who had retired to rest. The phenomenon of a huge blazing fire, upon the opposite bank of the glen, again presented itself to the eye of the watchman. It was surrounded as before by figures, which, distinguished by their opaque forms, being between the spectator and the red glaring light, moved and fluctuated around it as if engaged in some mystical ceremonies. George, though equally cautions, was of a bolder character than his elder brother. He resolved to examine more nearly the object of his wonder; and accordingly, after crossing the rivulet which divided the glen, he climbed up the opposite bank, and approached within an arrow's flight from the fire, which blazed apparently with the same fury as when he first witnessed it.

The appearance of the assistants who surrounded it, resembled those phantoms which are seen in a troubled dream, and at once confirmed the idea he had entertained from the first, that they did not belong to the human world. Amongst the strange unearthly forms, George Waldeck distinguished that of a giant overgrown with hair, holding an uprooted fir in his hand, with which, from time to time, he seemed to stir the blazing fire and having no other clothing than a wreath of oak leaves round his forehead and loins. George's heart sunk within him at recognizing the well-known apparition of the Hartz demon, as he had often been described to him by the ancient shepherds and huntsmen who had seen his form traversing the mountains. He turned, and was about to fly; but, upon second thoughts, blaming his own cowardice, he recited mentally the verse of the Psalmist, 'All good angels praise the Lord I' which is in that country supposed powerful as an exorcism and turned himself once more towards the place where he had seen the fire. But it was no longer visible.

The pale moon alone enlightened the side of the valley, and when George, with trembling steps, a moist brow, and hair bristling upright under his collier's cap, came to the spot where the fire had been so lately visible, marked as it was by a scathed oak tree, there appeared not on the heath the slightest vestiges of what he had seen. The moss and wild flowers were unscorched, and the branches of the oak tree, which had so lately appeared enveloped in wreaths of flame and smoke, were moist with the dews of midnight.

George returned to his hut with trembling steps, and, arguing like his elder brother, resolved to say nothing of what he had seen, lest he should awake in Martin that daring curiosity which he almost deemed to be allied with impiety.

It was now Martin's turn to watch. The household cock had given his first summons, and the night was well nigh spent. On examining the state of the furnace in which the wood was deposited in order to its being coked, or charred, he was surprised to find that the fire had nor been sufficiently maintained; for in his excursion and its consequences, George had forgot the principal object of his watch. Martin's first thought was to call up the slumberers, but observing that both his brothers slept unwontedly deep and heavily, he respected their repose, and set himself to supply their furnace with fuel, without requiring their aid. What he heaped upon it was apparently damp and unfit for the purpose, for the fire seemed rather to decay than revive. Martin next went to collect some boughs from a stack which had been carefully cut and dried for this purpose; but, when he returned, he found the fire totally extinguished. This was a serious evil, which threatened them with loss of their trade for more than one day. The vexed and mortified watchman set about to strike a light in order to rekindle the fire, but the tinder was moist, and his labour proved in this respect also ineffectual. He was now about to call up his brothers, for the circumstance seemed to be pressing, when flashes of light glimmered not only through the window, but through every crevice of the rudely built hut, and summoned him to behold the same apparition which had before alarmed the successive watches of his brethren. His first idea was, that the Muhllerhaussers, their rivals in trade, and with whom they had had many quarrels, might have encroached upon their bounds for the purpose of pirating their wood, and he resolved to awake his brothers, and be revenged on them for their audacity. But a short reflection and observation on the gestures and manner of those who seemed 'to work in the fire', induced him to dismiss this belief, and although rather sceptical in these matters, to conclude that what he saw was a supernatural phenomenon. 'But be they men or fiends,' said the undaunted forester, 'that busy themselves with such fantastical rites and gestures, I will go and demand a light to rekindle our furnace.' He relinquished, at the same time, the idea of waking his brethren. There was a belief that such adventures as he was about to undertake were accessible only to one person at a time; he feared also that his brothers in their scrupulous timidity, might interfere to prevent the investigation he had resolved to commence; and therefore, snatching his boar-spear from the wall, the undaunted Martin Waldeck set forth on the adventure alone.

With the same success as his brother George, but with courage far superior, Martin crossed the brook, ascended the hill, and approached so near the ghostly assembly that he could recognize, in the presiding figure, the attributes of the Hartz demon. A cold shuddering assailed him for the first time in his life, but the recollection that he had at a distance dared and even courted the intercourse which was now about to take place, confirmed his staggering courage, and pride supplying what he wanted in resolution, he advanced with tolerable firmness towards the fire; the figures which surrounded it appeared more phantastical, and supernatural, the nearer he approached to the assembly. He was received with a loud shout of discord and unnatural laughter, which, to his stunned ears, seemed more alarming than a combination of the most dismal and melancholy sounds which could be imagined. 'Who art thou?' said the giant compressing his savage and exaggerated features into a sort of forced gravity, while they were occasionally agitated by the convulsion of the laughter which he seemed to suppress.

'Martin Waldeck, the forester,' answered the hardy youth; 'And who are you?'

The king of the wastes and of the mine,' answered the spectre; 'And why hast thou dared to encroach on my mysteries?'

'I came in search of light to rekindle my fire,' answered Martin hardily, and then resolutely asked in his turn, 'What mysteries are these that you celebrate here?'

'We celebrate,' answered the demoniac being, 'the wedding of Hermes with the Black Dragon. But take thy fire that thou camest to seek, and begone – no mortal may long look upon us and live.'

The peasant stuck his spear point into a large piece of blazing wood, which he heaved with some difficulty, and then turned round to regain his hut, the shouts of laughter being renewed behind him with treble violence, and ringing far down the narrow valley. When Martin returned to the hut, his first care, however much astonished with what he had seen, was to dispose the kindled coal among the fuel so as might best light the fire of his furnace, but after many efforts, and all exertions of bellows and fire prong, the coal he had brought from the demon's fire became totally extinct, without kindling any of the others. He turned about and observed the fire still blazing on the hill, although those who had been busied around it had disappeared. As he conceived the spectre had been jesting with him, he gave way to the natural hardihood of his temper, and determining to see the adventure to the end, resumed the road to the fire, from which, unopposed by the demon, he brought off in the same manner a blazing piece of charcoal but still without being able to succeed in lighting his fire. Impunity having increased his rashness, he resolved upon a third experiment, and was as successful as before in reaching the fire; but, when he had again appropriated a piece of burning coal, and had turned to depart, he heard the harsh and supernatural voice which had before accosted him, pronounce these words: 'Dare not to return hither a fourth time!'

The attempt to rekindle the fire with this last coal having proved as ineffectual as on the former occasions, Martin relinquished the hopeless attempt, and flung himself on his bed of leaves, resolving to delay till the next morning the communication of his supernatural adventure to his brothers. He was awakened from a heavy sleep into which he had sunk, from fatigue of body and agitation of mind, by loud exclamations of joy and surprise. His brothers, astonished at finding the fire extinguished when they awoke, had proceeded to arrange the fuel in order to renew it, when they found in the ashes three huge metallic masses, which their skill, (for most of the peasants in the Hartz are practised mineralogists,) immediately ascertained to be pure gold.

It was some damp upon their joyful congratulations when they learned from Martin the mode in which he had obtained this treasure, to which their own experience of the nocturnal vision induced them to give full credit. But they were unable to resist the temptation of sharing their brother's wealth. Taking now upon him as head of the house, Martin Waldeck bought lands and forests, built a castle, obtained a patent of nobility, and greatly to the scorn of the ancient nobility of the neighbourhood, was invested with all the privileges of a man of family. His courage in public war, as well as in private feuds, together with the number of retainers whom he kept in pay, sustained him for some time against the odium which was excited by his sudden elevation, and the arrogance of his pretensions. Now it was seen in the instance of Martin Waldeck, as it has been in that of many others, how little mortals can foresee the effect of sudden prosperity on their own disposition. The evil dispositions in his nature, which poverty had checked and repressed, ripened and bore their unhallowed fruit under the influence of temptation and the means of indulgence. As Deep calls unto Deep, one bad passion awakened another – the fiend of avarice invoked that of pride, and pride was to be supported by cruelty and oppression. Waldeck's character, always bold and daring, but rendered more harsh and assuming by prosperity, soon made him odious, not to nobles only, but likewise to the lower ranks, who saw, with double dislike, the oppressive rights of the feudal nobility of the empire so remorselessly exercised by one who had risen from the very dregs of the people. His adventure, although carefully concealed, began likewise to be whispered, and the clergy already stigmatized as a wizard and accomplice of fiends, the wretch, who, having acquired so huge a treasure in so strange a manner had not sought to sanctify it by dedicating a considerable portion to the use of the church. Surrounded by enemies, public arid private, tormented by a thousand feuds, and threatened by the church with excommunication, Martin Waldeck, or, as we must now call him the Baron Von Waldeck, often regretted bitterly the labours and sports of unenvied poverty. But his courage failed him not under all these difficulties and seemed rather to augment in proportion to the danger which darkened around him, until an accident precipitated his fall.

A proclamation by the reigning Duke of Brunswick had invited to a solemn tournament all German nobles of free and honourable descent, and Martin Waldeck, splendidly armed, accompanied by his two brothers, and a gallantly equipped retinue, had the arrogance to appear among the chivalry of the province and demand permission to enter the lists. This was considered as filling up the measure of his presumption. A thousand voices exclaimed, 'we will have no cinder-sifter mingle in our games of chivalry.' Irritated to frenzy, Martin drew his sword, and hewed down the herald who, in compliance with the general outcry, opposed his entrance into the list. A hundred swords were unsheathed to avenge what was, in those days, regarded as a crime only inferior to sacrilege, or regicide. Waldeck, after defending himself with the fury of a lion, was seized, tried on the spot by the judges of the lists, and condemned, as the appropriate punishment for breaking the peace of his sovereign and violating the sacred person of a herald-at-arms, to have his right hand struck from his body, to be ignominiously deprived of the honour of nobility, of which he was unworthy, and be expelled from the city. When he had been stripped of his arms, and sustained the mutilation imposed by this severe sentence, the unhappy victim of ambition was abandoned to the rabble, who followed him with threats and outcries, levelled alternately against the necromancer and oppressor, which at length ended in violence. His brothers (for his retinue had fled and dispersed), at length succeeded in rescuing him from the hands of the populace, when, satiated with cruelty, they had left him half dead through loss of blood, through the outrages he had sustained. They were not permitted, such was the ingenious cruelty of their enemies, to make use of any other means of removing him, excepting such a collier's cart as they had themselves formerly used, in which they deposited their brother on a truss of straw, scarcely expecting to reach any place of shelter ere death should release him from his misery.

When the Waldecks, journeying in this miserable manner, had approached the verge of their native country, in a hollow way, between two mountains, they perceived a figure advancing towards them, which at first sight seemed to be an aged man. But as he approached, his limbs and stature increased, the cloak fell from his shoulders, his pilgrim's staff was changed into an uprooted pine tree, and the gigantic figure of the Hartz demon passed before them in his terrors. When he came opposite to the cart which contained the miserable Waldeck, his huge features dilated into a grin of unutterable contempt and malignity, as he asked the sufferer, 'How like you the fire *my* coals have kindled!' The power of motion, which terror suspended in his two brothers, seemed to be restored to Martin by the energy of his courage. He raised himself on the cart, bent his brows, and, clenching his fist, shook it at the spectre with a ghastly look of hate and defiance. The goblin vanished with his usual tremendous and explosive laugh and left Waldeck exhausted with the effort of expiring nature.

The terrified brethren turned their vehicle towards the towers of a convent which arose in a wood of pine trees beside the road. They were charitably received by a bare-footed and long-bearded capuchin, and Martin survived only to complete the first confession he had made since the day of his sudden prosperity, and to receive absolution from the very priest, whom, precisely that day three years, he had assisted to pelt out of the hamlet of Morgenbrodt. The three years of precarious prosperity were supposed to have a mysterious correspondence with the number of his visits to the spectral fire upon the hill.

The body of Martin Waldeck was interred in the convent where he expired, in which his brothers, having assumed the habit of the order, lived and died in the performance of acts of charity and devotion. His lands, to which no one asserted any claim, lay waste until they were reassumed by the emperor as a lapsed fief, and the ruins of the castle, which Waldeck had called by his own name, are still shunned by the miner and forester as haunted by evil spirits. Thus were the evils attendant upon wealth, hastily attained and ill-employed, exemplified in the fortunes of Martin Waldeck.

THE ROSICRUCIAN

Among the numerous secret societies, the elaboration of the middle ages, which political agitation, the thirst of revenge, or the desire of knowledge, called into existence, none became more powerful and renowned than that body of men designated the Illuminati, who sought to pierce into the deepest secrets of nature – nay, far beyond into the sphere of the spiritual world: men who led a lonely and almost desolate life; men whose thin, pallid cheeks, and sunken eyes, which, however, shone at times with an almost unnatural brilliancy, white marble forehead, and altogether attenuated frame, gave indication of a student – life of that ardent, abstracted, enthusiastic kind, which wears away the vital spark of life, even as the oil in the lamp is devoured by the flame. Bright flashes and coruscations are occasionally struck out; but, on the whole, the light is calm, equable, and lucid, till when towards the last, the source of light and life is exhausted and becomes dim; so the worn soul, turning itself wearily from the world, perhaps in disappointment, disappears at last, and all that remains is dust and darkness.

Among the many branches of that noble and philanthropic brotherhood of freemasonry so widely extended throughout the world, is one known as the "Rosicrucians", though at the present day, they have little or nothing of the elements of their mysterious and profoundly erudite predecessors, save what tradition chooses to invest them with.

We may add, too, that the pursuits, employment, study, and course of life of the past and the present Rosicrucians, are as different as darkness from light. The one sought to unravel the mysteries of the invisible world, while the other is a good citizen in the tea line, deals in eggs and butter, or manufactures the chairs on which you sit – no whit the worse man, though less the scholar perhaps – for all that.

The stars which trace the destiny of each living human soul are not always evident to the sensible eye. Either the burning radiance which denotes their place or orbit, kindles up when life first dawns upon the world, or the lucid urns do not give forth their Promethean fire till the spiritual influence by attractive concord illumines it, or else it is shaded in the depths of an impenetrable darkness, which requires the fiat of unseen intelligence to make it palpable to us.

The great secret of the art is at first to acquire a knowledge which is in reality the star of the individual's destiny. By watching that shining oracle, then, in all its phases, the book of life becomes a mystery no longer; the future indicates itself whether in paths of danger or safety, in happiness or misery. Its dimming or its splendour denote the predominance of the good or the evil genius.

Few even with the most intense study can attain to this knowledge; many waste away life in the pursuit, and find they have been following a chimera; others again acquire this in an eminent degree; and among the numbers was one Count Arman, of the Rosegeberge, the representative of a noble house in the province of Suabia. The secrets of alchemy and magic, that other wondrous life which lies beneath the veil, was also known to him.

Quitting the court, and resisting the impulses of ambition, turning from the path which led to fame, honour, and wealth, he entered as member of a college in the old town of Nurnburg, where, in the secret fastnesses of an almost impenetrable tower, he passed away his youth, poring over those theurgic pages, in which erudition he became profoundly skilled.

He gave himself up to the amazing enchantments which he gleaned from the pages of Cornelius Agrippa and of Lilly; the bold empiricism of Paracelsus; the mysticism of Plato and Robert Fludd; or the more scientific, though loosely connected treatises of Sandivogius on mineralogy in particular. From those pages he learned that the elements of the philosopher's stone are sulphur, mercury, and salt; but in the method of their combination arose the difficulty. He found that air bears the seeds of all things, while water is the conveyancer, that fire is the germinator, and earth is the matrix: therefore the Sagani, or the spirits of the four elements, became the objects of his more daring pursuit; and the seven presiding intelligencies of Zoroaster were evoked, from time to time, but evoked vainly. He had not attained the grand secret; he stood as yet upon the threshold, though his advancing foot would soon lead him into the circle of mysteries, which it requires patience, study, and perseverance to reach.

He was still young, and it was rumoured that it was not alone the attraction of alchemy or magic that had led him into this unsocial path at the outset; but disappointment in the love he bore for a noble and beautiful lady, whose pride contemned his worship. He devoted himself to the wooing of the loftier powers, and learned to care no longer for the world that no longer could afford him aught but dim and saddening glimpses of an earthly happiness lost for ever. Let us, then, see in what manner his dark, stern studies repayed him.

Undismayed by the difficulties in the way of reaching the indescribable object for which he panted with all the powers of a great soul, now wholly roused, he still pressed on. In one of his rambles he met a tall, bearded man, whose majestic port and noble air awed him, and whose Armenian garment was marked all over with singular cabalistic figures. Without a word the man offered him a curiously bound folio, fastened with brazen clasps. The moon was up at the time, and the stars were out. Arman was so intensely occupied with the stranger and his wondrous book, that he looked not to the broad page that was unrolled sublimely above; for, had he done so, he would have found that his natal star was no longer visible among the shining sybils. He therefore took the book, when offered him the third time, and the unknown individual quickly turned away without breaking the silence, and vanished in the forest; and the count hastened back to devour the occult pages.

The windows of his tower were turned to that point of the heavens where the stars dawn first; and day and night he proceeded with his enraptured study, though he observed that each page he turned over, his star twinkled but faintly, and even when, at some tremendous revelation, its obscure glimmerings were almost totally lost, Count Arman persevered in his dark and awful task.

One night, when the moon was at the full, he went forth an hour before midnight, and in a neighbouring churchyard plucked up a quantity of certain herbs whose virtues, used under certain planetary aspects, had a Thessalian power. From thence he returned to his lonely chamber, and taking out a huge oak press, a number of ingredients, some liquid, some calcined, and others in a crude state, he kindled a fire in his crucible; and throwing in the materials waited patiently while their combustion went on.

The moon rose up to the meridian; a calm glory shone throughout the whole ocean of azure, while stars dotted it, like islands of light; but the count, as he glanced through the open casement, beheld not his own. Above, all was beautiful – below, all was black and murky; the streets, as seen from the tower, were like huge and yawning sepulchres. It was just on the stroke of midnight, the magical volume lay open, and Arman, gathering the herbs, flung them with muttered and inaudible words into the crucible. A thick smoke followed which filled the room, and, from the midst of the fuliginous cloud, there stretched forth a lean, terrible hand, clenched in menace. It bore a scroll on which were written some unutterable words. A pause ensued, during which Arman read them and he felt the blood curdling at his heart as their tremendous import became known to him.

'Show me thy face, dread being,' said Arman at last plucking up his courage: 'if I have summoned thee, I must not be daunted, nor shall mine eyes be daunted with a sight that might perchance turn other hearts than mine to stone. Appear!'

As he spoke, the clouds began to writhe and twist into shapes that were both ludicrous and horrible, till in the centre, a lambent blue flame began to broaden and spread out, then, as suddenly extinguished, and in its place there appeared the head of a dreadful being, so sublimely terrible, with its meteoric hair, dark brows, livid cheeks, and eyes where living fires flashed out with an intolerable blinding lustre. Arman shuddered, veiled his eyes with his hand, and said in a voice less bold than before, 'Spirit of fire, what can'st thou offer me if I will worship thee as thou demandest?'

'The mysteries that surround the world to thee shall be revealed,' was the answer, while the muffled thunder pealed with a sound of doom into the concave of heaven, as if in disapprobation of the Rosicrucian's unhallowed rites.

'I have the power already to call thee,' was the reply; 'and I can force thee to give me answers unconditionally: 'tis not sufficient – my soul is priceless, and if I serve thee, thou must give me more.'

'The gold of the sunless mine, the gems in the unseen caves, the jewels now elaborating in the crystallizing fires,' continued the terrible being.

'My art can transmute lead into gold, and I can crystallize the waters into starry masses,' replied Arman.

'Choose powers like those of eastern monarchs, and innumerable armies shall obey thee,' pursued the phantom.

'Man should be free and unfettered,' returned the count, growing bolder as he saw that the fearful eyes calmed their lurid fires. 'I will rule no slaves.'

'Wilt thou dwell in ancient cities, now all dead and silent? I will replace the stupendous temples and the marble and granite palaces shall be restored. The hundred–gated Thebes shall pour its thousands out to meet thee, roused from the slumber of centuries.'

The count made an impatient gesture. 'No – no,' he said, 'of all the fleeting things this feverish world can give, there was but one–'

'Behold that one!' interrupted the phantom; and then a singular change ensued, which shook the soul of the count, even as a reed is shaken by the wind.

Gradually and insensibly the fluent vapour assumed the forms of pillars, walls, ceiling, pictures, and furniture. It was the interior of a splendid chamber fraught with elegance and luxury. Seated on a couch was a young maiden of such a haughty and commanding beauty, that while gazing upon the magnificent face, the heart of Arman beat fast.

'It is she – it is Herminia!' he murmured, while tears came into his eyes. 'Spirit, why show me this? She is betrothed – nay, wedded to another: she loved me not. Thinkest thou, I had left the flowers and the sun, for these grim walls, if her smiles had but lightened up my path?'

'Thou did'st see greater beauty in those old tomes than in Herminia's face,' retorted the spirit, 'or neither thou nor I had been here.'

'False – false!' shouted Airman. 'I loved, but did not then seek to hold communion with the beings of your kind; but it was not till her eyes darkened upon me that I turned to these pages,' and he pointed to the formidable folios scattered about his chamber.

'Would'st thou be revenged on him who robbed thee of thy prize?' demanded the, frowning phantom.

'No!' answered Arman; 'and if I would, is not my arm as strong, my hand as powerful, my dagger as sharp as his? If I would thus heal up the bleeding wounds in my own heart, it is not to thee that I would turn for help.'

'I can give her to thee,' whispered the spirit.

'Hah!' ejaculated the count as he drew in his breath between his set teeth, and gazed upon the reclining figure so exquisitely lovely. 'Let me possess her and I am thine.'

The strong walls rocked; the towers shook as he spoke, while the sound of rushing winds swept by the window, and in the whirling clouds which he beheld were innumerable shapes floating here and there, some brightly beautiful, while others were as hideously ugly, until at last a scene of such unutterable horror broke upon his vision, that with a great cry he sank to the floor.

* * * * *

After this, Count Arman became still more absorbed, melancholy, even morose. His books were shunned and the unrevealed secrets of the massive volume were still bound up within its brazen clasps. He dreamed of Herminia, and thought not of the sublime secrets which his science taught him. Months passed away and he scarcely stirred from his old tower. He heard that Herminia was wedded long ago, and he did not demand the phantom to fulfil his part of the compact: but all this while his natal star shone out with all its wonted purity.

All at once it happened that one day, he suddenly started forth from some impulse he could neither comprehend or control, and unnoticed by any quitted the tower and the city, and striking boldly into the country, as if guided by his star alone, pursued with unfaltering limbs his dreary route till he arrived in the neighbourhood of an old castle belonging to his family.

It so happened that Herminia, with her husband, and two bright children, the fruit of their union, together with a group of their friends, were holding the anniversary of their wedding-day beneath the shade of the trees on a spreading lawn. The laughing eyes, the twinkling feet, the sound of the lute and the merriment of young and old, spoke of the happiness that pervaded every heart.

The husband of Herminia was a frank and loyal-hearted knight, who had wooed and won her hand. He had known the count as a moody, and as he thought, misanthropic man some years before, but their acquaintance was a slight one. He also knew of Arman's passion for Herminia, and when he gazed upon her face, he smilingly admitted, 'that it was no great marvel, for she was beautiful enough to bewitch anyone'; and with no pang of jealousy he lived contentedly, adoring his wife, and fondly loving his children.

Rumours only of Count Arman's studies reached them. It was

stated that he pursued alchemy, magic, and the profounder secrets of the Rosicrucians – and it was spoken truly; but more than this was not known. He had severed himself from the world and from mankind, with whom his communion was distant, cold and constrained. No one thought for a moment that in the bosom of the magician there burned the fires of a wild and fervid love, unchecked by time, distance, or coldness on her part; that his bosom glowed with all the delirious, headlong impulses of youth; that he had entered into a terrible compact to possess her.

When the mirth of the gay party was at the highest, their attention was suddenly called by one of their number uttering an ejaculation of surprise and fear; and turning their gaze in the direction, they beheld the figure of a man emerging out of the wood, with folded arms and imperious gait advancing towards them, and then, on perceiving them, suddenly halting. Herminia instantly recognized the count.

Count Arman seemed to have grown suddenly old after that fearful night. His form, naturally tall and majestic, appeared to be crushed; for no trace of decay was visible upon it, and his seeming age shrouded him like some tremendous mantle, whose ponderous weight clung to limbs of iron. His physiognomy, grave, handsome, and commanding, had an aspect at once grim and full of sorrow. The cap he wore, with its studded gems, gave it an appearance of barbaric splendour; and the dark mustachios, the flowing beard, the stormy ragged hair, together with the almost supernatural brilliancy of his eye, made him look like the being of another world, wilder, worse, and yet nobler than the world of man. His scathed brow was like the brow of a ruined archangel.

'It is Count Arman,' whispered the almost appalled Herminia to her husband.

'He looks as if he had made misery his companion for ever,' observed her husband in reply. 'Let the children go and welcome him – invite him to share our sports, and partake of food and wine.'

Arman was dreadfully agitated when he found himself thus abruptly cast into the presence of a woman whom he worshipped, witnessing the joy with which she gazed upon her husband, her children, her friends, while for him there were affrighted gestures and timid looks. His presence had damped the mirth of the party. He was evidently an unwelcome guest.

As these bitter feelings forced themselves upon him, rage and anger took in turn possession of his mind. Seeing the young children advancing towards him and guessing their errand, some emotion more human softened the ruggedness of his nature; but he dared not trust himself in the midst of the group, and abruptly turning upon his heel, with a proud and lofty step he vanished from their view; and having arrived at a spot, the gloom and horror of which was heightened by savage rocks, while the trees that clung to them were twisted and tortured into a thousand fantastically hideous shapes, the heavens above being obscured by a pall of inky blackness, the Rosicrucian tossed his arms aloft, and cried, 'Spirit of good or evil! phantom which my art hath raised! I call upon thee now – bring Herminia to my castle, but let her come willingly!' At this moment the sound of heavy wings fell sullenly upon the ear, as if some huge being were winnowing the air – and a voice replied:

'She is a wife, hath plighted faith to her husband, and willingly she may not come.'

'Hast thou, then, no power to rule her will?' demanded Arman.

'She is a mother,' said the phantom. 'Other spiritual essences are bound to her own spirit, by ties that no power can break.'

'Steep her senses in forgetfulness,' cried the count. 'Let some of thy potent essences work on her as they have worked on me. Dreams and images of fancy, hast thou no phantasies locked up in secret caverns, that can blind her for a space?', and the tortured man stamped in renewed rage and disappointment on the ground.

'It is All-souls' Eve,' returned the phantom, whose form was unseen, but whose lurid eyes, like dying fires of some extinguished universe, cast a spectral light through the profound gloom. 'It is All-souls' Eve; and brighter, purer spirits, though not more powerful than myself, are abroad. This night belongs to gentler influences. It is the turn of the enthusiastic worshipper of the mother of heaven to dream of the beatitudes of the blest, to behold in visions some apocalyptic glimpses, like those of the wrapt Ezekiel–'

'Juggling fiend,' shouted Arman, 'dost thou fool me to the brink of eternal ruin, and yet show me what I have lost? Fulfil thy compact, or, accursed one, depart for ever from me.'

'I dare not the first this night,' was the answer, 'and the latter I may not; for thou wilt not let me;' and with a low, bitter laugh the phantom departed, leaving the Rosicrucian almost stupified. Casting his eyes upward he beheld his radiant star shining through the trees; and as he crossed his arms upon his chest and gazed longingly upon it, he felt moved. Sadly and sorrowfully he moved away.

* * * * *

Ere the moon rose there went an alarm throughout the old castle that lights had been seen and sounds heard in the Count Arman's room, and that the retainers had fled in horror and affright from the spot. The news had rapidly spread abroad, and the father confessor who dwelt in the castle, conquering his fear and mastering his doubt, while devoutly crossing himself, boldly entered into the apartment, and found the count moaning upon his pallet.

'What, in heaven's name! is the matter with you, my son?' demanded the monk, grasping his crucifix.

'Little or naught, good father,' replied Arman collectedly, though the fever drops were oozing from his brow. 'I am about to expiate the tremendous secret that my studies have taught me.'

'Alas!' said the monk, 'I fear your knowledge is as unholy as it is profitless.'

'Not so, father,' replied the count, quickly; 'else why this passionate anguish of the soul to know? – why this diseased thirst for communion with the subtler spirits that people the element of fire and air, of earth and water? – why these devouring desires to be partakers of secrets locked from all human eyes, but to those who dare to lift the veil at any cost ?'

'At any cost, indeed, my son,' echoed the monk. 'Think of the peril of thy soul, and pray for aid in time.'

'I do,' groaned the man; 'but, look – behold!'

Dilating, broadening, spreading into a gigantic and colossal vastness, stood the evil spirit of the Rosicrucian in the air. Between him and the moon, between him and the holy stars; between him and the awful face of God, the features of the threatening phantom came.

'Awful shape what wantest thou?' demanded the monk.

'Ask him who bade me come,' was the reply, in tones that

made the flesh of the monk crawl upon his bones.

'I called thee not,' said Arman. 'False spirit, thou hast sought to juggle me out my soul; but thou wilt fail. Thou hast not kept thy promise, and so the bond is broken.'

'Hope till the morrow,' said the spirit, frowningly: 'again my power returns, and still Herminia shall be thine.'

'Herminia!' ejaculated the monk, a suspicion flashing across his mind.

'Avaunt with thy dark sorcery,' cried the count, rising up on his pallet, his features darkening in wrath. 'Avaunt! I defy thee!'

'Thou art mine,' muttered the phantom, with a ghastly laugh.

'Thou liest, spirit of evil, I am not; and yet,' he added, as he sank back, 'it may be so; but we shall see anon.' While he spoke the phantom vanished, and all was bright again.

'Father,' said the Rosicrucian, 'send to the Lady Herminia and her noble husband. Say to them that a dying man would see them and crave pardon of them.'

'Dying,' repeated the monk in amazement.

'Aye, father, dying. If in the night you hear sounds that may harrow up the soul, the rocking of the earth, the tolling of passing bells by unseen hands in the steeples, or shrieks in the air – but I am wandering. Will you do my bidding?'

'I will,' replied the monk, cowering, and quitted the place.

Not long after there stood around the dying man's bed the lovely lady, radiant as light, and her loyal husband. A change had come across the Rosicrucian at last, and on his haggard cheeks there wandered a quiet smile.

The wide window opened to a tranquil and lovely scene without. Streams murmured along the plains in the distance; the cottages peeped forth out of the trees; the far-off mountains were clothed in a soft and delicious haze of purple, and the breeze which passed with gentle sighings, rising and sinking, as breaths of air came in fresh vibrations through the Aolian strings, bearing some winged harmony palpable to the adept alone, who listened to it for a time in silent rapture. At last, turning his face to Herminia, he took her hand and said: 'Lady, forgive me: I loved you mightily, and I have wronged you, though you have been protected. Ere midnight goeth, I shall pass hence away.'

'Behold yon starry sky!' said Herminia, softly; 'you who have so often read its pages can trace upon the restless surface some footprints of the past and future. Has it never struck you that your science has one fatal error in it?'

'What is it that?' demanded the count, turning his bright and powerful eyes in surprise upon her charming face.

'You forget the present in following the future, and therefore have no life. You live by anticipation, and know not the season of the flowers, nor the joyous festival-time, when the snows are on the mountains, and the frost lies on the ground. You seek shadows of joys, and all your happiness is evanescent.'

The Rosicrucian groaned. 'True,' said he, 'true, in part only; for you know not the sublime attractions of the science I have sacrificed all for; but all is vain now. What see you out there?' he suddenly asked. 'Cover your face, avert your eyes, you may not gaze upon the dread shape.'

'What shape?' inquired Herminia's husband, approaching the bed. 'Compose yourself: there is nothing to be seen.'

'Be not too sure of that. You imagine those masses of fleece are cloudlets passing beneath the moon, do you not?' and he indicated with his hand the spot in the heavens he meant.

'I see naught – the sky is clear as a fountain!' was the answer.

The Rosicrucian shook his head. 'Your eyes are sealed,' he replied: 'I heard the sounds of worlds rushing through the blue void; I see the restless orbs passing like shuttles to and fro; I behold the living fires traverse the blue ocean, and through the whole there streams sad melodies, with dirgelike accents – still, I say, do you behold naught there?' and he pointed with his finger across the fulgid landscape towards a cluster of bright stars that shone far beyond Orion. One in particular gave forth a radiant light as if it were diffused from the centre of a lucid globe, so clear and soft it was.

'My star shines forth,' again he shouted. 'My natal star, without a spot to soil its purity; but now, ah! now! What darkens it?'

From the distant plains, from bog, and fen, and marsh, meteors tossing among murky vapours appeared to rise, to assume shape and form, till the whole took the aspect of the same terrible head which the Rosicrucian had called to life by the aid of his wondrous book with the brazen clasps. Wild, majestic, lightning-struck, but horribly vast, that head, filling up the whole space appeared, and fold upon fold, in gigantic masses trailed away behind it in the infinite distance, while the eyes flashed with a demoniac lustre upon the dying man.

His hands were clasped together, and his lips moved; but no word passed them. The features of the phantom writhed with hideous convulsions, it gnashed its teeth, it was infuriated – its doomed prey was escaping. Suddenly a blinding ray seemed to dart from Arman's star, and pierce the spectre in the forehead. In an instant the whole phantasma vanished, the starshine was dawning down again, the plains were lovely as ever, and the count was lying dead on the pillow with a radiant smile upon his thin lips.

When they examined his room in the mystic tower at Nurnburg, the book with the brazen clasps had vanished, and the whole of the remainder were burnt.